PRAISE FOR THE NOVELS OF KATIE MacALISTER

Memoirs of a Dragon Hunter
"Bursting with the author's trademark zany humor and spicy romance . . . this quick tale will delight paranormal romance fans."—*Publishers Weekly*

Sparks Fly
"Balanced by a well-organized plot and MacAlister's trademark humor."—*Publishers Weekly*

It's All Greek to Me
"A fun and sexy read."—The Season for Romance
"A wonderful lighthearted romantic romp as a kick-butt American Amazon and a hunky Greek find love. Filled with humor, fans will laugh with the zaniness of Harry meets Yacky."—*Midwest Book Review*

Much Ado About Vampires
"A humorous take on the dark and demonic."—*USA Today*
"Once again this author has done a wonderful job. I was sucked into the world of Dark Ones right from the start and was taken on a fantastic ride. This book is full of witty dialogue and great romance, making it one that should not be missed."—Fresh Fiction

The Unbearable Lightness of Dragons
"Had me laughing out loud. . . . This book is full of humor and romance, keeping the reader entertained all the way through . . . a wondrous story full of magic. . . . I cannot wait to see what happens next in the lives of the dragons."—Fresh Fiction

Also By Katie MacAlister

Dark Ones Series
A Girl's Guide to Vampires
Sex and the Single Vampire
Sex, Lies, and Vampires
Even Vampires Get the Blues
Bring Out Your Dead (Novella)
The Last of the Red-Hot Vampires
Crouching Vampire, Hidden Fang
Unleashed (Novella)
In the Company of Vampires
Confessions of a Vampire's Girlfriend
Much Ado About Vampires
A Tale of Two Vampires
The Undead in My Bed (Novella)
The Vampire Always Rises

Dragon Sept Series
You Slay Me
Fire Me Up
Light My Fire
Holy Smokes
Death's Excellent Vacation (short story)
Playing WIth Fire
Up In Smoke
Me and My Shadow
Love in the Time of Dragons
The Unbearable Lightness of Dragons
Sparks Fly
Dragon Fall
Dragon Storm
Dragon Soul
Dragon Unbound

Dragon Hunter Series
Memoirs of a Dragon Huner
Day of the Dragon

Born Prophecy Series
Fireborn
Starborn
Shadowborn

Time Thief Series
Time Thief
Time Crossed (short story)
The Art of Stealing Time

Matchmaker in Wonderland Series
The Importance of Being Alice
A Midsummer Night's Romp
Daring in a Blue Dress
Perils of Paulie

Papaioannou Series
It's All Greek to Me
Ever Fallen in Love
A Tale of Two Cousins

Contemporary Single Titles
Improper English
Bird of Paradise (Novella)
Men in Kilts
The Corset Diaries
A Hard Day's Knight
Blow Me Down
You Auto-Complete Me

Noble Historical Series
Noble Intentions
Noble Destiny
The Trouble With Harry
The Truth About Leo

Paranormal Single Titles
Ain't Myth-Behaving

Mysteries
Ghost of a Chance

Steampunk Romance
Steamed

A Tale of Two Cousins

A Papaioannou Novel

Katie MacAlister

Cover by Racing Pigeon Productions & Ninth Moon
Formatting by Racing Pigeon Productions

For everyone who's hung in there while I wrote other books: this is your thank you. You're the best!

ONE

"My room is an utter and complete crap hole. What's yours like?"

I looked around the small room. Despite the bright sunlight of Athens in a late spring afternoon, the room felt oddly gloomy. There was a distinct air of glory days long relegated to the past, but despite that, I liked it. "It's fine," I called back through the connecting door to Maggie's room. "Not great, but the online reviews say that the owners are diligent about keeping the hostel clean. And it's cheap."

Maggie appeared in the doorway clad in only her underwear, her face expressing mingled sadness and disappointment that made me feel like a heel. "I know you did the best you could, but I really wish you could have found us somewhere nicer, Thyra."

"Nicer costs more money." I pushed down the guilt, and shook out the gold lace cocktail dress that had been my mother's, thankful that vintage garments were in style again. "Of which I have none."

Maggie gave a little snort before withdrawing into her room, leaving the door open so we could talk. "I thought the magazine paid you?"

"An advance only," I reminded her.

"So? That's still money, and we could have been staying somewhere that reeked a little less of a low-class youth hostel."

"The advance was spent. This is all I can afford. If you want to stay somewhere else, you're welcome to, but I simply don't have the money to pay for it." I hoped that would stop her from continuing the gentle stream of complaints that had drifted my way during the last hour, which was the entirety of the time we'd been in Athens. This was our first venture, and already I was regretting having agreed to her plan.

Dammit, I told myself, this is what comes from depending on other people. This is why it's better to just do things by yourself rather than rely on others.

"What did you spend it on?" What sounded very much to me like annoyance tinged her words. I was a bit surprised—Maggie had always been so supportive in the past that now her sense of unhappiness prickled on my skin. "It can't have been clothes."

"Transportation to the airport, plane tickets for two from London to Athens, transportation from the airport, and two rooms at this hotel for four days," I said, peeling off my t-shirt, which was glued to my back with sweat. Although neither of our budget hotel rooms had its own bathroom, we did each have a sink, and I had a quick wash at it to clean off the worst of the sweat and dirt of travel. "Not to mention food and the incidentals you wanted."

"That was five hundred euros? Somehow that doesn't seem right."

"Well, it was, and we're here." I looked out of the window, excitement driving away the sudden worry and misgivings about my cousin. "We're in Athens, Maggie! Exotic, glorious Athens! On our first job! Aren't you excited?"

"I'd be more excited if I was in a proper hotel. A princess doesn't stay in a budget hotel. A princess stays in glamorous places with room service, and fresh towels, and chocolates on the pillow."

"I'll buy a candy bar and put it on your pillow tonight," I promised, hugging myself with the joy that filled me, determined to enjoy myself even if Maggie's unhappiness was a bit wearing. Although I hadn't seen much of Athens on the ride in on the bus, what I had seen made me itch to be a tourist.

But first I had to get through the events of the evening that Maggie insisted were necessary. I dug through the meager belongings of my suitcase and for a moment, thought I'd lost my purse. "Do you still have my bag?"

"The black one that wouldn't fit in your little carryon? Yes, it's locked away in my suitcase. Do you need it now?"

"Well, it does have my passport, although I don't suppose I will need that for a cocktail party," I said, pulling the gold lace dress over my head, and immediately snagging my hair on a metal hook and eye. "Ow. Ow ow ow."

"What on earth is the … oh." Maggie bustled into my room, where I spun around with my hands over my head, my arms partway through the dress, flailing ineffectively as I tried to remove the hook from my hair. "Honest to God, Thyra, you're the only woman I know whose hair deliberately does things to make itself difficult. No, stop struggling—I see where it's hooked … there."

"It's just because there's so much of it," I said, pulling the now freed dress down onto my torso before rubbing at a spot on my head where Maggie had inadvertently pulled my hair getting it untangled. "Mom always said unruly hair was the curse of the Patoise family, although your hair never seems to fight you like mine does me."

She patted the shoulder-length old-gold-colored hair that lay in perfection framing her face. "Maybe you and Aunt Sunny got some bad hair genetics from Grand-mère Patoise, but Mom and I didn't. Are you ready?"

"I suppose," I said, taking the small beaded coin purse I used on those rare occasions when I went out for an evening event, and stuffing the entirety of my bankroll—less than one hundred euros—into it. On second thought, I removed half of it, and hid the remainder in my bra, under one of my breasts.

Maggie had been admiring herself in the small mirror over my sink, turning this way and that before giving a big sigh. "It's just not what a princess should have," she told me.

"It may not be, but it's what we can afford, so let's stop focusing on the negative and enjoy our time while we're here. Are you sure you need me tonight? I'd be happy to just wander around the city while you gate-crash the party."

"It's not gate-crashing if you know about a party," she said, flashing a smile before hustling me out of the narrow room.

"It is if you aren't invited, and we aren't," I pointed out.

"Meh. We would have been if people had known that Her Serene Highness Princess Juliane of Sonderburg-Beck was in town." Maggie sailed blithely ahead, completely missing the fact that I rolled my eyes.

"It's just that … well, you know how I am at parties." I followed her down the narrow stone stairs, emerging into a small but clean reception room, where two young men with backpacks were checking in. I gave a little wave to Nita, the co-owner who had welcomed us earlier, and hurried after my cousin when she charged out the door, pausing to glance up and down the busy street.

"I know you're insular, yes."

"I'm not insular!" I protested, catching up to her.

"Oh?" She tipped her head to study me. "How many friends do you have?"

"That's a silly question. I have friends," I said, lifting my chin to attempt to look down my nose at her. This was a move that never worked, mostly because she was taller than me, but also because I had to look through glasses to see her.

"How many?" she repeated, arching one eyebrow.

"I have four roommates—" I started to say.

"Those are roomies, not friends," she said, waving them away. "You don't hang out with them for fun, do you?"

"Well ..." I didn't want to continue on with the subject, because I had a horrible feeling she was right.

"Uh-huh. What friends—other than that weird group of computer geeks you live with—do you have?"

"Well, Chris, naturally—"

"Chris is your brother," she interrupted. "Other than family members and your roomies, who do you consider a friend?"

I thought for a minute, swearing under my breath before waving a vague hand. "I don't see what your point is. OK, I'm particular about how many people I consider friends. It's not like that defines me as a person."

"No, but the fact that you don't let anyone get close to you does." She softened the words by giving my arm a brief squeeze. "I'm not trying to pick on you, Thyra, I'm really not, but other than family, you don't really let people know you, the real you. I just want you to see what others and I see."

"Others? What others?" I asked, narrowing my eyes. I was extremely uncomfortable with the discussion and would happily have changed the subject if I thought she'd let me. "Who are you talking about me with?"

She was silent, looking away, her gaze scanning the cars that drove past us.

A horrible thought struck me. "Oh, Maggie, you didn't."

"I did. He called me. He's been very worried about you."

I groaned aloud. "I don't know why, since he's done everything he can to make my life a living hell."

"Kardom?" She whirled around to give me a little frown. "Are you crazy? He's wild about you. Why would he try to make you unhappy?"

"Because he wants to be top dog in Beck, and he's doing everything in his power to make that happen. No, don't tell me you've fallen for his line of bull; I don't want to discuss it. I just want to enjoy Athens and do this interview right. If the magazine likes it, it might lead to other things in addition to the column."

"I like that!" She whapped me on the arm. "You get to drop statements like your own cousin Kardom is trying to do you a nasty, and then forbid me to talk about it? This is exactly what I'm talking about, Thyra—you put up barriers between yourself and everyone."

I took a deep breath, and reminded myself that arguing was not how I wanted to spend the evening. "I have a lot of reasons for protecting myself, as you well know, but I admit that perhaps I might go overboard once in a while. If you're done dissecting my psyche, can we go?"

"Yes, but just remember that I know all about you, and how you are. And you can't be standoffish and isolated if you want to be the secretary to a princess."

"Personal assistant," I corrected, resigning myself to an evening spent in an introvert's hell—a cocktail party. Afterward, I promised myself, I would take one of the free walking tours that were available around town. There had to be some that ran at night. Perhaps even a ghost tour ... "Not to argue the point, but I think royal assistants are isolated and standoffish. It goes with the job."

She gave a ladylike snort, then asked, "Where are all the taxis?"

"Is that what you've been looking around for?" I shook my head, and gave her a little push in the direction of the address she'd given me the day before. I'd looked it up at the library and memorized the location. "We don't have money for a cab. Come on, it's only about twelve blocks."

"Twelve blocks!" She gasped and looked appalled, but hurried after me when I set off at a brisk pace. "I'm going to have blisters if I walk that far."

"Don't be silly. Twelve blocks is nothing on a nice night like this. It's cooled down, there's lots of people out, and mmm, just smell the smells from the restaurants. You did say there would be food at this party, right?"

"Of course there will be food, cocktail party food. Little nibbles of this and that, but, Thyra, promise me you won't scarf down great big platefuls of appetizers."

"I haven't eaten since this morning, so if there is food, I'll be partaking, but I promise I won't let anyone see me making a pig of myself."

She chatted for almost the entirety of the twelve blocks, telling me how much fun the party was going to be, how much she was going to enjoy being seen as a princess, and that if I wasn't comfortable, I could find a quiet spot to sit. She finished with a reminder of, "Just remember that these people are going to be very impressed by having a princess in their midst."

I made a face at that. "Assuming they have even heard of Sonderburg-Beck, which most people in the world haven't."

She whapped me again on the arm. "It's a perfectly fine title. It's just a little ..."

"Outdated?"

"No."

"Irrelevant?"

"Of course not."

"Landless? Worthless? Impossible to cope with?"

"Now who's being negative?" she asked, giving me a quick grin.

"Just you remember that if this party is as elite as you were told it's going to be, it's likely there may be some real royalty there, like one of those Middle Eastern princes that are all over the society magazines. If you take my advice, you'll steer clear of anyone who looks important," I warned her. "Oh, I think that's the hotel there on the next block."

"Damn," she said, pausing to fret. "I hate to just walk up to it. Look at all those limos and expensive tiny sports cars. What sort of a princess arrives on foot to a hotel like that?"

"One who is flat broke." I glanced down a cross street and noticed a smaller, less busy entrance. "Let's go in the side entrance. That way we will be in the hotel before you make your grand entrance."

"All right, but I really wish we could have gotten a car. Appearances matter so much."

I managed to not comment on that, but it was a near

thing. Just as I passed the dark entrance of an obviously closed shop, a girl of about ten or eleven popped out, holding a large cardboard box in her arms.

"I hear you talking. You are English lady?" she asked me, her eyes red as if she had been crying.

"Oh, hello. I live there, yes." I hoped Maggie would stop with me to help the distraught child, but she proceeded on, obviously unaware of the girl.

"You like cats?"

I looked at her box. "Uh … sure, but—"

"I give you cat. Papa say Valentino has to go, but he will die if he is in the street. English like animals, I saw this in TV we watch at school. You take him. I love him. Maybe you love him, too?" Her dark eyes filled with tears that spilled over, making my own eyes prick painfully.

"Wait, I can't take a cat—"

"He is very good cat. You look like nice lady. You will love him, and treat him well, and then he will have a better life than with me, just like on the English TV shows," she said, and, with a heart-wrenching sob, turned and dashed down the street.

"Hey, I can't—I'm not the best person—well, hell."

No one else was around on that side of the street, certainly no one who looked like a suitable home for an unwanted cat. I flipped open the lid of the box to find an orange cat curled up on a ratty Bugs Bunny blanket. His head tilted back to give me a long, assessing look. There was a black splotch that completely covered one ear and dribbled down the back of his head a little bit. He was wearing a harness, and included in the box were a plastic bag filled with dried cat food, two small cans of what looked like tuna, and a couple of beat-up toys.

"Oh, God," I told the cat, my heart breaking at the thought of a young girl driven by desperation to find her beloved kitty a home. Then I thought of what it would take to care for a cat properly, and my heart broke a little more, because I knew I couldn't do it. I didn't have the time or situation or money. "I can't, Valentino. I just can't. Tell me you understand."

The cat stood up, stretched, then sniffed where my fingers were curled through the cutout handle of the box before giving them a head bonk.

My heart melted at the gesture. I'd always wanted a cat, but never could afford one … and with one rub of this odd cat's head, I was a goner, and we both knew it.

Still, how was I going to afford a cat? There was food, and litter, and vet visits, and toys. … I spent a moment imagining me turning the cat over to the local animal shelter, and almost flinched at the look in Valentino's eyes.

"You have no idea how much you've just complicated my life, kitty. Oh, stop looking at me like I'm a miser. I guess I'll eat ramen noodles for a month, but you have to do your part. You have to remain healthy, and not demand expensive food," I told him. "I hope that harness means you don't mind walking, because I can't carry a cardboard box with me into a cocktail party, and I'm certainly not going to leave you anywhere. Not since you're probably traumatized at being parted from your little girl."

The cat just gave me another long, considering look, his eyes blinking slowly.

"What are you doing?" Maggie called, her hands on her hips, when I hurried up to her. Her expression went from impatience to disbelief when she saw what was in the box I held. "A cat? Where on earth did you find that?"

"A little girl gave him to me. She said her dad was going to dump him on the street, and you've seen how people drive here. The kitty wouldn't last five minutes."

Maggie gawked at me. "Are you kidding? According to that Web site you read me, there's a whole neighborhood filled with cats in Athens."

"Yes, but that's not here." I clutched the box tighter, all my hitherto-unknown protective instincts rushing to the fore. I'd be damned before I did anything so callous as to abandon this poor, heartbroken cat.

"You can't keep a cat!" Maggie insisted.

I met Valentino's gaze, and once again melted under the effect of it. "Why not? Lots of people have them."

"How are you going to explain him to your flatmates?" she countered, and I had to admit she had me there.

"I don't know what I'll say, but I can't leave him here. It's inhuman." I could be just as stubborn as her.

"He looks healthy. He'll be fine on his own." She turned and walked quickly into the entrance of the hotel.

I looked again at the cat, who was curled up, his front feet folded under his chest. "She's right in that I don't know what I'll do with you when I get home. I don't suppose if I set you down, you'd find someone here to live with?"

He blinked at me again. I sighed. There was no further argument, and we both knew it. "Fine, but if you give me any grief, I will find the nearest Greek SPCA and hand you over." I took him out of the box and set him on the ground. His tail went up as he sniffed first my feet, then the mat outside the entrance of the hotel, then looked back up at me, clearly waiting for me to open the door.

"You sure? All right, but no peeing on anything." With the box in one hand, and the cat's leash handle looped around the other, I opened the door and he strolled in, just as calm as if he'd done that every day of his life.

Maggie stood just inside the door, clearly scanning the surroundings to make sure no one saw her arriving on foot. She turned to say, "It's all clear—oh, for the love of God! You're not keeping that!"

"You want me to fit in with the elite rich people of Athens," I told her, lifting my chin and pushing my glasses farther up the bridge of my nose. "They all have Chihuahuas and pugs and other little dogs they carry around in purses."

"That's in Los Angeles, and that is not a teacup Chihuahua. . . . Oh, never mind. If anyone complains, you're going to have to get rid of it."

I frowned, not appreciating the high-handed tone she'd adopted. I knew she wasn't overly fond of cats, but there was no reason to be so heartless about a poor homeless kitty. I dumped the cat's box of things at the concierge (who looked at it like it was filled with feces) and hurried after my cousin.

"Now remember," Maggie said in an undertone at the same time she slid into a hip-slinky walk down a hallway that led to various rooms used to hold events. "These people are the überest of the über. Don't mention anything about money."

"Or lack thereof," I said sotto voce to Valentino. His tail had a little curl at the end, so it looked like a shepherd's crook. My heart melted even more as he walked so nicely next to me.

"Don't forget to tell anyone who asks that you're my PA, and that I'm working for Noblesse International magazine. If they ask what I'm here to write about, say that you've been sworn to secrecy. That ought to pique their interests, and maybe we'll get invited to other parties."

"We're only going to be here for a few days," I reminded her. She stopped outside a door that had a sign in Greek and English that read *GEORGIO FOUNDATION OF THE ARTS.*

"Yes, and I expect to use every minute we're here to make valuable connections. OK, showtime! Oh, and remember to refer to me as Her Serene Highness."

I came close to rolling my eyes for a third time. "I know, Mags."

With a deep breath, she jerked the door open, and did a slow, exaggerated hip-action stroll into the room.

I looked at Valentino. He looked at me. "If we're going to do this, we're going to do it with style," I said, and hoisted him up, tucking him between my side and arm. I gave him a minute to protest, but he just curled his tail underneath my arm and adopted a regal expression.

"That's what I'm talking about." I nodded at him, and tried to move with something other than my usual shamble, striving for the sophistication and elegance that always seemed to fail me.

The room was full of the sorts of tables you see at wine bars, tall, with no chairs, dotted with candles and elegant floral arrangements. Mingling amongst the tables, chatting, laughing, calling to one another, and generally doing the cocktail party dance, were about a hundred and twenty people. They came in all shapes, sizes, and colors, but every single one of the men wore a suit, with the ladies in elegant short cocktail dresses that showed off long, tanned legs, or in the case of older women who obviously didn't wish to bare that much skin, silky garments that fluttered around them via the breeze coming in from an open patio.

Ahead of me, Maggie paused, posing. For a moment, I had a sense of her being a stranger. "Really," I whispered to the cat, "I had no idea she's such a good actress."

Valentino looked unimpressed. Maggie lifted a hand to wave at someone across the room all the while trilling light laughter.

"Do you see someone you know?" I hissed behind her, panic hitting me in the stomach. She'd sworn that she had no acquaintances who hung out in this set, but my worst fear was that someone would expose our subterfuge.

"No, silly. I'm just letting everyone think I do. Darling!" She laughed again, and started forward, bumping into a woman who appeared to be in her sixties, and who was chatting with two men. "Oh, I'm sorry. I was just waving to an old friend when my PA jostled me. Did I hurt you? No? I'm so glad. I couldn't forgive myself if her clumsiness resulted in you being hurt. But you look familiar. Did we meet at Bunny's party last year?"

"I don't know anyone named Bunny," the woman said with some suspicion, eyeing first Maggie, then me, and finally the cat. Her lips pursed. "And I don't know you."

"Of course you don't, and here my PA had me almost running you down. Thyra." Maggie gestured toward the two men and the obviously disapproving woman, waiting for me to do my thing.

My stomach tightened, and for a moment, I thought of

refusing to go through with the charade, but the weight of the cat on my arm reminded me that I badly needed the money that had been promised for the article. I'd be able to pay my flatmates all the back rent I owed, and put a little into my nonexistent savings account. I'd be able to afford food and litter for the cat. I might even be able to shop somewhere other than thrift stores. And most of all, I might be able to present my case to Beck. "Good evening. May I present Her Serene Highness Princess Juliane of Sonderburg-Beck," I murmured, and, with a glance that I hoped told Maggie a good deal, backed away. The two men—one of whom was older, the other probably in his early fifties—murmured politely and kissed her hand.

Maggie smiled flirtatiously at the younger one, who whispered something in her ear that had her throwing back her head and giving another trill of laughter.

"Oh, brother," I muttered to the cat, and, with a quick glance around the room, hurried over to where I could see waiters emerging through a door, laden with trays of hors d'oeuvres. My mouth watered at the same time my stomach rumbled ominously.

One waiter paused, a handsome dark-eyed devil in a plain white shirt and black pants, offering me a flute of champagne. "No, thank you," I murmured, adjusting Valentino so he could glare at the waiter when he tried to get a glimpse down my dress. The possessor of substantial cleavage, I was no stranger to men trying to do that, which is why my mother's old dress was so perfect. It left my shoulders bare, but the band across the chest was almost leer-proof.

I spied an unattended table that bore a tray of snacks near the waitstaff entrance, and made a beeline for it, ignoring all the bright chatter around me. "Yum, Valentino. These look tempting. I hope no one sneezed on them or otherwise did something to take them out of the running." I examined the hors d'oeuvres carefully, but they looked OK, and I quickly popped three phyllo pastries filled with goat cheese and herbs into my mouth, moaning softly to myself. "Oh, lord, I could eat a whole tray of just those. But I suppose I should find something you can eat. Let's see. … That looks spicy." I tried a little samosa, saying around it, "Yup, spicy. This looks like some sort of slider. Let's peel the meat off it and see if you like it."

Valentino, who'd expressed haughty interest when I started stuffing my face, snuffled the little blob of what I assumed was lamb before licking it off my fingers. With a furtive, quick glance around me, I picked up the platter and took it over to where a couple of chairs had obviously been tucked away forgotten in a corner. It was partially hidden by the door that led to the depths of the hotel, which suited me just fine. I turned my back on the room and hurriedly picked the meat off the three other sliders, feeding it to the cat.

A brief gust of air, making my skirt flutter out around me, preceded a thump on my back that sent me flying forward into the wall. "Bloody hell!" I hit my head on the back of one of the chairs when I stumbled into it, clutching the cat to my side so he wouldn't get crushed when I half fell onto the chair seat.

"Christ! I'm sorry, I didn't see you standing behind the door—are you hurt?"

I slid off the chair onto the ground, using one hand to rub the spot on my forehead while I set Valentino down and held tightly to his leash. "Not seriously, no. And it's not your fault. I shouldn't have been there. I was just feeding … er …" I looked up when the man who'd spoken squatted next to me, words drying up on my tongue at the sight of him. He looked to be in his late thirties, had short curly black hair and olive-green eyes, and could very easily have graced the cover of the magazine for which I had promised to interview an up-and-coming desirable bachelor. His cheekbones were just high enough to make his jawline angle down to a gently blunted chin in a way that made me feel first hot, then chilled.

"Your cat?" he finished my sentence, smiling as he gave Valentino a little pat on his head. Valentino considered him with his yellow-eyed gaze for a few seconds, then strolled over and sniffed cautiously at his shoes.

I stared at the gorgeous man for a few seconds, my attention on the two indentations that appeared on either side of his cheeks when he smiled. They weren't exactly dimples, but they were cute enough to remind me that I wasn't there to ogle the waiters.

"My what? Oh, Valentino. Yes, he's mine. Newly so. A little girl gave him to me outside the hotel," I said, managing to get myself under control enough to allow the man to give me a hand. I got up, brushing off the full lace skirt, hoping the crinoline petticoat that I wore underneath to give it the proper shape wasn't stuck in my underwear, or some other embarrassing circumstance. "I was just giving him a little meat. I think he's hungry."

The man looked at first the cat, then me. "Someone gave him to you?"

"A little girl. It was heartbreaking, but I guess he's my responsibility now."

"How very thoughtful of you. You have the most amazing eyes."

I was a bit taken aback by the abruptness of the statement, but then, I was just ogling the man's jaw and almost dimples, so I guessed I didn't have much to complain about. "I do?"

"They're amber. I've never seen amber eyes before. And now I've offended you." He smiled again, making me feel like the air-conditioning needed to be cranked up a couple of notches.

"You haven't, actually, although I've always thought of my eyes as a boring old light brown. Yours are very nice, too. They're kind of a sage, olive green."

"That would be my mother's influence. She was Irish. Are you by any chance American?"

Valentino tired of smelling the waiter's shoes and hopped onto the chair to consider the tray of snacks. I pulled him back, giving him the last of the slider meat. "No, although I grew up in Ottawa. Until my parents died, that is."

"Ah, that would explain why you sound like my cousins' wives." He smiled again, and then stuck out a hand. "I'm Dmitri."

"Hello, Dmitri. I'm Thyra. And this is Valentino."

"He looks like one. Er ... TEER-uh?" he asked, looking hesitant as he carefully pronounced my name.

"Yup, it's an odd one, huh?" I spelled it for him. "It's a family name that my parents insisted I have. I actually have four names, and this is the best of them, so really, it could be worse.."

He laughed. "My father insisted I be called after him, so I completely understand. Luckily, my family lets me use Dmitri—my middle name—instead. Now, I've just about knocked you silly with the door, and we've exchanged name secrets, so I believe we should progress to the point where I ask if I can get something for you. For your cat? A glass of wine? A bowl of water? A piece of paper so you can give me your phone number?"

I gawked at him for a moment. "Are you insane?"

"Not that I know of," he said, his cheeks doing that almost-dimpling thing again.

"Wait ... I just need to be sure because this doesn't happen very often. ... Are you flirting with me? Oh, God. You weren't, were you? You were just being funny, and because I like your eyes, and you have those almost dimples, I thought you were, but you weren't, and now I want to die. And now my mouth won't stop telling you everything I'm thinking. Gah! Please go away so I can die of embarrassment here in the corner by myself. Well, with Valentino, because he has no one else to take care of him."

"I was most definitely flirting with you," he answered, his smile growing into an outright grin. I liked what that did to his face. It made little laugh lines spread out from the edges of his eyes. "Although I doubt if that doesn't happen very much."

"I'm short, wear glasses, and am probably the most introverted and socially awkward person you will ever meet,"

I said, giving him a wry smile. "You'll have to trust me that men don't often give me a second look." I hesitated, not wanting to lie to him. He seemed so nice, so friendly, that it just seemed wrong. "Not ones who don't have an ulterior motive."

He was silent a moment. "I don't quite know how to respond to that. I want very much to compliment you and say that you aren't short, that your glasses are charming, and that I don't find you awkward at all, socially or otherwise, but I suspect you might not take that in the spirit that I intended, so I'll simply ask you if you would give me your number so that we might continue the conversation at another time. Say, tomorrow? Perhaps over coffee? Lunch?"

"I'd like that," I said before I remembered that I shouldn't be spending money on meals out … and then there was the matter of the interview. We were supposed to meet the Greek playboy the following evening. However … after a moment's consideration, I decided that given Maggie's attitude, I was due a little fun before I had to fall into step for the interview. "But I was going to go sightseeing tomorrow. I only have a couple of days in Athens, and I really want to see everything I can."

"That's perfect!" he said with another eye-crinkling, almost-dimpling smile. Something inside me felt girlish and giggly, a bolt of excitement cheering me up despite the awkwardness of the party. "I'm known for my ability to show off Athens, if you would like me as a tour guide."

I glanced toward the door behind him, which opened to allow two more waiters to emerge with fresh trays of snacks. "That would be awesome, so long as you can take the time off."

"I think that can be arranged." He pulled out his cell phone. "Will you give me your number?"

I shook my head. "I don't have one. A phone, that is. But if you give me yours, I can borrow my cousin's phone."

He hesitated, but held up his phone to show me the phone info on it. "I'll write it down for you."

"No, it's not necessary. My brother and I have this weird mental thing with numbers—he can do mad math problems in his head, and I remember strings of numbers."

"That must be convenient. Is your brother here in Athens?"

"No, he's a homicide detective in Scotland," I said, wincing a little at the pride in my voice. "Sorry, that sounded smug, didn't it? I didn't mean that his job was better than anyone else's, although I am very proud of him. He's … happy."

"And you're not?" The laughter faded from his pretty green eyes.

I hesitated, torn between telling this handsome stranger everything and knowing that even though he had an easy manner and I liked him, it wasn't wise to go baring my soul when I knew nothing about him. "My life is a bit complicated at the moment."

"Then I hope that seeing Athens tomorrow will bring you some pleasure," he said with another pat on Valentino's head. "What hotel are you staying at? I can meet you there about … shall we say nine?"

"Uh …" I thought quickly. It was on the tip of my tongue to tell him that I was staying at this hotel, but I didn't want to lie to him. "It's a small one; you probably wouldn't know it. How about if I meet you here?"

"As you like," he answered, his voice smooth, but I felt like he'd just withdrawn from me. I realized with a stab of guilt that he probably thought I didn't trust him, but before I could rally some sort of excuse for not giving him the name of the hotel, he added, "I should get back to it. I'm sorry again for bumping into you, although I look forward to seeing you tomorrow."

"So do I," I said lamely, feeling even more awkward when he gave me a little nod and moved into the room, probably to pick up some of the empty glasses that had been left on the tables.

It was if the sun had gone behind a cloud, dimming my joy a little. I badly wanted out of there, so I could sit and think about Dmitri, and remember the warmth in his eyes when he smiled, but knew Maggie expected me to be at her beck and call, as befitted a princess.

"Oh, screw it," I said after a few minutes of inner struggle, and went in search of her. I found her in the center of the room, surrounded by people, her face shining with pleasure. The satisfaction in her eyes gave me a guilty twinge in my belly, but there wasn't much I could do about my regrets now.

"Can I have a word?" I asked softly when Valentino and I managed to nudge aside a couple of men in expensive suits in order to get to her side.

She shot me a look that was rife with a warning. "Someone on the phone for me?" she asked, giving another lilting laugh, and said with a big smile to the circle of men and women who were evidently hanging on her every word, "Unless it's His Serene Highness—my brother, the crown prince, you know—I don't wish to be disturbed."

I ground my teeth for a few seconds, managing to bite back everything I wanted to say in order to murmur in her ear, "I'm done."

"Thyra, no!" Her eyes filled with a plea that made me feel like a heel. "You can't stop now. I've only just started, and you said we'd have several days. It's unfair of you to expect me to walk away before I've had any fun!"

"I don't mean you have to go, too. I'm going to take the cat and go buy him a litter box and some food, and then go back to the hotel. You don't need me here. Just please remember Beck, and don't do anything that they wouldn't like."

She beamed a smile at me that could have lit up half the city. "I won't do anything you wouldn't do," she answered before turning back to the group of beautiful people. "So sorry about that interruption. Thyra is an excellent PA, but so moody. I think she's just a bit overwhelmed."

"Oh, yes," I said under my breath, hoisting the cat higher as I marched out of the room, my temper getting the better of me. "I'm so overwhelmed by you pretending to be me.

How on earth am I going to stand another four days of this, Valentino? How am I going to get through it without cracking or yelling at Maggie to stop acting like she's so much better than everyone else? What if word about her behavior gets back to Beck, and that just adds fuel to the fire Kardom is trying to start?"

The cat had no answer. I sighed, feeling a kinship in that respect, and took us off before it got too late to visit a pet store.

TWO

"You're welcome to borrow a car of course, although Harry and I will be flying up in a few hours, so if you could leave us the BMW—"

"I'll take the Jeep, then, if you don't mind," Dmitri said, looking out of the window at the people who bustled down the sidewalk, the view from the tenth floor making them look like tiny animated beings. Idly, he wondered what Thyra was doing at that moment. Was she one of the tiny beings who flowed past the building? Or was she still curled up in bed? It was only a little after eight in the morning—perhaps she was snuggled into bed, her long, glossy black hair fanned out on a pillow around her, while her beautiful amber eyes were filled with sleepy contentment. "Hell, I suppose I should just rent a car if it's going to take long to repair the damage on mine."

Iakovos, his cousin and once employer, now partner, said abruptly, "Take the Jeep. Use it with my blessing. Harry would like to know how the interview went."

"What inter—oh, the one for that magazine with the bachelor list?" He allowed an irritated expression to pass over his face. "It hasn't happened yet. I think it's supposed to be tonight. Alexis?"

The young man whom he'd employed some two years

before as his assistant hurried into his office, a tablet computer in hand. "You bellowed, sir?"

Dmitri fought the urge to smile. He'd found Alexis working in a legal department of Iakovos's business, and recognized the same analytic sort of mind and love of order that had made him such a sterling assistant himself. Except now, he reminded himself, he was a full partner, and heading up the newest Papaioannou venture. "What's on my calendar for the day?"

"Er …" Alexis tapped the tablet a few times. "Well, you canceled all of your meetings, so there's just an interview with a journalist from the Noblesse International magazine, and later you said you will be having drinks with a woman who is a friend of Ms. Patricia Perry."

"Oh, that." He made another face, waved off Alexis, and said into the phone, "You heard?"

"Yes. Why on earth did you let Patricia set you up on a blind date?"

"Is there any reason I shouldn't? She's not still trying to steal you away from Harry, is she?" Dmitri smiled even as he asked the question. He knew well that his cousin was head over heels in love with his wife, and not even the lovely Patricia could shake that devotion.

"Not since you hooked her up with Bentson," Iakovos answered. "I gather they are still together?"

"So far as I know, yes, and I didn't so much set them up as I mentioned to Bentson when he was in town pitching his new cooling system that I knew of someone who loved the opera as much as he said he did, and boom. They were off and running. Are you bringing the kids with you when you come up here?"

"No, Harry needs a break. She's been looking a bit tired. I thought a few days away from our brood would let me pamper her as she deserves. You'll come to dinner tonight?"

Dmitri hesitated. "I would, but I might have plans."

"With Patricia's friend?"

"No, that's later. There's someone I met last night, at the Georgio Foundation party."

"How was that? Harry wanted us to go, but changed her mind two days ago, deciding that if Patricia was there, then she would be happier being elsewhere."

"It was the usual—lots of people trying to impress each other. There was a princess in attendance, some minor European royalty swanning around like she owned the place. At one point she flung her hand out to make a dramatic statement and knocked my glass of red wine all over me, but luckily the hotel staff had club soda, and had the stain out and the coat cleaned by the time I left."

"And the someone you met?" Interest was rich in Iakovos's voice. "What sort of a someone was she? Anyone I know?"

"I doubt it. Her name was Thyra ... er ... damn. I didn't get her last name. She said she grew up in Canada, but was from ... hell. I guess I didn't ask where she lived, either, although she has a brother in Scotland."

"That sounds promising," Iakovos said, humor lacing his voice. "What do you know about her?"

"Not a lot," Dmitri admitted. "Just that she wears those little round glasses that make me think of John Lennon, she has a soft heart—she'd found a big orange cat on the way to the party, and I suspect she's going to end up keeping it—and for some reason, she didn't want me to know where she was staying."

"If you just met, that's hardly surprising."

"Possibly, although she didn't seem to be reticent about other subjects." He remembered the sting of the insult that was her obvious reluctance to tell him what hotel she was at. "I did think it was curious that she doesn't have a mobile phone. Do you know anyone who doesn't have one?"

"No," Iakovos said slowly. "That is a little odd."

Dmitri shook his head at the feeling that Thyra was hiding something from him, then chastised himself. Of course she was keeping things from him—they had chatted all of ten minutes. Still, he couldn't shake the impression there was some point in their conversation where she had started to say something but stopped, and that intrigued him. "Perhaps I'll figure it out today."

"The phone situation?"

"No, sorry, I was talking to myself. I'm going to show Thyra around Athens this morning, so I'll have a better chance to assess what it was that bothered me."

"There's bothered, and then there's bothered," Iakovos said, a hint of humor in his voice. "I hope it's the latter. Harry is starting to make noises about finding you a woman now that Theo is married, and given that her idea of the perfect woman for you is her aunt, I'd suggest that if you like this someone, you act on it."

"Just because you and Theo fell immediately for the loves of your respective lives doesn't mean I'm going to do the same," he said with a laugh.

"You're a Papaioannou," Iakovos said. "It's in your blood. Take my advice and don't fight it. When the right woman comes along, of course."

"Of course," Dmitri murmured, and after discussing how the newest arm of Papaioannou International was moving forward, he rang off, and did a little work reviewing notes from a building engineer and taking a couple of video calls with vendors in India. "I'll check back in a few hours," he told Alexis when he strolled out to fetch Iakovos's Jeep. "Don't forget to keep on the back of the local council in Anyi. We need those permits."

"Aye aye, mon capitaine," Alexis said, saluting him.

Dmitri reviewed the work done to launch Papaioannou Green, the branch that would focus solely on building self-sufficient, low-carbon-footprint housing, but found his mind wandering to the events of the past evening.

He couldn't help but smile at the memory of Thyra's horror when she thought she had misinterpreted his light flirtation. The way she spoke, her thoughts appearing to tumble out unfiltered, reminded him of Harry, a woman he admired greatly. "But I'm not going to follow the same path," he said aloud. "I might be a Papaioannou, but I have yet to fall in love at first sight, and I have no plan to change that."

Still, he had to admit that there was something to the thought of settling down with one woman, one perfect woman. Iakovos had been married for almost ten years, and Theo for almost a year, and Dmitri was very well aware of just how happy both of his cousins were. Perhaps if Patricia's friend was as enticing as she'd hinted, that might be a possibility. She knew well that he had a weakness for redheads, and swore that her friend had a fiery personality that matched her hair.

A vision of a laughing woman rose in his mind, her golden eyes smiling behind the little round lenses of her glasses, her hair as black and glossy as the wing of a raven. Thyra might be delightfully unconventional to talk to, but she wasn't at all what he liked in a woman. He, like Theo and Iakovos when they had been single, preferred women who were what Harry once referred to as "ethereal little sprites who could easily be underwear models."

Thyra was very much not an ethereal little sprite. She was solidly built, with the high cheekbones that hinted of some Slavic blood in her ancestry, two thick black eyebrows that were almost perfectly straight, and a direct way of looking at him that bespoke a woman who didn't know how to play the seduction game. He had no desire to get entangled with an innocent, one who didn't understand the rules of attraction, and ultimately how to part ways with a minimum of fuss. No, she was not at all what he was looking for.

He imagined her in his bed, that black hair spread around her, all her smooth, ample flesh waiting for him, the heat of her body calling to him, tempting him into exploring all her secrets. . . .

The honk of a horn at a green light recalled him to the fact that he was almost at the hotel where he'd agreed to pick up Thyra. He pulled into the front entrance, scanning the few people that were emerging from the hotel, but didn't see her. "I just hope she's not one of those women who feels she has to be fashionably late—"

"Dmitri!"

Just as he was about to hand over the keys to a valet attendant, he caught sight of Thyra waving on the other side of the street, the cat on a leash walking beside her while she stood waiting to cross the street. The wind ruffled her hair, lifting a few tendrils as if by an invisible hand, and Dmitri wondered if he wasn't being too hasty in ruling out women with dark hair from his preferred type. Certainly the long, straight curtain of black that flowed around Thyra when she bent to adjust the cat's harness wasn't anything to dismiss. And then there were her soft rounded arms and shoulders that were exposed in a red-and-white striped sundress, not to mention the way her breasts—abundantly apparent in the tight bodice—drew the eye to their lush roundness.

No, he definitely was being too restrictive in his view of the ideal woman. There was nothing displeasing about Thyra's shape even if it was opposite those of his usual companions. It would be downright discriminatory of him not to broaden his horizons to include her.

Damn, but the way her hips moved when she walked was almost sinful.

"Sorry, Valentino doesn't seem to know he's a cat, and he wanted to smell everything, so it took a lot longer to get here than I anticipated. … Oh, thank you."

He picked up the cat and, after a moment's thought, set him in the back, and slid one side of the seat belt through his harness, effectively strapping him in while still giving him the ability to sit or lie down. "I think this ought to hold him."

"Smart thinking. They have a car seat belt for cats at the pet store that I went to last night, but …" Thyra looked around her with pleasure, and changed the subject. "Isn't it a glorious day? Not too hot, but boy, I could get used to having this sort of sun all the time. I put on tons of sunscreen, so if I smell like coconut, that's why. I like your car. It lets you see everything."

"It's my cousin's, actually. He's letting me borrow it." Dmitri helped her into the front seat before getting in behind the wheel. "But what?"

"Hmm?" She watched with apparent interest as a long limo pulled up, dispersing from its depths a Middle Eastern family.

"You decided not to get the cat seat belt?"

"That's right. I have a list of places that I thought would be fun to visit." She pulled a scrap of paper from a small bag strapped across her chest. "Let's see. ... There's the Museum of Greek Popular Instruments, and a botanical garden, and I heard it's fun to watch the changing of the guard outside the parliament building, and there's a museum about Greek costume that looks super fun, and another one at Athens University that covers history, and a postal museum, and one for an artist who was named Yorgos Gounaropoulos that's supposed to be fabulous."

Dmitri laughed, amused by her choices of tourist activity. Why was he not surprised that what he was coming to realize was a very unconventional woman would want to see sights that many tourists didn't care about? "That's quite the list. I'm not sure we can fit in all of it in just one day. How about if we start at the Parthenon, and then perhaps see the changing of the guard, and then we could have lunch. After that, there's an excellent archaeology museum, if you are interested in that sort of thing, followed by the Monastiraki flea market. It's very quirky. I think you'll like it."

"Oh, I'm sure I would, but I can see a flea market anywhere." There was a note to her voice that he puzzled over, not being able to place it. Was it disinterest? Reticence? If he didn't know better, he'd say there was a tinge of anger to the words, which made him wonder if she disliked him changing the plans she'd obviously made.

"Do you like to sail?" he found himself asking, despite not intending on doing so. He didn't have time to take her out sailing, not if he had to go to that blasted interview in the evening.

"I don't know. I've never tried it."

"Perhaps tomorrow we could go out on the water. We could go to—"

"Oh!" Her involuntary exclamation interrupted his offer of taking her sailing. She twisted in her seat, her head almost out of the car in order to peer upward at the Acropolis. "Wow, this is just so … is that the Parthenon?"

"At the top, yes. The Acropolis itself is a complex of temples, far too much to see in the time we have, but I do recommend a visit to the Parthenon. I've been to it numerous times, and I am still amazed by its beauty. There's a very good museum near it. Shall we start there?"

"You know, I think maybe I'll save that for another day," she said, and once again, he heard that odd tone in her voice. This time, however, he got a distinct feeling it was embarrassment. "We could do the costume museum, if you like. Or the folk music one. Then maybe see the garden? Valentino will probably be ready for a potty break by then."

"I'm afraid he won't be allowed in the museum," he said, his mind busy with the puzzle that was Thyra.

She was silent a moment. "Damn. I didn't think of that. It's way too hot to leave him in the car." She chewed her lip, then sighed. "Well, I guess we'll just have to do the botanical gardens."

"We could leave him at my apartment," he offered. "My housekeeper loves animals, and I'm sure she wouldn't mind taking care of him for a few hours."

She bit her lip again, but shook her head. "That's sweet of you to offer, but I wouldn't feel right about leaving him with a stranger. He has to be grieving for his little girl, and the home he knew, and I wouldn't want him to have any more anxieties than what he already has."

"Has he shown signs of anxiety?"

"Well … not so much, although he looked so pathetic when I was going to the shower that I ended up taking him with me. He stood outside it and monitored the water flow."

Dmitri had a sudden mental vision of soapy water sliding down her lush curves, of her wet, sleek hair pointing straight down to her ass, and was immediately aware of that he was becoming hard. He cleared his throat, telling himself he really needed to avail himself of a woman if he was having that sort of reaction after having been in Thyra's company for less than an hour. In order to distract himself from just how long trails of soapy bubbles would wind themselves down her legs, he asked, "Since Valentino doesn't mind walking, there are several interesting ancient neighborhoods we could stroll through. Do you have an interest in history?"

A little smile made her lips curl. "You could say that. My family is very big on it."

What the hell did that mean? He shot her a quick glance, but she was exclaiming over the scenery. Was she deliberately trying to pique his interest with curiosity about the odd things she said? He didn't think so. She seemed to be unaware that her comments were anything but normal. He continued to study her while they toured the botanical gardens, relishing her delight with everything despite the fact that he wasn't actually interested in plants.

After an hour of that, he lured her to the Anafiotika neighborhood. "It's very scenic," he told her when they climbed one of the narrow white stone staircases, surrounded by white stone houses and walls, and bougainvillea that seem to spill down over every available surface. "There are several cafés right on the stairs … ah, yes, Valentino, and many cats, too."

Thyra giggled when Valentino came face-to-face with an indifferent cat. He stared at it for a moment, his yellow eyes unblinking until the lazy white-and-gray cat got up, stretched, then sauntered off down the stairs. "Valentino! Why do I have a feeling you just glared at that cat until he moved out of your way?"

Valentino strolled forward, his tail held straight up with its little shepherd's crook bend at the tip giving him a jaunty air.

They roamed the area for another hour before Dmitri's subtle suggestions of having lunch in a cool taverna took a more direct bent. "I'm going to drop if I don't get something cold to drink, and what's more, your cat is bound to be thirsty. You may not feel the need for refreshment, but Valentino and I do. Ah, this one looks pleasant." With a hand on her back, he all but pushed her into the small fenced garden area crowded with white metal wrought iron tables and chairs, and umbrellas that gave much desired refuge from the midday sun.

"Well … I suppose a little lunch would be OK," Thyra said reluctantly, picking the cat up to carry him through the crowd. "I brought his food so that he can have a meal. The woman at the pet store said he is probably used to eating throughout the day."

When a waitress came to see what they wanted, Dmitri asked for a pitcher of water for them, and a bowl of the same for the cat, while they perused the menu. She gave him a little flutter of her lashes that he had no difficulty interpreting. To his surprise, Thyra commented on that after the woman left to get their water.

"Does that get old?"

"Does what?" he asked, looking up from the piece of paper that listed the day's offerings.

"Women ogling you like that. That waitress was all but drooling on you. I just wondered if you're flattered by that sort of thing."

Dmitri considered that for a few moments. "I don't really think much of it, to be honest."

She made a face. "Which means you secretly like it, but you don't want to say that because you're afraid I'll think you're egotistical."

"Not exactly. I would be lying if I said that I don't notice the attention that I get from women, but that's just something that happens to us, so I don't spend much time worrying about it." He looked back at the menu.

"Us?" Thyra asked, her straight eyebrows rising a little.

"My cousins. They are … were … very popular with the ladies before they were married. If you want to see ogling, you should see them in public without their wives. Women have been known to go to great lengths to get their attention, and that, I assure you, has not happened to me." He smiled at the memory of the times Iakovos and Theo had been all but dripping with women.

The waitress returned with a pitcher of water containing a few ice cubes and several slices of lemon floating in it, which she set down before placing a separate bowl of water on the floor for the cat. She made sure that the side of her breast brushed Dmitri's arm when she leaned over to pour a glass for him, before leaving him with a sultry smile.

His gaze met Thyra's. She had a hand over her mouth, but her bright amber eyes were dancing behind the lenses of her glasses. "Oh, sure, it doesn't happen to you."

"That was unfortunate timing," he admitted, then, unable to keep from asking, added, "What about you? How do you cope with men who ogle you?"

"I'll let you know when that happens," she said, picking up the half sheet of paper, and frowned at it, her lips moving when she sounded out the Greek letters. After a moment she glanced up, her brows pulling together a little when she asked, "What?"

"I was just wondering why you pretend that you're not attractive. I know that many women have body issues that keep them from realizing just how beautiful they are, but you seem to be very in touch with your emotions, so I don't think it's that."

She shrugged. "Oh, I wish I was thinner, and taller, and could wear contacts without my eyes getting irritated, but once I hit thirty, I decided life was too short to worry about crap like that. It doesn't mean I delude myself, however. Men don't seem to be overly interested in me. Most men."

"Now, that is a very cryptic statement, one I will want to return to in a moment, but first, do you need help with the menu? I can translate for you if you wish. I think we'd better have our order ready before the waitress returns, lest she feel the need to refill my glass again."

"Well . . ." She bit her lip, hesitating before giving a little sigh. "I'd like a salad if possible."

"After walking around all morning? You can't tell me you're not hungry. Or are you slimming? Er . . . dieting?"

"I should be, but eh." She made a face. "I actually do like salads. I'm not one of those women who pretend they don't eat anything in front of a man, and then go home and binge on a pizza, in case you were worried."

"Very well. I am most definitely an omnivore, so I believe I'll have something a bit more substantial. Shall we get a bite to eat for Valentino?"

"I have his kibble here, but maybe I could swing . . . maybe just a tiny bit of plain chicken breast," she answered, tucking a small packet of cat food into her purse. "The woman at the pet store said not to give him too much people food, but they have plain chicken in cat food, so I can't imagine that would hurt him."

The waitress returned for the order, retreating without rubbing herself on Dmitri again. But Thyra's odd statement remained in his mind, and when she had finished talking about how much she enjoyed this neighborhood, he gently returned her to the topic that interested him. "Would you consider it rude if I asked what you meant by most men not being attracted by you?"

She looked down at her glass, giving it a swirl before taking a sip, after which she bent over to check on Valentino. The cat was sitting in the shade of the table, his eyes mostly closed. "That's kind of a long story. And one that I shouldn't . . . but I hate this, I really do, and I'm not any good at lying. Chris always said that I had the worst poker face he'd ever seen."

"Chris?"

"My brother, Christian." She made a vague gesture, looking anywhere but at Dmitri, clearly distressed by something.

"Thyra, you don't need to tell me anything that would make you feel uncomfortable," he said, reaching across the table to give her fingers a friendly squeeze. That was his intention, but the way her fingers curled onto his made him aware once again that she possessed a many attributes that he would greatly enjoy exploring further.

"I know, but we've had such a nice day, and I just hate this. I really do. I didn't think I would, because I always thought it doesn't matter, you know? It was always there, and it doesn't mean anything, but then Maggie had this idea that she could take my identity temporarily, because I'm such an introvert and am so bad with people, and she's just the opposite, and she eats up attention."

"Maybe we could start at the beginning," he said, confused. "What didn't you think you'd hate?"

She hesitated, bit her lip again, drawing his attention to her mouth. A rush of blood hit his groin when he watched her little white teeth bite what were sure to be sweet, sweet lips. "Have you ever heard of a country called Beck?"

He dragged his mind off the idea of tasting that delectable lower lip that she insisted on abusing, digging through his memory. "Beck … no, I don't … oh, wait, yes I do. It's a small Russian country that recently declared its independence?"

"Not quite. Beck was part of Prussia originally, then belonged to Poland, and after World War I was given to Germany. The government there has declared independence from Germany, and has applied to the United Nations and European Union for recognition."

"Is your family from there?" he asked, guessing there was a reason she knew so much about what he recalled was a tiny principality of no particular importance either politically or geographically.

She nodded. "My brother and I were born there despite the fact that my father was exiled. …Well, his grandfather was, and on down the line to Dad. And Chris, I suppose. But Dad said it was important we were born in Beck, even if it wasn't really Beck at the time, so he dragged my mother there when she was about to pop both times with Chris and me."

"That must have been difficult on her." He was confused by the importance of her birthplace, but was content to let her tell the story in her own time.

"I'm sure it was, but that's all part of why this just seems so wrong now. Dad ..." She shook her head. "Dad would have had kittens if he knew what I've done. He was always insistent that we knew who we were, and honored our family. But Maggie can be very persuasive, and it seemed to make sense at the time. I was desperate for the job the magazine offered, but I couldn't do what they wanted me to do, parading around like ... ugh. I just couldn't. But Maggie could, only she kind of let it go to her head, and last night ... last night was just so awkward. She loved it, but I didn't, and heaven only knows what the people in Beck are going to think if they ever hear about it. Not to mention the fact that Dad is probably rolling in his mausoleum."

Dmitri wasn't quite sure what she was talking about, or what a charity party had to do with the small country of Beck, but figured that if he was patient, she'd explain. "Last night at the party?"

She nodded, her expression miserable as she played with the water glass, her gaze firmly affixed to it. "It was awful."

"Did someone say something to you?" he asked, deciding right then and there that if anyone had made an unkind comment, he'd have a word or two to say to the person in question.

"No. Yes. Maggie did."

"Maggie is ... ?"

"My cousin. Actually, second cousin once removed, but her mom and my mother were best friends, so we grew up fairly close." She glanced up at him, her lovely eyes almost glowing in the sunlight. "Maggie came to Athens with me. Her name is Margaret Colton. Except last night, she told people at the party that she was Princess Juliane of Sonderburg-Beck."

Dmitri thought back to the blonde who had knocked the glass of wine onto his chest. "I believe I saw her. She was quite the ... er ... life of the party."

"That's Maggie for you," Thyra said with a sigh, her shoulders slumping, pouring a little of her water into the now-empty cat's bowl. Valentino sat up and promptly stuck a paw in the water, patting the edge of the bowl until he dragged it closer to him. "She always has been a bit of a ham. She should have been an actress, but she doesn't stick to things for very long. I hope she didn't do anything embarrassing last night."

"Nothing out of the norm for a woman who clearly enjoyed being the center of attention ..." A thought occurred to him, one that had him narrowing his eyes on her. "You said that she was pretending to be you?"

She nodded, chewing on an ice cube.

"But if she told people she was this princess, that would mean you ..." He stopped, unable to continue.

"It doesn't mean anything," she told him. "Not really. Beck hasn't existed for almost a hundred years, and although Dad's family maintained the titles, they are basically meaningless. Just an anachronism held by a bunch of stubborn men who refused to admit that times had changed."

"You're a princess?" he asked, not believing that it was possible.

She nodded. "But like I said, it's not—"

"A real princess?" he asked, trying to wrap his brain around the idea that the quirky, unconventional, completely unique woman before him was a royal. An actual royal princess. One whose ancestors ruled a country.

No. It couldn't be. She had to be pulling his leg. If there was anyone less like nobility than Thyra, he had yet to meet them. For some reason, she was trying to beguile him into believing her incredible story, and that left him moderately annoyed. He'd enjoyed the day spent with her, enjoyed thinking about her all soapy and wet, her flesh silky smooth as he stroked his hands along her curves, but if she expected him to even consider wanting to kiss and touch her after she'd filled him full of such obvious lies, she was very mistaken.

"You don't believe me, do you?" she asked, a little smile curling up one side of her mouth.

It took him a moment to find a response that wasn't downright obnoxious. "It's an incredible story."

She rummaged around in her bag for a moment before pulling out a passport. "I'm glad I got this back from Maggie this morning." She held it out to him.

He took it, staring deep into those amber eyes, seeing only their clear depths. Slowly, he flipped open the first couple of pages until he came to her picture. Below it, was her name.

Juliane Thyra Friederike Luise, Princess of Sonderburg-Beck.

"Hell," he swore in Greek, then looked up to meet her gaze, her eyes now filled with amusement. "You're a bloody real princess."

"If you get all weird on me and start calling me Your Serene Highness, I will dump this pitcher of water on you," she said, taking back the passport.

"You're a serene highness? Not even just a regular highness?" he asked, feeling as shocked as if she had, in fact, dumped ice water on him.

"Right, don't make me sorry I told you," she said, her brows pulling together again. "This is exactly why I don't tell people. They get so weird around me once they know. I'm no different than I was ten minutes ago, Dmitri. I'm unemployed. I live in a small flat in London with four other people, because I'm broke. The money the magazine is willing to pay me to interview some hotshot Greek businessman is the only thing that's going to feed me for the next month. So you can stop looking at me like I'm something special, because I'm not. I just have a title that goes along with my name, that's all."

"On the contrary, I think you're very special," he said, adding before she could voice her protest, "But it has nothing to do with your ancestry. I'm confused about one thing, though: if your title is tied to Beck, why aren't you there living the royal life?"

"It's a long story, one involving a man named Kardom. He's trying to convince the Beck powers-that-be that he should be named crown prince over my brother, who actually is the crown prince. Kardom's doing his best to make everyone think that Chris and I aren't worthy of taking on the job of being the new royal family." She wrinkled her nose. "And to be honest, Chris doesn't want any part of it."

"But you do?" he asked, intrigued.

"I wouldn't mind it, if . . ." She hesitated and bit her lower lip once more. He wanted desperately to taste that lip. "Well, it's a moot point. The leadership of Beck doesn't seem to be overly interested in having me take the job."

"It doesn't work like that, does it?" He thought of what he knew about other small principalities, which admittedly wasn't a lot. "If you're the heir, doesn't the government have to recognize you as such?"

"Yes, but they can choose simply to not recognize us and forgo having a royal family. I heard that they did want a royal family, though, for reasons of tourist revenues, but the minister I talked to said that Kardom was deep into the government's back pockets, and was handing out bribes like crazy to be recognized over us. Over me." She drew little circles on the top of the table, not meeting his gaze.

"So, what are you going to do about that?"

"Do about it?" Surprise was evident in the glance she shot him. "About Beck not wanting me, you mean?"

He nodded.

Her back stiffened. "Nothing. There's nothing to be done. Kardom's work is done."

"Who exactly is Kardom?" he couldn't help but ask, not wanting to upset her, but disliking the feeling of confusion.

"He's a cousin. A very distant cousin," she added with emphasis. "He's descended from another line, not the direct line like Chris and me, and thus his claim to the title is much, much weaker. But he's not letting that stop him, the bastard."

"Hmm." He rubbed his chin as he thought. He didn't know why he felt so invested in Thyra's problem, but he accepted the fact that he did, and moved on. "You're going to fight him, naturally."

"There's no naturally about it," she said with a shake of her head. "I told you: Kardom's poisoned the administration against Chris and me. That's why they won't have me. Right now the government is in transition while they work out everything. There are twelve ministers on the council who makes the decisions about this sort of thing, and the woman I talked to, one of the twelve, said that she and another woman were fine with recognizing me as crown princess, but that Kardom had five other ministers who wanted him."

"What about the other five?" Dmitri asked, wondering whom he knew in the north of Europe.

She gave a little shrug. "Undecided either way."

"Still, there's a hope you can change their minds. You'll just have to fight for it."

"You don't understand," she said, shaking her head again. "It's not that easy. I can't make them recognize me."

"No, but you can inform the government that your cousin is spreading lies about you. If you are the heir presumptive—or rather, your brother is—then, assuming they wish to have a royal family for purposes of bringing income to Beck, they will have to recognize you, and not your cousin."

"I've tried to point out that Kardom is lying up one side and down the other, but no one believes me."

"Why?" he asked, studying her face. It didn't make sense that a government that needed an influx of tourist dollars would turn down such a lovely woman to act as figurehead.

A little flush warmed her cheeks as she looked down to rub a finger down the damp curve of the water glass. For a moment, he had a mental image of her fingers doing the same to his penis, and for what seemed like the fiftieth time that day, he hardened. "It's … it's complicated," she said softly.

He wondered for a moment if her revelation that she was a bona fide princess had anything to do with his attraction, but realized it didn't. He'd been aware of her all day, and aware of a subtle sensation of pleasurable anticipation that seemed to hum around them. She was nothing like the women he was normally attracted to, and yet the thought of touching her, and tasting her, increasingly filled his mind.

But all thoughts of indulging in any of the things he'd like to do now had to be dismissed. She was a princess, and despite her claim that the title meant nothing, others would take a different view. He'd be accused of chasing after her for the fame she'd bring to him, to Papaioannou Green. He couldn't risk damaging the company before its first project was even finished.

No, he told himself while the waitress brought their meal. He'd have to let the intriguing Thyra go on her way without any further interaction between them. He'd simply sate the desire he felt for her on Patricia's friend, and his life would remain as calm and even-keeled as he planned it to be.

A voice in the back of his mind laughed and laughed and laughed at that.

THREE

"Are you sure you wouldn't like something else?"

Dmitri looked concerned when I finished my salad, and he still had half a plate of something meaty left. "We could get another order of chicken. Or would you like some of my moussaka?"

"No, thank you, I'm fine," I said, glancing around us. "I'm just a fast eater. It comes from having an older brother who felt it was fair to pillage food from my plate because he had what my mother called a hollow leg. This is such a nice area, but not for claustrophobics, huh?"

He smiled at the change of subject, but let it pass. I was still a bit worried that he was going to treat me differently now that he knew the truth, but I was prepared for it if he did. I'd simply tell him I'd had a nice day, and would leave.

Valentino had finished his bit of poached chicken breast and, after cleaning his face extensively, was now curled up with his front feet tucked under his chest, watching the world go by with an expression that, if not contented, was at least no longer testy.

When Dmitri finished his food, there was a tussle—which I fully expected—over the bill.

"Please let me pay for my lunch," I told him when he

frowned as I tried to give him a few coins that would cover the cost of the salad and chicken breast.

"Why would I do that when you've given me so much pleasure today?" he countered, giving the waitress a couple of bills. She gave him one last seductive look and wiggled her way off. Dmitri rose.

I shoved the money toward his plate. "I appreciate that, but my father taught me that it was very important that I pay my own way. Here."

He shoved the money toward me. "With all due respect to your father teaching you proper manners, I have yet to take a lady to lunch and make her pay for herself. Take your money back."

I stood up, too. Valentino stretched, and moved out from under the table, sliding an expectant glance up to me. "This isn't about manners—it's about who I am. I would never have agreed to have lunch if I knew you were going to be this stubborn and let your male ego get in the way. Just take the money, Dmitri."

His frown got a bit darker. "I am not stubborn, and you haven't done anything to my male ego other than make me appreciate just how reasonable men are. If I take a man to lunch, he allows me to pay without any sort of a fuss. Keep your money." He shoved it back across the table to me.

"Papa always said that it was important that I not let others do things for me when I'm capable of doing them myself," I said with dignity, picking up the money and slapping it in his hand. "I know you aren't trying to use me, because you aren't that sort of person, but I can't remember the number of times Papa warned Chris and me how wrong it was to accept gifts and favors that were offered because we were who we were. I know lots of actors and royals do otherwise, but Papa was adamant about us not allowing ourselves to be swayed by such temptations. I've lived my entire life by those dictates, and I'm not going to go against that now, just because I've dinged your pride a little bit."

He reached across the table and shoved the money into an open edge of my purse. "It's not a matter of my pride. I asked you to lunch. Therefore, it is my right to pay for it. Surely even your father would recognize that gesture, and not attribute to it any ulterior motive."

"I just said that I don't think you have an ulterior motive," I protested, pulling out the money and slapping it down on the table. "But I went into the lunch with the intention of paying for it, and I will. Now, please, take back your money."

"I would sooner light myself on fire than take that damned money," he said in a low growl, turning and walking away.

"I'm going to leave it there until you take it," I said loudly, scooping up Valentino and stalking after him.

"Fine," he called back without even turning to look at me. "The waitress can have it as a second tip. Your Highness."

"That's Your Serene Highness, you ignoramus! And you can't leave that for the waitress—it's way too much for a tip!" I protested. He continued walking. I hesitated a minute; then my frugal self got the better of me, and I ran back to the table and snatched up the money, muttering things under my breath. By the time I caught up with him, he was next to his cousin's car, and looked mad enough to spit.

"Don't you even think of giving me attitude," I told him, shaking the money at him. "I'm the injured party, here. You have no right to look like how I feel!"

He stared at me for a minute, his lovely black eyebrows pulled together; then suddenly they smoothed and he tipped his head back and laughed. To my utter and complete surprise, he took both my arms in his hands and, despite Valentino being clutched to my chest, leaned forward and kissed me.

I was so startled for a moment that I missed the first few seconds of the kiss, and by the time my brain registered the feeling of his mouth on mine, not to mention the heat that pooled in my belly and rippled outward, it was over and he was smiling down at me, his almost dimples making my legs suddenly feel weak.

"Thyra, I can honestly say that you are utterly delightf—"

I lunged before he could finish the sentence, the desire that had burst into instantaneous life consuming my every thought. I grabbed his shoulder with my free hand and stood on my tiptoes to plant my lips on his, nipping his lower lip.

He jerked backward, and I realized with horror what I'd done: I'd just thrown myself at the handsomest man I'd ever seen. My cheeks burned with shame at the look of surprise in his eyes.

"Oh, God," I said, all that desire and need and little spurts of lust smooshed together, making me sick to my stomach. "I didn't just … I'm so sor—"

It was his turn to lunge, and lunge he did. This time Valentino objected, squirming between us when Dmitri's mouth closed on mine, claiming it. I'd read of such things in books, but never had anyone taken over my mouth like they had the right, but Dmitri did just that. He didn't politely nip at my lips asking for permission to come in and say hi; he was just there, making my lips part, his tongue all bossy on them before it marched into my mouth and told my tongue that it was now in charge.

He tasted lemony and hot and spicy, and the sensation of his mouth worked magic on my breasts and belly and lady parts. My nipples went from boring, mundane parts of my breasts to highly sensitized demanding bits of flesh, feeling both needy and heavy, and wanting badly for me to place them into Dmitri's hands.

My stomach fluttered with a thousand little butterflies of excitement, while my lady parts went from quiet business as usual to bring that man's parts to us immediately mode. It was disconcerting, and arousing, and set off all sorts of warning bells in my head.

It was Valentino biting my wrist that had me pulling back, my mouth immediately singing a sad little dirge about the loss of Dmitri's tongue from its premises.

I stared at him, absently noting that those lovely olive-green eyes had gone a bit darker, my brain struggling to make sense of Dmitri kissing me a second time, and failing to parse it in any meaningful way.

"That was … hoo," I said, setting the cat down when he began to struggle in earnest.

"It certainly was hoo, and possibly a wow, as well," Dmitri answered, an odd look on his face. "Are you … you're not seeing anyone, are you?"

"Yes," I said, stupidly, I realized a few seconds later. "Oh, you mean other than you standing there with your really nice lips, and those almost dimples that make me feel all squidgy inside? I'm not dating anyone, if that's what you meant." I gave a little wry smile. "I wouldn't have kissed you if I was. No, don't put him in yet—I think he may need to go potty, and there's a stretch of dirt over there that he might want to use."

He put the cat down, and I walked him around on a tiny bit of dirt until Valentino, his gaze firmly locked on mine, squatted and piddled.

I had a mental argument with myself about what to say once we were back at the car. Valentino was once again strapped into the backseat, at which point he took care of a little personal grooming, leaving me free to watch Dmitri when he got behind the wheel and stared for a moment at nothing, before starting the car and driving us out of the neighborhood, heading to the north.

"I was worried for a few minutes that you might let the thing about who I am affect you, but you don't care, do you?"

He blinked a couple of times like his thoughts had been a million miles away. He slid me a look that I couldn't read. "No. That is, I do, because it's a part of you, but it doesn't make me want to fall on my knees and propose to you, if that's what you were implying."

"Good," I said, relaxing back into my seat. "Because I don't believe in marriage."

I had no trouble reading the startled look he sent me. "For any particular reason?"

"I just don't think it's necessary." I gave a one-shouldered shrug. "I'm not a religious person, so I don't believe in marriage for those reasons, and once you take that element out of it, all that's left is a legal convenience. And these days, you can set things up legally with a partner, so why bother?"

"That's a rather unique opinion," he said in a noncommittal tone of voice.

"Uh-oh. I think I just offended you," I said, trying to assess if he was being so distant with me because of the kiss, or if I'd stepped all over his beliefs. "I'm sorry, if that's the case."

"It's not. As it happens, I'm not any great believer of marriage, either." His cheeks did their thing when he smiled. "Despite my cousins telling me how badly I need to find a woman and settle down so I can be as blissfully happy as they are."

"Bah. You don't need to be married to be happy. I was very happy when I was kissing you, but that doesn't mean I want to marry you."

"Likewise," he said. "That said, I wouldn't mind if you … if we explored that kiss a bit more. In private."

I stared at him with wide eyes before whacking him gently on the arm. "Dmitri! Did you just proposition me?"

His eyes danced with amusement when he glanced at me. "Perhaps. Do you want to be propositioned?"

I thought about that for a bit. "I'd like to kiss you again, so I guess so. Although only if you let me pay you for my lunch."

"No," he said evenly.

"It's important to me," I said, the pleasurable, tingly sense of excitement that seemed to wrap around me fading just a little.

"As it is to me." His jaw, that delicious jaw that made my fingers itch to touch it, tightened, warning me he wasn't teasing.

"Fine," I said, thinking of sliding the money under the seat, but remembering in time that it wasn't his car. I'd just have to get it into his pocket somehow without his knowing. Maybe if I was to kiss him again? I eyed the patterned navy-blue shirt he wore. It had a tiny breast pocket, but I doubted if I could get the money into it without him noticing. That left his jeans, and those seemed to be fairly tight.

"If you continue to stare at my cock like that, I'm going to find the nearest hotel, carry you into it, and proposition the living hell out of you," he said in a conversational tone of voice.

My gaze snapped up from where I was, in fact, wondering if he was just unusually beefy in the genital department, or if he had been aroused by our kiss. "Oh. Sorry, I didn't mean to ogle. Well, all right, I did mean to, but I didn't mean to be so obvious that you'd notice me. I will allow you a reciprocal ogle of my bosomage if you like."

He laughed, and reached over to pat my thigh. "I will take you up on that, although perhaps not while I'm trying to get through this traffic without killing us. Would you like to see Athens from Mount Immitos? The view is one of my favorites."

"Sure, but if it's very far away, we might have to hurry. Maggie doesn't normally get up until one or two in the afternoon, so she won't have missed me this morning, but she'll want me to be back by four or so in order to get ready for the interview."

"It's not far, and I will have you back in time to do whatever you do to get ready for an interview."

"I don't intend to do anything other than let Maggie schmooze the guy, and take notes on his answers. Say what I will about her pretending to be me—and I'm really starting to think of a lot of things to say—she is very charming and always has men eating out of her hands. I don't know why she hasn't caught some rich dude who wants a pretty woman parading around making him look good, but she hasn't. Yet."

"Most men are wary of women who pursue them merely as a means to an end," Dmitri said, driving us through the city and out to the east, where a big hill dominated the horizon. I assumed that was Mount Immitos. "Who is the man you are interviewing?"

I dug through my memory, it not being as good with words as it was with numbers. "Christos … um … Papaioannou?"

The car jerked to the side while Dmitri swore, glancing quickly at me before checking the rearview mirror. "Sorry. Are you all right?"

"Yes." I turned to check on Valentino, but he was happily snoozing in the sun. "Did you get stung or something?"

"No." He was silent for a few minutes until we left the Athens outskirts and started up a winding hill, pulling out at a spot that I assumed was for people who had car trouble. He turned to me then and said, "Christos Papaioannou?"

"Yeah, that's the name. Do you know him?" I thought the odds of that were pretty unlikely, but then, how likely was it that I'd kiss a man I'd met only the day before?

"You could say that. I am Christos Papaioannou. Christos Dmitri Papaioannou, to give my full name."

I felt my jaw drop a little at his words. "But … Christos Papaioannou is an important businessman. He's, like, über-rich. And the editor said that he's being considered for some world's most eligible bachelor list. You're … you're a waiter."

"I am not."

"But … at the party, you were dressed just like a waiter, and you came out of their area. …" Was he yanking my chain? Maybe he was flat out trying to deceive me. I hadn't gotten that feeling at all from him, and yet what he said didn't make sense.

"Your cousin had just spilled wine on my suit jacket. I'd taken it in for the hotel staff to clean, and bumped into you when I returned to the party."

We stared at each other. "So, you're not a poor waiter?" I finally asked.

"No. You were sent to interview me?"

"I guess so." I readjusted my view of him to this new

Dmitri, and instantly felt all shades of uncomfortable and awkward.

A Dmitri who was a workingman, one who had to borrow his cousin's car to take me sightseeing, was one thing. But a Dmitri who was so desirable that an international magazine wanted to put him on a most wanted bachelor list was a whole different matter.

"Well, that solves the problem of getting you back in time for the interview," he said, smiling and pulling out onto the road. "We can do it any time we like. Not that I'm anxious for it. I agreed to do it only because it will be good press for Papaioannou Green, not to be on that damned list. Both my cousins were on it, and they said it was a pain in the ass."

"Papaioannou Green?" I asked, my mind running around in circles. I liked Dmitri, I really liked him. My body wanted to like him a whole lot more, but my body was a notoriously bad judge of men. After all, it had driven me into a relationship with Kardom when I was only twenty, and that had been the biggest mistake of my life.

"It's the name of the company my cousins and I run. I'm in charge of the eco-friendly branch." His voice was filled with pride as he told me about how he wanted to make housing that had limited negative impact on the environment, envisioning entire cities that were reliant upon renewable energies, available to compromised populations who seldom had such things as housing, medical care, and schooling. He told me about the inspiration—a place in Rio de Janeiro that was trying to provide for the poorest citizens—and how he wanted his arm of the family company to lead the way.

With each mile we drove up the side of that mountain, I felt more and more disconnected from him. Oh, he was fascinating, and charming, and clearly was filled with passion for making the world a better place, but he lived in a world that—despite taking a job with a magazine that catered to the world's one percent—I'd only seen depicted on TV. Dmitri's life with its glitz and limos, penthouses, and private jets was as foreign to me as an alien was.

The view of Athens was truly outstanding, I will hand him that. Valentino enjoyed the stroll we took along a dirt path to a vantage point that laid the city out like a relief before us, occasionally pouncing on a stray leaf or pinecone, but almost immediately regaining his dignity. The mountain itself was gorgeous, green and cool compared with the heat of the city below, with firs, oaks, and poplars giving shade over the pathways. People dotted the picnic areas, clearly enjoying a day out into the wilderness, while others hiked over to a monastery and ruined eleventh-century Byzantine church.

Dmitri continued to talk about his projects while we strolled, Valentino maintaining an interested air, condescending to allow other visitors to stop and pet him.

It was a gorgeous spot, in a gorgeous country, with a gorgeous man, and I was utterly miserable.

Stop it, I lectured myself when we sat on the grass to look at the city. You're acting like someone has taken away your piece of candy. Just because Dmitri isn't what you thought he was doesn't change anything.

But it does, I argued, suddenly angry. It changes everything.

"You've been awfully quiet this last half hour. Have I talked your ear off?" Dmitri asked, tickling Valentino with a long piece of grass, which the latter immediately pounced on and wrestled before suddenly sitting up and licking his shoulder just as if the playful episode had never happened.

"It's all ... gone to hell in a handbasket," I told him.

He narrowed his eyes at me. "I suspect you're talking about something other than Papaioannou Green."

"I am." I struggled with my emotions for a few seconds, but with an exasperated click of my tongue said, "I've never been good at this. I hate trying not to say something that I badly want to say. It just makes everything bubble up inside until I feel like I'm going to explode."

"Have I made you feel like you're going to explode?" he asked, the smile fading from his pretty green eyes.

"Yes. No. Partly. Mostly it's me, because I know you're

no different now that you're not a common working person, but your life is so remote from what I know, and that does matter. You live around and with and in a world that's way out of my league."

"Do you know," he said after a minute's thought, leaning back on one arm, turned so he could face me, "if I had said the same thing to you an hour ago, you would have lectured me about treating you differently because you are royalty."

"Of course I wouldn't," I scoffed, then because I try not to lie, even to myself, admitted, "All right, I would have, but the two things truly are not the same."

"I don't think they are, no. You're a princess, an actual living, breathing princess. Descended from kings, I assume."

"Beck was a principality, so they were all princes. Although supposedly there were some kings if you go back far enough, but millions of people can say that. I know, because my mom did a lot on the family genealogy before she died. Besides, I can't help being born into a family that had titles."

"No more so than I could help being born into a family that consisted of two very smart and savvy cousins who taught me everything they knew about real estate development," he parried, and I had to admit he had a point.

"But it's a different world."

"You're absolutely right," he said, to my surprise. "In the normal course of events, you would be so far above me, I wouldn't have the chance to even meet you, let alone show you Athens, and kissing you would probably be a beheadable offense."

"Now you're being pedantic," I said, frowning as I looked back at the city.

"If I am, I apologize. I'm simply trying to point out that you can't help being what you are any more than I can, and we're both still the same people we were an hour ago. Except perhaps now I have a finer appreciation for my desire to kiss you."

I couldn't help a little smile at his words, but I felt like I had to make it clear what bothered me so much. "What might be in the normal course of events, as you put it, doesn't have any relation to reality. Your situation in life is wholly different from mine."

"It's not. I might have made enough money to keep me comfortable and in a job I love, but you're a princess."

"A poor one." I struggled with what I wanted to say, part of my brain marveling that I was so open with things that I normally kept private, but Dmitri was different. I had a feeling that if I could just explain it, he'd understand. "You asked me why I'm not going for the position of crown princess of Beck."

"I did." He tipped his head. "It seems to me that it would be a life worth fighting for."

I swallowed hard, looking off into the distance so I didn't have to see his pretty green eyes. "What I said was true—they don't want me, mostly because of the lies Kardom's been pouring in their ears. But … well, it's also because I'm so … so …"

"Tempting?" he asked.

"No." I ignored the faint note of amusement in his voice. "Poor."

His eyebrows were raised when I glanced over to see how he took that.

"Broke. Flat busted," I added, so the eyebrows would understand. "That's why doing this interview is so important. If it goes well, then the Noblesse people will give me a column, and I will be solvent again. Not rich by any means of the word, but at least I could support myself, and then I can prove to the Beck ministers that I don't want the position so I can suck up all their limited funds, as Kardom claims. I don't want or need them to support me, but getting them to believe that when I've got sixty euros to my name is downright impossible."

"That does seem quite the problem," he agreed in a neutral tone.

I slid another glance his way. "That's why it's just so wrong us being here. Together. Your world is miles away from mine, Dmitri."

"So?" He traced a finger down my arm. "Your ancestry is miles away from mine, and yet, I still want to lay you down on this grass and kiss you until the sun sets."

"That sounds awfully good to me," I said with a sigh, wishing I could shove away all the woes of my world.

"I was hoping you'd say that." He pulled me down until I was lying on my side facing him, my head resting on his arm. He brushed my cheek with a hand, frowned, and asked, "How well can you see without your glasses?"

"I'm farsighted, so I can't read without them, but for the most part, I can see."

"Ah. Good." He gently took off my glasses and set them on a flat bit of rock behind us. "I wouldn't want to smudge them with the amount of kissing I'm about to conduct all over your face."

"Ooh," I said, excitement rippling through me. I let him pull me up against him, my hand tracing out the line of his bicep through his white shirt. "I shouldn't ... I just got through pointing out how different are lives are ... but honestly, at this moment, I don't care. Would you think I was a hussy if I said I wanted to kiss you silly?"

"Not at all. I'd think you were simply as interested in me as I am in you."

Interested, yes, my mind warned, but we had no future together. We were from worlds that were too far apart.

I tried to think of something witty or profound or even halfway sensible to say, but the second his lips touched mine, all thoughts but those of an extremely carnal nature left my mind. Aware that we were in a public place—even if no one was on this particular stretch of mountain slope—we remained on our sides facing each other. I looped Valentino's leash around my foot so I would be able to give Dmitri my full attention, and by the time he was done checking out each and every one of my teeth, I was glad I'd had that foresight, since my thoughts were as scattered as leaves on an autumn wind. "You are really good at this," I said at one point when we both came up for air. "Either you have a natural talent for it, or you've been with some very instructive women."

"Both," he said, his hand, which had been resting on my hip, sliding up to cup the underside of my breast through the fabric of my dress. "But I have to admit that you're inspiring me to new heights."

"Can I … I don't see anyone around us. … Can I touch your chest?"

"Only if you let me touch yours," he said, but before he could do so much as slip his hand inside my bodice, I pushed him onto his back. I hesitated over straddling him, as I wanted to do, but contented myself to simply kneel beside him, tugging the tail of his shirt out of his pants, and sliding my hands underneath. He moaned when I spread my fingers out across his flesh, his eyes closing for a few seconds.

He was warm. Very warm. And the way my fingers moved over the various swells of his chest and belly made the fire that he'd started inside me with his kisses burn even hotter. "I want very badly to tell you that my crotch feels like it's on fire, but since that is only going to sound wrong, I'm going to simply say that your chest feels wonderful. More than wonderful. Your chest hair is baby-bottom soft, too. I'd rip your shirt right off you if there weren't families with small kids here. Oooh, tiny little nipple nubs. Do you like it if I …"

He sat up suddenly when I gave his nipples a gentle squeeze, pushing me backward until he loomed over me. "You, Princess, do not play fair. There's no way I can return that sort of attention to you here, but be warned, the next time you find yourself in a private location, you will pay the price of tormenting my tiny little nipple nubs. But for now, I'll have to content myself with kissing you until you can't think."

I held open my arms. "Yes, please."

By the time a family, complete with grandparents, three small children, and a couple of giggling teenagers, emerged at the top of the slope above us, I was not only thoughtless; I was breathless, witless, and damned close to just ripping Dmitri's clothes right off his delicious body.

I stared at him when he pushed himself off where his chest lay across mine. He said something to the people, all of whom laughed and gave us cheery waves. I panted for a few seconds, desperate to get breath back into my lungs, wondering how I could meet someone the day before and want him so badly now. My body ached, positively ached for him. I wanted him touching me. Tasting me. I wanted him burning inside of me, my intimate muscles almost cramping at the thought.

"If you keep looking at me like that, I'm going to strip you naked and make love to you right here," he said in a low, harsh voice, his hair, which normally lay in tidy curls, now standing on end after I'd had my hands fisted in it.

"Is that supposed to stop me somehow?" I asked, having to clear my throat twice before I could speak.

He stood up, grimacing as he did so. If I'd thought he was looking a bit full in the fly department before, now he was positively bulging. He stood with his back to me, his hands on his hips. I thought for a moment he was admiring the view, but when I got to my feet, fetched my glasses, and separated Valentino from a small green lizard he was tormenting, I realized Dmitri was trying to get himself under control.

And as my desire and lust and need all faded with the return of sanity, I reminded myself that anything but a little flirtation would be foolish.

Why? my inner voice asked. Because you're so proud?

I hushed her and moved over to stand next to Dmitri. "You OK?"

"Yes. Just badly in need of a cold shower." He slid a glance toward me that was so heated, it made me want to throw myself on him. "Or some time alone with you."

"If I told you that my girl parts were yelling at me for not encouraging you to do more than kiss me, would that make you feel any better?"

He laughed, and took my hand in his as we started down the path to the parking area. Secretly, I was thrilled by the fact that he did so, enjoying the way his fingers twined around mine. His hand was warm and strong, and it gave me little girlish skitters of excitement that heightened what was already arousal-tinged anticipation. "No, but you can tell your girl parts I feel the same way. I don't suppose you'd care to stop by my apartment before I return you to your hotel? And yes, that was another proposition."

I sighed. "I wish I could, but I'd better get back. Maggie is bound to be up, and she'll want me there so she can go over the questions to be asked. Just so you know, she fully intends to twist you around her little finger at the interview."

"She can try, but she won't succeed. Not when there's a pretty journalist taking notes who I'd rather get alone."

"Pretty," I said in a scoffing tone, flattered nonetheless. I wanted to protest the word, but my mother had taught me that it was rude to dispute a compliment, so I simply murmured a thank-you, and let the subject drop.

On the drive back to my hotel, Dmitri offered to pick up Maggie and take us to his cousin's apartment, where he had arranged to have the interview. "You'll like Iakovos and Harry," he said, his attention on the rush hour traffic. "Harry's American, and is very outspoken. You remind me of her, or at least, your way of straightforward speaking does."

"Oh, lord, another person whose brain doesn't vet things before she says them," I said with a faux moan. "And thank you for the offer, but I think it would be better if Maggie doesn't know we spent the day together."

"Oh?" He risked a quick, curious glance at me before returning his attention to the road. "Why?"

I couldn't put the feeling into words, not even to myself. "It's just a vague worry that I have," I said slowly. "Last night she was ... different. If she thought I'd broken her cover, she might refuse to do her bit, and then I'd lose the job. And I really need this column, Dmitri."

"I'm more than happy to be interviewed by you without her," he said.

"Yes, but it's not just you. The editor was thrilled to have a princess writing for them, and said that if I did well with this interview, the column would be a go. And I really, really need that."

He said nothing, but his jaw tensed, and I wondered if I'd somehow insulted him by reminding him that I was doing the interview for the money. "Not that I wouldn't love to interview you anyway," I added, the words sounding lame even to me.

He didn't respond to that, just asked me for the hotel address, and after a moment's struggle with my pride, I gave it to him. "It's a budget place, but very clean inside," I said, feeling like the worst type of reverse snob.

"Is that why you didn't want me to pick you up?" he asked, glancing at me, since we were stopped at a light.

I gave another one-shouldered shrug. "Maggie is mortified at being there. I figured even a waiter would think it was a dump."

"I suspect that attitude also has something to do with why you wouldn't let me take you to the Acropolis."

"The entrance fee is like ten euros. Ten euros, Dmitri! That's outrageous," I said, with a little righteous sniff.

"And you don't have ten euros?" he asked, his voice carefully neutral.

"Of course I have ten euros," I said, thinning my lips at him, although he didn't see it since he was driving again. "I have much more than ten euros. I just simply chose not to spend my many-more-than-ten euros on things like entrance fees."

"My intention was to treat you."

"Are we back to this? I'm sure all the other women you hang out with don't have a problem with letting you pay for things, but I was taught differently."

He burst into loud laughter that I would have found insulting except it rolled over me, calling forth the desire to join him in such an expression of pure joy. "I didn't mean to start that argument again, Thyra. I understand that you feel your point is valid, just as I feel mine is. No, you don't have to explain it again. I'll just say that you are very much going to like Harry. And Kiera, for that matter, although I don't think Theo is in town. Theo is Iakovos's brother, and Kiera is his wife. They've only been married for a year, but Kiera and Harry both give my cousins hell when they try to give them anything valuable."

"Good for them," I said with approval. "It's nice to know that other women have standards, too."

He gave a little shake of his head. "I believe, in interest of harmony, and the hope that you'll let me take you to dinner after the interview—and yes, I mean I will pay for your dinner without any unseemly wrangling over the check—I will let the subject drop."

"I guess if you're loaded, then I don't need to offer you gas money for driving me around in your cousin's car—hey! I didn't say I would let you buy me dinner."

"Dammit," he swore under his breath. "And now I find myself in an embarrassing situation."

"You do need gas money?"

"No." His expression was grim. "I promised to meet a friend of a friend for drinks at the marina later, after the interview."

"Gotcha. Maybe we could do dinner another time." I tried to keep my voice as free from disappointment as possible. He had a date. Of course he did; he was gorgeous, rich, and probably going to end up on that world's most adorable bachelor list. "For the record, I would have let you buy me dinner without even looking at the prices on the menu. Not only that, I would have had a glass of wine, and we both know how restaurants charge up the ying-yang for that."

"How am I supposed to resist such an rare event as that? I will simply arrange to have drinks with Patricia's friend another time." He sounded annoyed and determined at the same time.

"Don't cancel on my account," I said quickly, reminding myself that I'd just made a big deal about him living in a different world from me, and I couldn't be disappointed to find it was true. "I'll have Maggie to deal with anyway."

"Do you have the address?" was all he said five minutes later when he double-parked in front of the narrow hotel entrance door, helping me down out of the Jeep before lifting out Valentino.

"Of your cousin's house?" I recited the address that I'd memorized.

"That's it. It's an apartment building. Tell the concierge you want the penthouse. I'll see you in two hours, then."

"Thank you for lunch even though I really would like to pay for it. And for taking us around everywhere," I said politely, back to feeling awkward and gawky and highly, highly desirous of kissing him again and again and again.

"It was my pleasure." He started to turn away, then made an annoyed noise and, grabbing me by my free arm, pulled me sideways up to his chest, his mouth as hot as I remembered as he gave me a fast, hard kiss. "That was just in case you were thinking I'd rather have drinks with someone else than dinner with you."

He was gone before I could gather up my wits. "That man," I told Valentino when I led him inside the hotel and up the stairs to my room, "has magical lips that make my brain stop working when they touch me. Hoobaby. It's a good thing we aren't having dinner with him, because I'd spend the whole time thinking about touching him all over."

"Who are you thinking about touching all over?" a voice asked me when I closed the door to my room on the last of my words.

I stared in stark surprise at the man who stood at the window, his hands clasped behind his back, my skin prickling unpleasantly at the possessive way his gray-eyed gaze crawled over me.

Kardom was here? In Greece? In my room?

I slumped against the door. Now what the hell was I going to do?

FOUR

"Juliane, you look well."

Kardom was the only person who called me by my first name. I swore he did it just to annoy me.

"And you look like the piece of shit that I know you are," I said in a polite voice that belied the actual words, then picked up Valentino and stormed into Maggie's room. She was standing before her tiny mirror, applying eyeliner and mascara. "Why the hell did you let that rat bastard into my room?"

"Kardom?" She eyed me in the mirror. "He asked to wait for you. I figured you wouldn't mind."

"You figured wrong. Maggie, you know full well what he's been doing to me—the lies he's been spreading!"

"I know he's been asking to marry you. Why is that so bad?"

I waved that away. "He's lying to the Beck ministers about Chris and me. Mostly me, because Chris has no interest in taking up the crown prince duties."

"You say that, but I've never actually seen any proof that you're being slandered," she said, turning back to her reflection and dabbing at an errant eyelash. "All I see is a very devoted man who has bent over backward trying to get you to marry him."

"Gah!" I said, filled with frustration. How could she not see what was so obvious? "He's not devoted. Not to me, anyway. He wants to be recognized by Beck so he can exploit them for every cent he can wring out of them."

She waggled a hand. "Well, if it comes to that, why shouldn't he want to make money off the country that did him wrong?"

"He was not done wrong. My great-grandfather Christian was done wrong when a group of leaders of other countries booted him out of his own homeland and handed it over to Germany. Kardom is not descended from Great-grandpa Christian."

"No, but I am descended from Christian's younger brother Friederich," Kardom said, strolling into the room. Just his presence made me twitchy, as if I'd been covered in itching powder.

"Via an illegitimate son," I snapped. Normally, I wouldn't give a hoot about whether someone's parents were married, but I made an exception for Kardom. "One who, by laws of cognatic succession, could never inherit the throne, even if Great-grandpa Christian didn't have sons. Which he did."

"I'm fully cognizant of the details of our family tree," Kardom said calmly, gliding toward me in that creepy way he had. He was a little taller than Dmitri, but very thin, and had pale white hands that made my skin crawl just thinking of them touching me. "I have spent a good deal of money researching it."

"And a whole lot more trying to bribe parish priests to alter their records. Oh, yes, I know about that. Didn't I tell you? One of the priests who you tried to pay to modify the registry listing your great-grandfather's birth from illegitimate to legitimate contacted Chris. He was very appreciative of the fact that the priest refused to do so, and told him that he was glad that a group of German genealogists had digitized the records a few years before. Just so that if anything happened to the original records, there were copies. Safe. And undoctored."

Kardom stiffened with anger, and for a moment, I marveled that I had ever allowed him to seduce me. My only excuse was that I was young, stupid, and flattered that a sophisticated man ten years older than me was interested in me romantically.

Only he wasn't, of course.

"That was a small misunderstanding, nothing more. I was attempting to get a copy of my great-grandfather's birth records to present to the Council of Beck in order to prove my heredity. I don't know why you insist on being so antagonistic toward me, Juliane. I want only what is best for you and your brother. When you marry me, the council will not be able to resist the joining of the two royal lines into one, and will be happy to accede to your brother's request to be passed over in favor of you. You will be a rich woman."

"Rich? From what source? Certainly not Beck. Even if I did marry you—and I am not going to, under any circumstances—I wouldn't take money from them. And I certainly wouldn't sit around and watch while Beck was raped of every natural resource you could get your hands on."

"The use of resources would naturally fall to the government to decide," he said with an unctuous smile. "Although we will be the royal family, we will likely have limited powers to influence the government. To start, at least. Later … well, that's best left for another discussion."

I wanted to slap him, but instead clutched Valentino tight until he wiggled to be free. I set him down, keeping a tight hold on his leash. I didn't trust Kardom further than I could spit. "I don't have the slightest doubt that you will bribe and threaten and do God knows what until you convince the government to exploit anything and everything, just like you are bribing and threatening them to believe I'm a soulless wretch who just wants to be supported by the money they can ill afford to spend. You may not give a damn about the people of Beck, but I do. They've suffered a lot, Kardom, and I will not do anything that will hurt them."

"You will naturally do as you please after we are married," he said, his eyes reminding me of those of a snake. A particularly loathsome and heartless snake. One that ate baby bunnies.

"I really don't like you," I couldn't help but tell him.

He brushed something off the sleeve of his suit. Kardom always wore suits, no matter how hot it was, or what sort of environment he was in. Unreasonably, that irritated me almost as much as his repeated attempts to get me to marry him. What an insufferable, stuck-up prig. "As to that, you do not top my list of favorite people, but we do not need to view each other with favor in order to have a successful marriage. You will wed me, ensuring that I am recognized by the government of Beck, and I will naturally disprove all those pesky rumors going around about your mercenary intentions with regards to their budget. In addition, I will pay you a generous allowance every year that you remain married to me, enough for you to support as many bleeding-heart causes as you like."

"You truly are a pus-filled boil on the buttocks of the world," I told him, picking up Valentino, who was snuffling around his shoes. "No, kitty, you don't want to smell him. You don't know where he's been. You might get some horrible disease."

"Thyra!" Maggie gasped, shocked. She'd been quiet, watching us with a wary look, but she came over and put a hand on my arm. "You don't have to be rude. Your cousin is just trying to do right by you."

"He's doing nothing of the sort." I took a deep breath and turned to face Kardom, hoping he could see the conviction in my eyes. "This is the last time I'm going to say this, so listen up: There is nothing on this good, green earth that would convince me to marry you. No amount of money, no campaigns to make Beck believe the worst of me, no attempts to browbeat me, nothing. I will not marry you. Not now, not ever. If you continue to pester me, I will lodge a complaint with the police and take out a restraining order against you. I hope that's quite clear."

And with that, I spun around on my heel and stalked through the connecting door, slamming it behind me. I hated to leave Maggie to deal with Kardom, but I had reached the end of my patience with him. I set the cat on my bed and sat next to him, stroking him and rubbing his ears. Despite my brave words, I was shaking with the strain of having to deal with Kardom yet again.

The thought flitted through my head that I could borrow Maggie's phone and call Dmitri. Just hearing his voice would make me feel better. … "No," I told Valentino, giving a shake of my head when I got to my feet to fetch my gold lace dress. "I'm not his problem. He's going on a date later, and despite all that kissing and sexy talk about going to bed, I think he finally understood that we just aren't on the same playing field. Which is a damned shame, because just thinking about him makes me feel like I'm sixteen and in love for the first time—"

"Who makes you feel sixteen?" Maggie asked, coming through the connecting door. I swore at myself for forgetting to lock it.

"A man named Dmitri," I said. "I met him yesterday."

"At the party?" she asked, giving me a look I had a hard time reading.

"Yes." I hesitated, wanting to tell her the truth, but feeling that something was off ever since we had arrived. Instead, I said carefully, "He came out of the door the waiters use and knocked me into the wall. We drove around today and looked at the gardens and things."

"Oh." She lost interest at the word "waiter."

I couldn't help but wonder if her head had been turned by the attention she'd received at the party, and immediately felt another twinge of guilt. She'd simply done as we'd agreed and pretended to be me. Why did it matter if she enjoyed it so much?

"Did he leave?" I asked, telling the sense of unease that gripped me it was overreacting.

"Prince Friederich? Yes."

"Kardom is not a prince. Don't pander to his massive ego."

She rolled her eyes. "I think he's nice. He's certainly very elegant, and he dresses fabulously. Did you see his shoes? They were Italian."

"Probably made from the skins of baby seals," I snapped, shucking my clothing in order to pull on my dress.

"Now you're just being silly. No, don't lecture me; I'm not in the mood for it." She went over to the mirror and patted the French twist that emphasized her delicate bone structure. "Let's go over tonight so we both know what to do. And don't forget to introduce me properly. I know you don't like to have your title mentioned, but rich people love royalty almost as much as they do other rich people."

I listened to her chatter with half my attention, shaking out a little more kibble for Valentino, hesitating between leaving him behind and taking him with me. He didn't seem to mind going places at all, and although I knew he would probably be fine curled up on my bed, I decided I'd take him. I worried about him grieving the loss of his family, and felt stimulation would keep his mind occupied.

I finished dressing, and brushed my hair while I tried to think about what to do with it. It was down to my waist, nice enough except for the fact that it refused to curl no matter how many products I used with innumerable curling irons and hot rollers. I made a face at myself in the mirror; then with a glance at Maggie (who was demonstrating the proper way to make a curtsy), I quickly braided my hair and wound it into a crown on top of my head.

"You're not taking that thing with you," she asked when I scooped the offerings Valentino had just left in the litter box, then clipped the leash to his harness.

"I am. I don't want him feeling sad all by himself, and I don't know how long we'll be gone."

"But there's a party I want us to go to after the interview! You can't take a cat to a party."

"What party?" I asked, tidying up my room.

"One of the men I met last night invited us. It's going to be on a yacht, and he said only a few very select people will be invited. We can't miss that! You'll have to leave the cat here."

I made a face at myself in the mirror after checking my appearance one last time. "You know how I am about parties—you go if you want to, but I'd rather chill here, or maybe take a walking tour around the city."

"You really are the limit, do you know that?" she answered, shaking her head. "Even if you don't want to go to the party with me, it's going to look extremely unprofessional if you bring a cat with you to an important business meeting."

"We're going to interview a man in someone's apartment. That's hardly a business meeting," I said calmly. "Besides, Valentino likes to go places. Look, he's already at the door."

Maggie heaved a put-upon sigh. "Where we are going to meet the elitist of the elite. I heard a lot about this Christos Papaioannou last night, and everyone said he was super rich, and about to launch some company that is going to revolutionize something. Buildings, I think. Also, he's hot. Like, really hot, the sort of hot that has women ripping off their underwear and writing their phone numbers on them."

I pursed my lips, wondering how many women had given Dmitri their underwear, and more, why I was so furious at the thought of that. "What sort of woman would be so low-class as to write her number on her underwear?"

"It happens," she answered with a shrug, waggling her butt at me as she marched to the door. "I'm not wearing any, so I certainly won't be doing so."

"For the love of Pete, Maggie, what would your mother say if she knew you were going out commando?" I asked, following with Valentino marching alongside me, his tail up, and his expression one of reserved interest. There was something about his dignified manner that made me giggle to myself. Once we were outside, I added, "Hang on, I'm going to let Valentino have a few minutes at the base of this tree, just in case he wants to scratch around and pee."

"He just pooped!" Maggie protested. "I saw you cleaning it out of the box!"

"Yes, but he didn't pee. It won't take but a few minutes."

"For heaven's sake! I do not know you," Maggie said, ire dripping off every word. "I suppose you're going to make me walk all the way to this appointment, too?"

"No, it's too far to walk. Oh, good kitty, Valentino. See? He seems to like free-range dirt as opposed to his box."

Maggie turned her back when I helped Valentino kick a bit of dirt over where he'd peed.

"If we aren't walking, I assume we're taking a taxi? Or did you call for an Uber car?"

"Neither." I smiled and gestured down the road. "We're taking the underground. There's a station only two blocks away from the apartment where we're going. Shall we?"

Maggie had many things to say to me about my parsimonious ways, but I let most of it wash over me. I was too busy feeling excited about seeing Dmitri again, even if I would have to pretend to be Maggie's lackey. What was it about the man that put me in such a state? I mused when we entered a stylish block of apartments. A reception desk sat squarely in the middle of the room, manned by an elegant woman in a dark blue power suit.

A part of me, a tiny little part of me, wondered if Dmitri's apartment building was as nice as this one, but immediately I dismissed the thought. It didn't matter. He was out of my league, and we both knew it.

"Thyra," Maggie said in a terse voice, gesturing abruptly to me. She was standing in front of the concierge, who I assumed was waiting for us to announce ourselves, and I stared at her for a few seconds, wondering why Maggie wasn't giving the woman our names, but after a very pointed look, I realized that she was waiting for me to do the honors. I fought back the urge to tell her that she was irritating, if not downright obnoxious.

Instead, I slapped a smile on my face, and strolled over to the woman who was clearly waiting for Maggie to speak. "Hello. Her Serene Highness Princess Juliane of Sonderburg-Beck is here to see Mr. Christos Papaioannou."

"Ah, indeed." The woman looked with new respect at Maggie, who gave a cool smile. "You are expected in Mr. Papaioannou's penthouse … er … Your Highness."

"Oh, this is going to be such a long interview," I told Valentino when I bent down to pick him up before entering the elevator with Maggie. He smelled my chin. I took that as a sign of agreement.

A small woman with salt-and-pepper hair opened the door to the apartment. We didn't have to knock, leaving me to assume the concierge had called to tell her that we were on our way up.

"Hello," Maggie said graciously to the woman who held the door open for us, then cast an expectant glance at me.

I stared stonily back at her, hoping she'd realize that I would draw the line at introducing her to what was probably a housekeeper. She glared at me.

I lifted my chin.

"You'd better not ruin this," she whispered to me, then beamed at the woman and, with her head held high, did her exaggerated hip-walk into the room.

I pushed aside the hurt caused by her comment. She was no doubt just a bit salty because she didn't want to stop playing princess, and knew the charade would be over once the interview was done.

"Hi," I told the woman, setting down Valentino and holding out a hand. She shook it gravely, her eyebrows raised at the cat. "My name is Thyra."

"I am Mrs. Avrabos," the woman said, her gaze still on the cat, who eyed her in return. After a moment's thought, he head bonked her ankle, and strolled in.

"Sorry about the head bonk. I hope you're not allergic to cats. He's very chill, and seems to have exceptionally nice manners. Much nicer manners than some people I could name, but I suppose that's really more than you wanted to know. Is Dmitri here?"

"Dmitri?" Her eyebrows rose even higher as she gave me a quick once-over. "Not yet, no, but Kyrie Papaioannou is home."

"OK." I took a deep breath. I disliked meeting new people as a rule, more or less turning into a big tongue-tied oaf when called upon to interact with people who were powerful. And rich. And, according to Dmitri, really good-looking. "I can do this. It's just people. The worst they can do is yell at me."

Mrs. Avrabos gave me a long look, then gestured behind me. "They are waiting for you on the patio. You will go, yes?"

"Yes," I said with another deep breath, then turned and walked through a spacious living room filled with blue-and-green furniture, inviting-looking couches and chairs, with the sort of thick carpeting that you sink into when you walk on it. I made a mental note that, at all cost, I would keep Valentino off the carpet, and passed through a bank of wide glass doors that had been thrown open to a patio area, which—since this was a penthouse—had a mind-blowing view of Athens.

"—and of course, we are delighted to be in such a lovely city," Maggie was saying when I approached where she stood facing a tall woman who was heavily pregnant. "Ah, here is my assistant. Thyra will be happy to do the honors, since most people like to be formally presented to me."

She steadfastly ignored my attempts to catch her gaze. I looked past her to the woman, studying her to see if Dmitri had told her the truth about me. The woman held her mouth closed tightly, like she was biting her lip, but her eyes brimmed with humor.

Dammit, he'd told her who I was.

"Thyra!" Maggie whispered with added emphasis, her eyes filled with meaning. I opened my mouth to just say it, say the words she wanted, but irritating though she was, I didn't want her making a fool of herself. And she'd be doing just that.

"THYRA!" This time, the word was accompanied by a pinch on my arm.

"I'm sorry," I started to say, planning on adding, "I don't want you to be embarrassed," but at that moment, a man strolled out of the apartment onto the rooftop patio. I assumed he was Dmitri's cousin despite not having even the slightest resemblance, but then, I mused, Maggie and I didn't look at all alike.

This man was tall, probably a good six inches taller than Dmitri, with dark hair and eyes, and although he was nice to look at, I didn't think he held a candle to Dmitri. He didn't have green eyes, or almost dimples, or curly hair, and most of all, his gaze was coolly impersonal when it swept over first Maggie, then me.

"Thyra—" Maggie said warningly before blasting the man with a smile when he came to a stop next to the pregnant woman, his arm sliding around her.

"I see the journalist has arrived," the man said, giving Maggie a quick nod before giving me a slight bow. "It is our honor to meet you, Your Serene Highness."

"What?" Maggie asked, disbelief overflowing the word. She stared first at the man, then turned to me, her brows pulling together. "What is going on? Do you know these people?"

"No, I've never met them before," I said softly, then held out my hand to shake theirs. "My name is Thyra. I don't use the title, but it is a pleasure to meet you. I assume you are Iakovos and Harry Papaioannou?"

"That's us," the woman said, smiling, her hands resting on her belly. "We really are pleased to meet you. Dmitri swore to me that I'd enjoy talking to you. Oh, hello there! What an adorable cat. We just got a pair of chocolate Labs for our kids, but they've been yammering for us to rescue a few of the village cats. Goodness, your kitty wears a harness just like a little dog. How very interesting. It's very well behaved, not at all like ours. The puppies, that is, not the children. Those are hellions. You must be Thyra's cousin Maggie, who kindly took over dealing with people so she can be shy and introverted."

I shot Harry a grateful glance before introducing Maggie to them.

Maggie, whose eyes were still narrowed, her mouth held tightly, managed to gather herself together enough to greet the couple. "I didn't realize we were going to tell everyone who we were," she said with a pointed look at me.

I kept my own expression as placid as was possible. "I didn't intend on doing that; it just turned out that the man I met last night is also the man I was sent here to interview."

The look in her eyes promised a discussion in the very near future, but regardless, she turned back to accept a glass of wine that Iakovos offered her, taking a seat next to Harry on a couch that overlooked an infinity pool. Beyond it, the sounds of the city rose, the night air still bearing the warmth of the day, but with slightly cooler breezes picking up to drift past us.

"I'm afraid Dmitri is held up by traffic," Iakovos said, holding a chair for me. I took it, feeling uncomfortable, unsure if he was just naturally polite, or if he was being overly so because of what Dmitri had told him. "But he should be here shortly."

"I've never met a real princess before," Harry said, studying me. "I thought you guys lived in Monaco, and hung out on yachts and in casinos, and villas in the Caribbean."

I wrinkled my nose. "I'm afraid I don't much look like one, I've never been to Monaco, and I probably can't even spell Caribbean, let alone have visited it."

"I've been to the Bahamas," Maggie said. "It's very nice. I liked it."

She shot me a quick glance as if daring me to deny it.

"Maggie has seen a lot more of the world than I have," I said in an attempt to placate her. "That's one reason why we thought the idea of having her pretend to be me was the answer to my problem—she's so much more what people think of when they think royalty."

She looked pleased, and took a big swig of the wine.

"I don't know," Harry said slowly, her gaze going from me to Maggie. "No disrespect intended, of course, Maggie, but people come in all shapes and sizes, so why shouldn't princesses?"

There wasn't much I could say to that, even if I wasn't feeling as if everyone was staring at me, judging me for not being at all what a real princess should be, so I just smiled, and wished that Dmitri would arrive.

I didn't know why that thought shocked me so much, but it did until I realized that I wanted him there because his presence offered me a sense of comfort that was lacking even with Maggie. Iakovos and Harry carried on a polite, if uninspiring, conversation with Maggie while I tried to tell myself that I would not, under any circumstance, allow myself to fall for Dmitri. We had no future together, absolutely none, and there was no sense in pretending otherwise.

I really hate it when I'm pragmatic.

FIVE

Dmitri heaved a sigh of relief when he finally—after two delays due to accidents, and one caused by construction—strolled into Iakovos's apartment, his eyes immediately going to the patio, where he could see Thyra sitting in a chair that was at a distance from the three other people present. He wasn't an expert on psychology, but he'd done enough wining and dining of potential clients to be fairly conversant with body language, and the way Thyra was sitting with her arms wrapped around herself, her back pressed firmly against the chair, her head angled slightly away from the others, told him everything he needed to know about how well things were going.

She was clearly miserable.

The big orange cat with her stood up and strolled over to greet him, nudging his leg with his head until, absently, Dmitri scooped him up and held him while he greeted everyone. "My apologies for being late, but traffic is its usual horrendous nightmare. Harry, you look as radiant as ever."

"You only say I'm radiant when I'm pregnant," she said, giving him a warm smile nonetheless. "It's a good thing we have so many kids, or I'd never hear it."

"Jake," he said, giving his cousin a swift hug, only slightly impeded by the cat.

He felt the curious look Thyra cast at him. She was on her feet now, too, and he turned to explain, "Iakovos is Greek for Jacob. He hates the name, so of course, his brother and I use it whenever we can."

"You can be replaced, you know," Iakovos said, sitting back down next to Harry, his arm draped over her shoulders. "You're not as indispensable as you think you are."

"I'm not your assistant any longer," Dmitri answered with a grin. "You made me a full partner, and only an act of God is going to get me out of your hair now. Thyra, you look charming."

The look she gave him was full of mingled wariness and pleasure. It was an odd combination, but that seemed about par for this woman who was filled with contradictions. "It's nice to see you again. This is my cousin Maggie."

"Ah, is it?" he asked, glancing quickly from Thyra to Harry.

"It's my fault," the latter admitted, making a vague gesture toward Maggie. "Blame the pregnancy hormones."

"It's a pleasure to meet you, Maggie. Thyra has told me how grateful she was that you offered to help her," Dmitri said, expending some charm on the woman who clearly had ruffled feathers. He lifted her hand and gave it a quick peck. She smiled, fluttering her lashes a little.

Thyra gazed at him with amazement chased quickly by approval, which almost immediately melted into a little frown when she glanced at Maggie.

"I hope you all can stay long enough for us to have some dinner," Harry said when Iakovos gave him a glass of whiskey. "Iakovos has to take an important videoconference call at nine, but I heard of a great new Italian restaurant in town, and we can bring him back a doggie bag."

"California?" Dmitri asked his cousin.

"Reynolds, yes. He's finally willing to talk about that piece of land in Fiji."

"Ah, that's good news. Unfortunately, Harry, I'm afraid you can't count on me for dinner." Dmitri tried to keep the regret out of his voice. "I have … I'm meeting someone later for drinks."

Harry narrowed her eyes on him. "You've got a date? Tonight?"

"With Thyra?" Maggie asked, her voice curiously flat.

"Alas, no. One of Iakovos's friends has asked me to meet an old friend of hers."

"You're talking about Patricia, aren't you?" Harry asked, her nostrils flaring. "She isn't Yacky's friend. She's a work associate. A really annoying one."

"Yacky?" he heard Thyra say under her breath.

"It's Harry's equivalent to 'Jake,'" Dmitri explained to her. "And when he wants to retaliate, he calls her by her proper name, which is Eglantine."

Harry glared at Iakovos, who kissed the tip of her nose before asking, "Will the interview take long? Harry will need to eat soon, and if I don't ensure she's fed frequently, she threatens to eat the most unhealthy foods she can find in an attempt to hurry the labor."

"Oh, certainly," Thyra said, glancing worriedly at Harry. Dmitri wanted to reassure her that Iakovos was joking, but to be honest, he wanted the damned interview over with as soon as possible, as well. If there was enough time, he fully intended on talking Thyra into having dinner with him. "Let's see, I have some notes the editor sent me. … Oh, lord, that's right."

He raised his eyebrows at the apologetic look she sent him. She readjusted the cat, who had jumped into her lap as soon as Dmitri set him down, and, taking a deep breath, said so quickly the words almost ran together, "The editor would like to know what sort of things you're looking for in a woman, what turns you on, what are deal breakers, and what your ideal woman looks like."

"Wow," Harry said, looking at Iakovos. "Is that the *Tiger Beat* sort of questions they asked you?"

"*Tiger Beat*?" he asked, frowning.

"It was a teenybopper magazine in the seventies. Think David Cassidy and the Bay City Rollers."

"Ah. Yes, unfortunately, I recall being asked similar questions." He looked at Dmitri. "I didn't answer them."

Dmitri was about to say he would decline to answer them, as well, but one look at Thyra, her head bent as she stared down at a tiny notebook, a pen in her hand poised to write, reminded him that what he thought of as a silly, ridiculous waste of time was a serious matter to her. She was counting on the money from the interview.

A sudden spurt of rage at the idea that she had to demean herself in such a manner just to earn a living took him by surprise. He wanted to call up her brother and ask him why the hell he wasn't doing something to help his sister; then he wanted to yell at the editor for the repugnant idea of trading on Thyra's title just to sell a few magazines.

Instead of doing any of that, he answered almost as quickly as she had spoken, "I want a woman who is honest, above all, but who also has a good sense of humor, and an appreciation of others. Turn-ons are what I just mentioned—honesty and humor. I like a woman to be real, not what she thinks others want her to be. Turnoffs are people who aren't comfortable with themselves." He realized the second the words left his mouth that Thyra had admitted she was socially awkward and an introvert, and quickly added, "That is, I dislike people who try to change themselves to be something they aren't. Deal breakers are too many to list, and my ideal woman …"

She slid him a glance from the corner of her eye. He wanted badly to say he liked brunettes with glasses, and curves that made his mouth water to taste them, but he confined himself to saying simply, "I have no specifics with regards to ethnicity, body type, or hair color."

Iakovos shot him a quick look, one eyebrow raised, before his gaze moved to Thyra in lengthy speculation.

"I know about your company, but perhaps you could tell me what it is you find so intriguing about making buildings that work with the environment instead of against it?" Thyra's golden gaze was solemn on his, and he knew that was one of her questions, not a prepackaged mindless query submitted by the editor.

"We only have one planet," he said slowly, leaning forward to stroke the cat's head. "And while Iakovos has always been careful that any construction he puts up is as environmentally friendly as possible, I wanted to go a step further. I think it's important that people who don't have much are able to live in a home that doesn't cost them everything they earn just to keep it up. I want to see self-sufficient communities where even the poorest people have a decent home, access to health care and schools, and can raise their families with hope, instead of the prayer of mere survival."

"That's quite the populist philosophy, isn't it?" Maggie asked, her voice sweet, but it grated on Dmitri nonetheless.

"Maggie!" Thyra said, staring at her cousin in obvious horror. "That's rude."

"It's also unfair," she answered.

"Unfair how?" Iakovos asked, frowning.

"You're talking about third world countries, aren't you?" Maggie asked Dmitri.

"Some, yes, but we have intentions of building in other areas, as well—"

"Right, so all the people who have lived for generations as rice farmers or cattle herders or whatever are to have all the advantages, but what about us? What about those of us who can't catch a break? Don't we deserve a nice house, and someone to take care of us when we're sick, and that sort of thing?"

"Maggie!" Thyra's glare was truly a thing of beauty to behold, but Dmitri wasn't about to let her fight his battle. He opened his mouth to set her cousin straight, but he hadn't counted on just how contrary Thyra could be. She got to her feet and stood over her cousin, saying hurriedly, "You are speaking of underprivileged people who have severely limited opportunities, not people who live in countries where there are a variety of options for self-support. Dmitri is talking about people whose own governments treat them as refuse, disposable and not even human. For you to compare their plight to your own is out of line."

Maggie rose, as well. "Pfft. You can spew that liberal crap to Kardom, but it's bull, and you know it. The second the Beck government gives you the nod, you'll be living in a palace, with lots of clothes and jewels and cars, and royalty and celebrities falling over themselves to meet you. So you can pretend you're some sort of Sister Teresa to everyone else, but it doesn't fool me. I know why you really want Beck to recognize you, and it has nothing to do with helping them."

"First of all, it's Mother Teresa, and second, no, I do not view Beck as a means to an end," Thyra answered, her face flushed but her eyes stricken. "My family owes them our dedication, and if Chris is unable to fulfill that duty, then I will."

Dmitri rescued the notebook from where the cat—clearly put out when Thyra leaped to her feet—was swatting at it.

"I told Kardom he was crazy for even trying to make you see reason." Maggie's lip curled when she glanced over to Dmitri. "I can see your boyfriend doesn't see anything wrong with the way you think, so I'm going to take myself off to that party I mentioned. The very exclusive one, where people aren't ashamed to be capitalists."

"Maggie, please—" Thyra started to say, obviously trying to placate her cousin, but the other woman would have none of it.

"Good night," she said stiffly to Harry and Iakovos. "It was a pleasure to meet you."

Dmitri wondered with amusement if he was supposed to be wounded by her obvious cut, but rose politely when she hurried off without so much as a backward look at any of them.

Thyra stood staring at the ground for a few seconds before she made an apologetic gesture at Iakovos and Harry. "I'm mortified by the things my cousin said, and really sorry you had to see that. Things have been a bit dicey between us the last day, and I kind of snapped. I'm very sorry that I lost my temper in front of you."

"I'm not sorry in the least," Harry said, giving Thyra a warm smile. "It was most excellently done. I couldn't have ranted better."

"Oh, God, I did rant, didn't I?" Thyra said, sitting down suddenly, one hand over her eyes. "In front of everyone."

"I forbid you to be embarrassed," Dmitri told her, giving her shoulder a little squeeze until she uncovered her face and looked up at him. He smiled down into her eyes, the gold of them now dulled. He didn't like to see them so unhappy. He much preferred it when her eyes were dancing with humor and pleasure. "You did nothing wrong, and Harry and Jake don't think the worse of you."

"I made a scene," she said in an almost whisper.

"A righteous one. I enjoyed it greatly."

"I hope I'm not the only one who is curious about who this Kardom is, and what the bit about the palace and celebrities are all about," Harry said.

"I suppose I owe you an explanation after Maggie acted so rudely," Thyra said, taking the notebook Dmitri handed her. "Kardom is another cousin, a distant one, but unlike Maggie, he's from my father's side. He's descended from an illegitimate nephew of my great-grandfather, and he's using that as the basis for having the provisional Beck government name him as the crown prince. He's also slandering me to whoever he can in an attempt to keep them from recognizing me."

"Is there a crown prince now?" Harry asked.

"Yes. My brother."

"That's kind of mind-blowing," she admitted, then, looking a little confused, asked, "Wait, where's Beck? I've never heard of it."

Thyra briefly explained the history of the country. "The people forming the government feel that the best way to kick-start the economy is through tourism, and they figure if they make a big deal about the royal family being welcomed back to Beck a hundred years after they were booted out, it would get world attention, and tourists would flock to see them."

"And you and your brother are the royal family?" Harry looked impressed. "That's seriously cool."

Thyra gave a delicate shrug. "It is and it isn't. To be honest, I don't look forward to being on display as the token royalty, assuming, that is, that Beck wants me. But at the same time, it is my family's role to do just that, and since Chris is really happy in his job, then the responsibility falls to me. Or it would if Kardom wasn't trying to do everything he can to swing things his way."

"Are there no other family members who feel differently about being in the limelight, so to speak?" Iakovos said.

"There's just Chris and me," she said, her expression closed. "We do have a first cousin descended from the legitimate line, but she's a Buddhist nun, and the last time I talked to her, she wasn't at all interested in giving that up. Other than her, there is no one else except a handful of people descended from illegitimate lines, and of them, only Kardom has made a push to be recognized. Wow. I really got off topic, didn't I?"

"Only because we dragged you there." Iakovos glanced at his watch. "Was there much more to the interview? If so, I'm afraid I will have to go take my call, and Harry will need to eat before she falls over faint with hunger."

"You know me so well," she said, smiling at him.

"I can finish later," Thyra said, putting her notebook into her bag. She didn't meet Dmitri's eyes when she added, "If Dmitri doesn't mind, that is. I have a few more questions, but they can wait, since I know he has plans for tonight."

Dmitri bit back the desire to tell her that he'd happily throw over his plans to meet Patricia's friend, but he reminded himself that he had no cause to be rude to the woman just because his libido wanted to spend more time with Thyra.

"Potty break! But also, I have an idea. Why don't you have dinner with me, Thyra, since the men are abandoning us?" Harry allowed Iakovos to help her to her feet, pausing while she waited for Thyra's response.

"Oh, uh ..." She glanced at Dmitri for a moment, and he knew she was struggling for an excuse to refuse the invitation. He was just about to intervene when she surprised him. "That sounds wonderful. I love Italian food."

"Excellent. I'll be right back. The baby shifted and I swear she's sitting right on my bladder."

"We have three daughters already," Iakovos called after her as she hurried into the house. "It's only fair that you give me another son to balance out all that estrogen."

"Are you sure you don't mind going with Harry by yourself?" Dmitri asked Thyra when Iakovos, with a murmured excuse, went off to take his video call.

"Of course not. You were right—I like her. She says what she thinks."

Dmitri was pleased. He wasn't sure why it was important that Thyra like Harry and Iakovos, but it was. "I'm afraid I have meetings tomorrow morning, but if you'd like to go sailing in the afternoon, I believe I can get away for a bit. If you had any other interview questions for me, I could answer them then."

Her face lit up with pleasure. "That sounds like fun. Do you mind if Valentino comes, too?"

"Not at all. I'll even treat him to a flotation device."

"Oh." Her expression clouded over for a moment; then she said, "I guess you could keep it on hand for any other cats who sailed with you."

"That's right," he answered, amused despite himself. "Shall we say two? I will pick Valentino and you up at your hotel. Wear a swimsuit if you want to swim."

"Two is fine. Dmitri ..." She bit her lip, and once again, he had to fight to keep from rubbing his thumb across it. "I'm really sorry about Maggie. There's no excuse for how rude she was to you and your cousin and Harry, but I'm even more ashamed of my own behavior."

"Don't be," he said, then, unable to stop himself, swore under his breath, "Oh, to hell with it."

"To hell with wha—" Her eyes widened when he pulled her forward, his mouth on hers in the kiss that he'd been wanting to give her since he'd seen her sitting so obviously miserable. Her lips were soft and sweet, and when they parted, he took advantage and deepened the kiss, her heat seeming to sear his blood. She moaned into his mouth, her hands going up to tangle in his hair at the same time her hips moved gently against him in a way that ensured he was fully aroused in less than three seconds.

"That was even better than the last time," she said when he finally managed to pry himself off her. "I don't know where you learned to kiss—or rather, from whom—but I really want to thank whoever it was, because man alive, Dmitri."

He smiled down into her eyes, now molten with passion, and was on the verge of inviting her back to his apartment, but he'd put off this meeting with Patricia's friend too many times. Regretfully, he released her and, with a pat on Valentino's head, said simply, "Two o'clock."

"I'll be there," she said.

He left, finding it harder and harder to come up with reasons why he shouldn't pursue a relationship with her. He'd first thought she was the opposite of everything he wanted, but now he was beginning to see that she not only ticked every box on his desired-companion list; she added several attributes that he hadn't before thought were important.

He had a feeling he was getting in over his head, but there didn't seem to be much he could do about it, and what was more, he wasn't absolutely sure he wanted to.

SIX

Maggie wasn't in her room by the time I got back from having Italian food with Harry, or at least she didn't answer when I knocked at her door. I suspected she was still off at her party, and wondered idly if Kardom was there with her. She hadn't said he would be, but he had a way of showing up at swanky parties that led me to suspect he'd make a showing.

"Which brings up the question how he found out I was here in the first place," I mused aloud to Valentino when we took an evening walk around the block. I discovered that he enjoyed the bedtime walks, his tail held high while he marched along, periodically pausing to sniff a bit of weed poking through a sidewalk, and stopping to allow people to pet him. "He must have maintained contact with Maggie, because there's no way Chris would have told him where I was, and Maggie's known for a month. And that's just a creepy thought, since it means he's deliberately keeping tabs on me."

I had a vague memory of more than a decade before, after I finally managed to get myself away from Kardom, when I told Maggie how emotionally controlling he was. Her response that he was just naturally dominant, and that if I hadn't been so oppositionally defiant, our relationship would have gone much smoother, still rankled. It occurred to me now that in the years since, she had never supported me whenever I spoke of how much I disliked him. "I wonder if she's been doing more than just keeping him up to date with my plans."

Valentino had no answer for me, or at least none that I didn't have to wrestle away from him and toss into the trash, lecturing him about the unhealthiness of picking up bits of abandoned food he found on the sidewalk.

I spent a restless night thinking about Dmitri, wondering how his date was going, and whether he was at that moment with his ideal woman, having wild, steamy sex with her. It wasn't until the small hours of the morning that I admitted that I might just be falling for him, and that I really wished I had done something to stop him from keeping that date.

"I'm not that sort of person, though," I said, flipping my pillow over and sighing heavily, my mind going over yet again how much I wished I had the nerve to simply make a move on a man in whom I was interested.

Valentino, who was sleeping on my belly, narrowed his eyes in warning at my restlessness.

By morning, he was annoyed with my sleepless ways, while I was flat-out miserable, my mind full of images of Dmitri laughing with another woman, his almost dimples making her melt the way they did me. I pictured him touching her arm when he helped her from the car, the warm brush of his fingers against her flesh making little fires start deep inside her, just as they did me. Worst of all, I imagined him tumbling her into bed, his hands and mouth busy on her body, stirring the need and want in her to the point where she was thrashing restlessly on the bed, her legs tangled with his, his breath hot on her.

"This is stupid," I snarled to myself, and, after giving Valentino his breakfast and cleaning his box, took a few coins from my precious stash of money and marched downstairs to the tiny hotel lobby. "Is it possible to use your phone? It's a local call, and I can pay for it," I asked the young man who was watching reception. I vaguely recalled the owner saying he was her brother, helping her out because he'd lost his job at a nearby restaurant.

He pulled out a cell phone. "Sure. But you have to pay me in pets, not money."

I laughed and took his phone while he squatted down, gently scratching Valentino behind his ears. The latter gave him a slitty-eyed look of enjoyment, leaning into his hand, and rubbing his teeth on the man's fingers.

I moved a few feet over to the corner of the lobby, one eye on the cat while I dialed Dmitri's number.

It rang through to voice mail.

"Damn." I thought for a moment, gnawing on my lower lip, thinking about sending him a text message, but it seemed a bit too presumptuous using someone else's phone for that. Still, Dmitri had said he was going to be in meetings in the morning. ... I sighed and tried the number again. "Hi, it's Thyra," I said when the voice mail beep sounded. "I just thought I'd say hello, and how much I enjoyed last night. The interview, that is, not the part where Maggie acted like an ass. Er ... I hope the rest of your evening was pleasant." But not too pleasant. I hesitated, wanting to ask how the date went, but not sure if he would think that was too invasive or not. "Harry and I had dinner. She had no problem letting me pay for my own meal. Did your date go well? Oh, hell, I didn't mean to say it right out like that, like I'm being nosy, although I guess I am. I just wondered. How it went, that is. Your date. I hope she was ... nice. Because you're nice, and if you have to be with someone, it would be nice if she was also nice. Jesus. Now I'm babbling. Also, I'm using the word 'nice' too many times. Oh, just ignore me. I'm ... I'm ... gah!"

I hung up, calling myself an idiot. What sort of woman left a babbling message to a man who she'd spent all night imagining was having sex with another woman?

"A crazy one, that's who," I told myself. After giving the young man—whose name turned out to be Giorgi—back his phone, and chatting with him a bit about how he wanted to go to England and study history there, I managed to pry Valentino away, and took the cat out for a long walk, partially to give him a little exercise but mostly so I could try to get away from my own thoughts. Two hours later, we returned to the hotel hot, sweaty, and exhausted. To my surprise, as soon as I got back to my room, Maggie tapped on the connecting door and opened it, poking her head into the room.

"Hey, you're back."

"Yes," I said, getting Valentino a bowl of fresh water. "We went out for a walk."

"That cat is so weird. I've never known one that likes walks just like it was a dog. Er … I … I want to apologize for last night." She moved partway into the room, her face wary while she watched me splash my face with water. I was red from the sun and exertion. "I don't know what came over me. I just kind of flipped out, you know?"

I gave Valentino his water, silent for a few seconds. It was on the tip of my tongue to say that I didn't know, but decided that wasn't charitable. Maggie was apologizing, after all—the gracious thing would be to accept it. "I'm sorry things turned out that way, but I didn't do anything to intentionally ruin your fun or make you angry. I had no idea who Dmitri was until after I told him about my family."

"I know. I wish we could have kept up the plan a bit longer, but I guess I'm just not meant to be a princess, huh?" she asked.

I felt about as low as a slug's belly. "I'm sorry," I said again, desperately trying to think of a way to make her happy, but before I could do so, she gave a little wave of her hand.

"It's OK. You hungry? I have a peace offering. I was waiting for you to get back, and was just about to dive in because it smells so good."

"Starving," I said, collapsing exhaustedly onto my bed next to Valentino, wondering if she'd gotten something more substantial than her usual makeup offering of coffee and a pastry.

She came back into my room with a bag and two drink cups. "I think the ice has melted a little, but it still feels cold. Lemonade for you, and iced tea for me." She handed me a cup, then pulled over the sole chair in the room before spreading out a couple of paper bags of fries, and two gyros. "I got chicken for you, because I know you won't eat lamb."

"Thank you, that looks wonderful," I said, touched that she'd gone to so much trouble. It made me feel even worse how things had turned out. Maggie, I reminded myself as I stuffed a couple of fries into my mouth, had always envied my title, and now I'd ruined her chance for a little pretend fun. I racked my brain for a way to make it up to her.

The food was delicious, although the lemonade had suffered in the half hour that she'd evidently waited for me to return. I didn't want to hurt her feelings by telling her I thought it was off, since she'd gone to the trouble of bringing it back to the hotel for me, so I waited until she ran to the bathroom before dumping the half of it that I hadn't drunk down the sink.

"How did the interview go after I left?" she asked ten minutes later, when Valentino graciously accepted a tiny bit of chicken I'd saved for him.

The lack of sleep and the long walk were getting to me, making me yawn before I answered. "It didn't. He had a date, and I went to dinner with Harry. I'll be seeing him later today, though, so I can ask him the rest of my questions. What time is it?"

She pulled out her phone. "A little after noon. You OK? You've yawned three times in a row."

"Just a bit tired and a little dizzy. I probably spent too much time in the sun. I think there's time for a nap before I have to meet Dmitri. What are you up to today?"

She smiled as she put back the chair. "I'm going to see Kardom later. He was at the party I went to last night."

"Ha. I knew he'd be there."

"We had a great time. There were so many interesting

people there, and of course, they were all thrilled to see two royals."

"I just hope you didn't do anything that will get back to Beck," I said, uncomfortable with the idea of her continuing her impersonation of me, but too tired to work up enough energy to really get upset. "I wouldn't put it past Kardom to spin our deal to make me look horrible to the Beck ministers."

"That's your opinion. I find him delightful. You look sleepy, so I'll let you nap. See you later."

It seemed to take a huge effort to scoot myself over on the bed so I could lie down, my body feeling oddly heavy. I wondered if that was a sign of heatstroke, but it was too much trouble to make the words go from my brain to my mouth. "Thank you," I managed to say. "For lunch. Was … really … nice …"

I must have fallen asleep immediately, although I think there was a moment where I suddenly woke up and found myself sitting upright in a car, Valentino's warm weight on my lap.

"Why did you bring that damned thing?" a man's voice asked.

I felt like my whole body was floating, but at the same time, it seemed to be made of something infinitely heavy, like cement or lead, because I couldn't turn my head to see who it was who spoke.

"She takes it everywhere. It would be suspicious otherwise."

I slipped back into a nothingness that in itself was troubling, but my brain seemed to be filled with an odd sort of molasses, thick and black, slowing everything in my world.

"Thyra, you have to answer the priest. Just say yes."

My eyes opened suddenly, my vision rolling up and down in waves, like I was floating on the ocean. "Huh?"

"Say yes." A blob danced in front of my face that slowly resolved into my cousin's face. "That's all you have to do. Just one word."

"Huh?" I asked again, confused, a sense of panic starting to grow deep inside me. I felt like I was bound up like a mummy, to the point where I looked down, my vision still blurry, but as it focused, I could see nothing amiss.

At least, not with my body, but there was definitely something wrong with my mind. My gaze slid along a patterned stone floor until it came to two black shoes, which led to black pants, and up to a yellow shirt under a black suit jacket, up farther to a long, narrow face and dark hair that had been slicked back.

Snake's eyes. The phrase rolled around in my head when I let my gaze move along the arm. It was holding a hand. My hand.

"Come on, it's only one word. Just say yes loud enough for the witnesses to hear, and you can go back to sleep," Maggie whispered in my ear. I turned my head slowly to look at her. She was smiling, but it was an odd smile, a satisfied one, one that made me want to recoil from it. If only my body wasn't bound ... but it wasn't, I reminded myself.

A man said something in a language that I didn't recognize. I looked at him. He stood in front of us, a little platter in his hand. On the platter were two gold rings.

Wedding rings. This was a wedding ... my wedding ... to Kardom.

"No," I heard a voice saying, but it came out slurred and slow. I moved my mouth again, hoping it would answer my demand to shriek and scream and call for help. "No."

I tried to step back, but Kardom held my hand, his fingers tightening painfully around mine.

Fury flared to life in his eyes, and I felt a jolt of adrenaline course through me. It triggered a brief moment of lucidity. He had drugged me somehow and was forcing me to marry him. I had to get out of there, get away from him and ... Maggie? How could she do that to me? How could she be a part of such a travesty? No, I thought to myself, pushing that away. No time to think about that. I had to get away. But how? My body felt like I had lead weights tied to my limbs. That had to be the drug, too. Drug … they drugged me. That meant I was sleepy. I could use that. "Sleep," I said, staggering forward onto Maggie.

Rough hands grabbed my arms, shaking me, but I let my body go boneless, which wasn't at all difficult, and heard Kardom swear. "How much did you give her? She's out again."

"Just what you told me."

"Lay her down while I reassure the officiant that she's not ill."

"Dammit, don't you mess this up for me," Maggie muttered while she hauled me over to where a couple of hard wooden chairs sat along a wall. "I've waited too long. Kardom! The witnesses are leaving!"

She dumped me face-first onto the chairs, my legs dangling off them at an angle that hurt. I shifted myself, rolling slowly onto my side, then slid down onto the floor. I still felt like I was bound by chains, but at least my vision was mostly working. I seemed to be in some narrow room with high windows. Kardom stood with his back to me, arguing with a man, his long white hands moving as he spoke. The man made an abrupt gesture and turned around, going through a door to another room, Kardom hot on his heels.

As he walked past a table, a couple of papers fluttered off it to the floor. Maggie was on the other side of the room, talking to an East Asian couple, who had the air of bewildered tourists trapped against their will. I looked around but didn't see Valentino anywhere, panic hitting me over what they'd done to my cat.

The fury that followed got me onto my feet, but when I opened my mouth to demand to know what they'd done with him, I saw that I'd been dumped next to a door. As silently as I could, I crept forward, snatching up the papers on the floor before staggering back to the door. I managed to slip through it, holding the handle carefully so it wouldn't click when I closed it. To my relief, outside the room was an open office space and an entryway, through which I saw a familiar disgruntled orange shape.

I lumbered across the room, ignoring the couple of people who sat working industriously at their desks, my joy at seeing Valentino tied up outside to a planter almost as great as his annoyance.

"Poor thing," I said, my tongue feeling as thick as a dictionary. "Sitting in sun without water. Come on."

I got his leash untied and, without thinking about what we were doing, or where we would go, stuffed the papers into my pocket and staggered across the street, my mind taking in vague images of a busy neighborhood in Athens, filled with traffic and people and noise and music. I don't know how long I wandered up and down the streets; I just knew I had to keep moving. Slowly, my mind cleared, and I entered one of the many small neighborhood stores that dotted the residential areas. A young woman of about eighteen sat behind a counter, playing a game on her phone.

"Hi," I said, panting a little. "Can I use your phone? I have money." I dug in my pocket and pulled out a collection of coins, not caring how much it was. "Someone kidnapped me. Need to call … need to call …"

The woman said something to me in Greek.

I slumped against the counter for a minute, my legs still wobbly, and my brain fuzzy. I had to focus, had to think, but it was so difficult. I needed help. I needed Dmitri.

"Dmitri," I said, and took a pencil from where it sat on the counter, and wrote his phone number on the edge of a newspaper.

The woman snatched back the pencil, tsking, and tried to erase the number, clearly lecturing me about writing on papers I hadn't paid for.

"Dmitri," I said again, pointing at the number, and shoved the coins at her. "Please call him."

She looked hesitant, her gaze going over me, then peered down to where Valentino sat at my feet. She gave a little eye roll but, to my relief, consulted the number I'd written, and called it. I sent up a prayer that Dmitri was out of his meetings and would answer his phone. If he didn't—

She started speaking, the suspicious look on her face changing quickly to one of curiosity. She shook her head, then held her phone out for me. "Dmitri?" I said into it, my words still sounding thick.

"Thyra? Where are you? I thought we were supposed to meet at two? It's almost four now."

"Roofied," I said tiredly.

"You're on a roof? What roof? Does this have anything to do with the message you left me?"

I took a deep breath. "I … was … roofied. Can't think. Kardom and Maggie drugged me."

He said something that I assumed was swearing in Greek. "Are you all right?"

"Yeah. Just out of it. Will you marry me?"

"What?"

I leaned against a tall glass-fronted beverage case, too tired to stand upright any longer. "Kardom tried to marry me. I need to get married. I like you. I like your mouth. Will you marry me so Kardom can't? I'll divorce you later. No one has to know."

"I think I will want to know a good deal more about what happened to you, but for now, I want to make sure you're safe. Put the woman on the phone again."

Tiredness swamped me. I could barely keep my eyes open. "K. But you have to promise to marry me first. Then I'll take a nap."

"I promise that I will do whatever will keep you safe, all right?"

"Deal," I said, and slid down the case to curl up on the floor with Valentino, who first sniffed my face, then patted it with one paw.

I heard the woman talking above me, slipped back into nothingness; then I came to again when a couple of men, neither of whom I recognized, carried me into a dimly lit room where I was put on a couch.

It seemed like just a minute or two, and I heard Dmitri's voice. I sat up, blinking and squinting at the sight of him handing over money to the two men, both of whom were smiling and talking rapidly.

"Oh, good, you're here. I hope you have a couple of gallons of coffee," I said, struggling to get up. He helped me, his arm strong and warm and utterly wonderful around my waist.

"Not here, but I will get you some. Can you walk?"

"Yes. Valentino?"

"He's out front with Athena. Evidently he's the hit of the shop. Here we go. Step down here."

Valentino was indeed sitting on the stack of papers, accepting pets from anyone who came into the store. I thanked the girl for her help, but I doubt if she understood. "Please thank her for me," I asked Dmitri.

"I have already done so. My car is around the corner. No, let Alexis have Valentino. He will take care of him until you are in the car."

"Alexis?" I eyed the skinny young man with a thick crop of curly hair and a pronounced Adam's apple.

"My assistant. This way."

"Hi," I told Alexis the assistant. "I was drugged."

"So I heard." He had an accent, but it wasn't nearly as nice as Dmitri's.

"I'm flattered you think so. I like yours, as well," Dmitri told me.

"Uh-oh." I put my hand over my mouth as I stumbled, Dmitri's arm keeping me from pitching forward. "I think my mouth is saying things without my brain telling it to go ahead."

"Probably, but a little rest should take care of that. No, you have to bend in order to get into the car."

He helped me get into the back of a shiny black car, handing Valentino in to me before taking the seat next to me. I went down into another sleepy period, waking up to find myself in an elevator with both men and Valentino.

"Where are we?" I asked, somewhat worried that I could go in and out of consciousness like that.

"We're going to my apartment. It seemed safer than your hotel room. I've called a doctor to check you over. We'll need her to test you for drugs if you want to file charges."

"OK." I stared at him for a moment, admiring the way his hair curled, his high cheekbones, and the black lashes that set off his eyes so well.

Amusement gave those eyes warmth as they considered me in return.

"Thyra?" he said while I was enjoying staring at his face, cataloging all the things I liked about it.

"Hmm?"

"We have to get off the elevator. Other people will want to use it."

"OK," I said, wondering what he'd do if I leaned over and kissed him.

"I'd kiss you back, but let's save that for once we're inside the apartment, all right?"

I frowned. "Sorry. Mouth is saying things again."

"I like the things your mouth says and does, but perhaps my apartment would be a better place to have that discussion." He urged me through the door, but before I could get a look around, I was sitting on the end of a bed with Dmitri peeling off my shoes. "The bathroom is through there," he said, pointing to a door. "I'll make some coffee for you, but I think you should let the doctor do a blood test before you have anything. She should be here any minute. Will you be all right if I leave you here?"

"Valentino?" I asked. "He needs water. Kardom left him tied in the sun."

"He had water at the shop, but I'll make sure that he has some."

"He might also need to potty," I said, fretting.

"I'll make arrangements for that. You lie down and rest until the doctor gets here."

I didn't, but not because I didn't want to sleep a good week or two. I used the bathroom, staring at myself as I passed a mirror. My glasses were askew, I had a smear of dirt on the side of my face, and my pupils were huge. "I'm going to get Kardom," I told my reflection, then reentered the room to find Valentino sitting on the bed, wearing his usual disdainful expression.

A half hour later, I felt much more human, and much more like myself.

"You have a nice doctor," I told Dmitri after she left. We were in the kitchen, sitting at an eating bar. Valentino squatted on the floor, occasionally reaching out one white paw to pat the lid to an empty water bottle that had evidently fallen on the floor. "She offered to loan me her boyfriend if I want him to rough up Kardom. Evidently the boyfriend is a bouncer at a club."

Dmitri's lips thinned. "You won't need him." He poured me out another cup of coffee.

"I think three cups is all I can take," I protested.

"The doctor said the more caffeine you had, the better you'd feel."

I sighed and sipped at the coffee. "Why won't I need Dr. Nina's bouncer boyfriend?"

"Because I have a few things I want to say to this Kardom."

I gawked at him. "That sounded almost possessive, Dmitri."

He looked surprised. "It did, didn't it?"

"Does that mean that your date didn't go well?" The words were out before I even realized I was thinking them. "No! Don't answer me! I have no right to ask you. Just ... let's move on."

"If I told you that your message made me laugh, would you be offended?" he asked; then before I could answer, he pulled me off the tall barstool I was sitting on, into his arms, his breath teasing my lips. "I thought about you the entire time I was with Audrey, wishing I was with you instead of where I was. Does that answer your question?"

"Oh, thank God," I said, sliding my fingers into his hair and pulling his mouth down the last half inch to mine. His kiss was as hot as I remembered, his tongue just as bossy, and his mouth just as sweet. I moaned, unable to keep from moving against him, my whole body demanding that I immediately apply my naked flesh to his.

"I think—oh, Christ, right there, Princess—I think maybe we should continue this conversation in my bedroom."

I stopped biting the tendon that ran up the top of his shoulder to his neck, and glanced toward the floor. "Valentino ..."

He had his phone out before I could finish the sentence. "Did you get her things? Good. And the cat's items ... well done. Was there any sign of the cousin? I thought not. The cat will be loose, so be careful about leaving the door to the balcony open. You can put his litter pan in the guest bath. There's a box in there now with shredded paper, but he hasn't seen fit to use it. Thyra is making gestures that I believe means she'd like you to put down some food for the cat, as well. Don't disturb me unless it's an emergency."

"Thanks," I said, stopping the sign language I was making, before I realized just what he'd said. "Hey, was that my stuff you sent him to get? That's kind of high-handed, isn't it?"

He cocked an eyebrow at me. Before I could say more, he scooped me up and carried me through the kitchen to a hall that ran to one side. "Perhaps, but I didn't think you'd want to go back to your hotel to get your things. Your cousin checked out, by the way."

"Oh. Wow. She did? Damn. I seriously misjudged just how angry she was that I took Pretend Princess Time away from her. Will Valentino be OK out there by himself? I don't want him to be afraid because he's in a new place."

With a sigh, he set me down just inside his bedroom. "Thyra, I very much want you in my bed, naked, with all your hair splayed out around you, so that I might do all of the things that I've thought about since last night, but I won't be able to do them if Valentino is sitting there watching me. And that would be a shame, because my list has grown in length, and I'm desperate to start working my way through the items on it."

"Desperate?" I asked, flattered enough that I trailed a finger down his cheek, where his almost dimples lay hidden. "I'm pretty desperate for you, too, but I don't know that Valentino should be alone."

He checked his phone when it pinged. "Alexis is almost here. He likes cats, so if yours is lonely, he'll be on hand. Now, do you need to use the toilet? Are you hungry? Should I run out and get some birth control?"

"Wow, that was direct," I said, giggling a little.

"I just want to make sure everything is covered, because the second you get into that bed, Princess, you're mine."

"Ooh, I like that lascivious look in your eye," I said, smiling, and pulling off my grubby T-shirt. By the time I was hopping on one foot, pulling off my shoes, Dmitri had closed the door and was peeling off his own shirt, revealing his chest.

I stopped, standing on one foot while I was pulling my other leg out of my jeans, staring at the glorious expanse of skin as it came into view. "Hoochiwawa, Dmitri! Your chest is ... woof! Do you go to the gym?"

"No, but there's a pool just beyond the atrium. I try to swim every day. It's a habit I picked up from Iakovos. Do you need some help?"

"No, I think I have it," I said, still hopping until I managed to get my foot out of my pants, after which the other leg peeled off quickly. "I am never again buying skinny jeans. I'm so not skinny."

He dropped his pants, getting out of them quickly and efficiently, whereas I had managed to catch one of the hooks on my bra on my hair, and was disengaging it. But at last we were both naked, and stood staring at each other, about five feet of distance between us.

"OK, you're downright impressive," I told him, wanting to cover the various elements of my pudginess, but feeling that was cowardly. "Can I touch everything?"

He laughed when I moved toward him, my fingers flexing. "Yes, but only if I am allowed to do the same."

"Oh, you definitely have permission for that. Oooh, it's that adorable nipple I saw earlier. And look, he has a friend."

"They are a matched set," Dmitri said, sliding his hands under my breasts until he cupped them, his thumbs gently sweeping across nipples that were suddenly needy and demanding. "I thought they'd look better that way."

"That was smart thinking," I said on a near moan. "Mine aren't so nice."

"On the contrary, they've taken to haunting my thoughts with their perfect roundness, but I think I'm going to want to admire them more closely from the comfort of the bed." He slid an arm behind my legs, hoisting me up and carrying me over to his bed before setting me down and pausing for a few seconds, just standing there staring down at me.

"What's wrong?" I asked, trying to adopt a pose that didn't leave me spread out like a smorgasbord. I tried first on my back with one leg bent, then rolled to the side and crossed my legs, and finally rolled onto my belly and with my heels kicked over my back.

"I was just wondering if you are well enough to do all the things that I want to do. The doctor didn't say you couldn't—what the hell are you doing, Princess?"

I'd flipped over onto my back again, this time sitting up, legs together and to the side in classic mermaid pose. "Trying to find some position where I don't look like a side of beef with breasts."

"I assure you that a side of beef is the very last thing I think of when I see you," he answered, crawling onto the bed with a look in his eye that had my girl parts celebrating. "I want to touch and taste and feel all of you, all of those glorious breasts, and your legs, and, dear God, woman, your belly."

I looked down at my belly, sucking it in for a minute. "I don't swim every day, which I think is apparent, not that I'm beating myself up for the way I look. Would you mind lying on your back so I can frolic upon your body?"

"Yes, actually, I would. Perhaps later, once I've had my fill of all the delicious bits you have to offer me, I will be able to lie back and let you have your turn, but not now. So long as you feel up to this, I plan on having my way."

A faint, foggy memory rumbled through my brain just as his mouth closed on one of my nipples, his tongue just as bossy there as it was in my mouth. I moaned, arching my back when he tormented it oh-so sweetly, the sensation of heat rippling upward to my face. "Other side!" I said on a gasp, tugging on his curls.

He stopped teasing my now-needy nipple and grinned. "Like that, did you?"

"Very much so." I frowned when he bent over the other breast, the pleasure of his mouth on it somewhat dimmed while I tried to catch the faint memory.

"Your breasts are ..." He bent down and nibbled on the underside.

"Large? I know. They make jogging impossible, not that I want to go jogging, but still, trying to contain them in a sports bra is never fun. Good lord, man, you're not heading where I think you're heading?"

He murmured something into my breastbone, his hands smoothing down my hips, his mouth following, trailing what felt like fire. I writhed on the bed, both highly aroused at the sensations of his mouth and hands and troubled by something I couldn't bring to focus. He gently bit my hip. "I know some women don't enjoy this sort of thing. I hope you are not one of them."

"Don't enjoy what—hooo baby!"

His fingers slid between my thighs, gently parting them before heading straight to ground zero, whereupon he immediately made my body feel like it had been turned into something fluid and very, very hot, like molten gold. "Ah, I see you are not one of those women. Do you like this?"

I grabbed his head when he bent to add his tongue into the party-zone fun, my stomach contracting at the same time my thighs wanted badly to tighten around him, but since I didn't want to have to explain to his cousin how I'd smothered him while he was trying to bring me pleasure, I forced myself to keep from wrapping my legs around his head.

The thought that slithered through my mind finally came forward, bringing with it a sense of horror, shame, and fear that leeched every bit of enjoyment from the moment.

"Oh, my God," I said, scooting backward until he looked up with a confused expression.

"What's wrong? Was I too rough?"

I stared at him in horror, shame filling me. Tears pricked in my eyes, making me blink rapidly as I tried to pull a sheet out from under me. "No, you were fine. I was enjoying it."

He frowned, watching me yank the sheet around until I had it up and over me. "Then why did you stop me? And why in God's name are you covering yourself up?"

"Because I can't think when you're touching me. You make everything go out of my mind except how much I like what you're doing, and how I want to touch you and taste you when it's my turn."

He gave an odd sort of exasperated sigh, and sat up, one hand on my sheet-covered leg. "Do you want to tell me what it is you have to think about that's so important that it stops what I had assumed was a mutually desired session of love-making?"

I closed my eyes for the count of seven. I knew it was that number, because I was counting to myself. "I asked you to marry me, didn't I?" I finally managed to get out.

A variety of expressions passed over his face: confusion, disbelief, and amusement that slowly turned into something heated. "Yes, you did, three times as a matter of fact, but I assume that was the drug talking, since we both discussed how marriage was not something either one of us was interested in pursuing."

"Yes, well, the thing is ..." I bit my lip, avoiding looking at his beautiful green eyes. "I've changed my mind. I need to get married. Right away. Like, tonight. And although my opinion of marriage hasn't changed—I still think it's a formality for the convenience of governments, and it's what's between two people that really matters—that legal formality is what I need. Desperately. And much as I want to have wild, sweaty bunny sex with you, because right now that seems like the best thing in the whole world, it seems kind of wrong to do that with you and then go out and try to find some man who doesn't mind getting married as soon as possible."

"What man?" he asked, frowning.

"Huh?"

"What man is waiting for you to leave my bed so he can marry you?" His frown turned into a scowl, and I was amazed for a moment that Dmitri, who seemed to have such a placid temperament, could suddenly go from mild to furious in the space of a few seconds.

"I don't know," I said, eyeing him. I had a temper of my own, so couldn't damn him for that, but if he was going to be the sort of man that got unreasonably angry, then it was best I find that out.

Not, I reminded myself, tugging the sheet a bit higher, that it mattered now.

Everything was ruined, and it was all because of Kardom.

SEVEN

Dmitri wanted to yell. He wanted to throttle the man who had dared to drug Thyra, he wanted to ask her roughly a million questions, and he very much needed her to explain why she had suddenly stopped him from bringing her what he assumed would be, if not exquisite pleasure, at least pleasurable enjoyment. But most of all, he wanted to change the look in her eyes from one of weepy unhappiness to the same shimmering golden passion that had filled them while he was taking great pleasure in exploring her nubile body.

But she was looking wary now, giving him odd little worried looks while she pulled on her clothing, so he tried to push back all the things he wanted to say and do, and instead focused on what was vital at that moment: understanding why she'd suddenly changed her mind.

"Did I do something that you didn't like?" he asked, trying to think of what he might have done to make her want to leave his bed. "I would never do something if you didn't care for it—"

"No, it's not you, don't you see?" she said, tears still swimming in her lovely eyes.

He shook his head. "I don't see. Would you explain it to me?"

"I want this," she said, gesturing toward the bed. He sat on the edge of it, his hands on his knees, his erection singing a sad little dirge at the turn of events. He knew just how it felt. "I want you. But I can't have you right now. That's what I realized when the memory stopped bumping around in the dense fog of my mind, and I remembered it."

"That you asked me to marry you?"

"Yes. I have to get married. It's the only thing that's going to stop Kardom from doing this again. Where is it? ... I had it when the doctor was checking me over. ..." She dug around in her pockets until she pulled out a wadded-up piece of paper. "Look what he did."

He took the paper, frowning at it before he looked up. "It's a marriage license."

"Yes. Your doctor said that bit in Greek is something called an apostille. Evidently her ex-husband is French, and he had to get it when they were married. It makes the license valid here."

"Why did you apply for a marriage license with this Kardom person if you didn't want to marry him?" Once again, Dmitri felt out of his depth, the sense of being caught in a whirlpool of confusion almost palpable.

"I didn't. That's not my signature. It's a fake that Kardom must have had made up. That's why I have to get married."

Dmitri shook his head again, trying to pick through the puzzle. "Even assuming he did forge a marriage license, and that looks real to me, why does it mean you need to be married to someone else?"

"Because if he went to this length—drugging me, convincing Maggie to help him, and obviously paying off some witnesses and an officiant—then he's certainly not going to give up just because I managed to escape his clutches." She stuffed the paper back in her pocket and sat on the bed next to him. "I think he has this idea that if we get married, it will seal the deal with Beck making him their crown prince, which is why I have to get married as soon as possible—so I can nip that plan in the bud. Once I find someone, then you and I can … then we can continue this. Assuming you aren't so turned off by my nefarious cousins that you still want to do all those things you were doing. And which I want to do to you."

"I think," he said slowly, wondering if she was baiting him into offering to marry her. The second he thought of that, he dismissed the idea—there was no sense of deceit in her. He'd been the recipient of such behavior by manipulative women before, and he knew what emotional blackmail looked like; she was genuinely distressed. "Perhaps you are jumping to an extreme action when a lesser one might suit as well. A restraining order, for instance."

She gave him a long, level look, the golden amber in her eyes dulled. "Do you think a man who clearly went to as much trouble as Kardom went to would honor a restraining order?"

"Well …" He had to admit that, upon thinking about it, it wasn't likely. Clearly this cousin of hers saw no goal but his own. "No, I don't. But marriage, even one where you don't intend on honoring it to the full extent of its meaning, is a serious step."

"The way I see it is that someone out there"—she gestured toward the window—"is going to want the ability to work and live in Britain."

He frowned. "You were born in Beck. I saw your passport, and assumedly, it will be part of the European Union."

"Yes, but my mom was British, and Chris and I have dual citizenship. And that's what I'm going to use to tempt someone—I was actually thinking about the hotel owner's brother—into marrying me, so they can work in England if they want."

He didn't want to say the words, but they were out before he realized just how insulting they were. "Why do I feel like you expect me to offer to marry you, instead?"

"Because that's the sort of thing that someone who didn't give a damn about you would do. But I'm not that person. I take back my request for your hand in marriage.

I've had time to think about it, and I see it's not a good idea," she answered. Far from being insulted, she patted his hand, just as if he needed to be comforted. "Dmitri, I want you to be my lover. My boyfriend. Hell, if things work out between us, my partner. But not my husband. That would just ruin everything."

"How so?" he asked, feeling slightly annoyed despite the fact that he had not wanted to be forced to marry her. He realized in a dim part of his mind that in the space of a few seconds he'd gone from being vehemently opposed to the idea of marrying to being unreasonably determined that if anyone was going to save her, it would be him; but that inconsistency of logic didn't matter. Thyra most definitely did. "I don't understand why you think it would ruin anything we have together."

"Because the marriage will be a business deal. It'll be a cold, lifeless convenience to keep Kardom out of my hair." Her hand slid to his bare thigh, her fingers trailing up it toward his belly. "What I want from you is much more personal. Intimate. Hot and sweaty and filled with me doing to you all the things you did earlier, and a whole lot more."

It made no sense, and yet, the second he realized that she would truly prefer to marry someone who just wanted to use her to get to England, he was determined that she should marry no one but him. "If it's just a marriage that you want so that your cousin can't force you into marrying him, then the answer is that I will marry you."

She'd been nibbling on his shoulder, her fingers spreading as she shifted her hand down, trailing fingertips that seemed to be dipped in fire along his (sad and forlorn at the state of affairs) length. She stopped touching and biting him to glare. "Did you not just hear me? I don't want to marry you, Dmitri. I want to make love to you. Lots of times."

"The two things are not mutually exclusive," he pointed out. "The contrary, traditionally speaking."

"Well, screw tradition," she said, releasing him, her eyes now glittering with golden lights as she stood up. "I'm not going to marry you and make everything that could be between us horrible."

"Why would everything be horrible? If marriage means so little to you, why would being married to me matter?" Dmitri asked, needing to get to the bottom of her sudden reticence. He had a feeling it was important.

She looked both defiant and frustrated, her hands gesticulating as she sputtered out, "It just would. It matters because—you would—it means that you—and then when you left me, we'd have legal crap to deal with. I don't want that, Dmitri! I just want you without all that potential for grief. I'll marry someone else who doesn't matter."

"Doesn't matter?" he said slowly, searching her face.

"Oh, that came out wrong. Of course the person I marry will matter. I'll give him a free pass to England, and then he can live there and I'll be here with you."

He was silent for half a minute, trying to pick through her words to the emotions that lay beneath. Discarding the obvious protestation that it was silly to worry about a breakup before they even started a relationship, he focused on an idea that was growing in strength. "Do you trust me?"

"What?" Her gaze skittered away for a few seconds, then returned to his when she nodded. "Yes, of course I trust you."

"I don't think you do," he said slowly, pushing down the little jolt of pain that accompanied that realization. His feelings didn't matter here—hers did. "For one thing, we've been acquainted a short time. I'd be surprised if you did trust me wholly."

"Do you trust me?" she asked, looking defiant again.

"Yes." He smiled. "But then, I'm different than you in that I don't share your fear of abandonment."

"What the hell is that supposed to mean?" she asked indignantly, whomping him on the arm. "That is so insulting!"

"It's not meant to be, and I apologize if it seems I'm criticizing you." He took her hand when she was about to pinch him, kissing the tips of her fingers. "Everyone in your life who you trusted and loved has left you. If I had lived through such tragedy, as well, I would no doubt feel the same way you do."

"I haven't been abandoned," she scoffed, but her gaze skittered away again. "My parents died in an accident. They didn't intentionally leave me."

"How old were you then?" he asked, stroking her fingers and hoping he'd make her understand just how much he admired her strength.

"Fifteen," she said, glancing back to him, her eyes wary.

"A formative time in anyone's life. How old was your brother?"

"Twenty-one, and if you're going to ask, yes, he was legally my guardian, although I didn't need him. I had a job. I rented a room from a friend's mom while I went to school. I was fine on my own. Besides, Chris was in England going to college, and he would have lost the scholarship if he had to come back to Canada."

Insight into her character deepened, giving him an understanding of why a woman as desirable as she was didn't have a string of relationships behind her. "So in other words, your parents left you, and your brother placed his education ahead of your well-being. No, you needn't say it—I know your parents were killed in an accident, but surely in your darkest moments, you must have felt like they abandoned you. My mother died in childbirth when I was just a year older than you, and despite knowing it was a tragedy and nothing more, I was angry at her for a long time for risking her life rather than being happy with my father and me."

She opened her mouth to say something, then closed it, only to open it again, her eyes a lovely old gold as she clasped his hand in hers. "I'm so sorry, Dmitri. That must have been awful for you to lose your mom in that way. And yes, if I'm being absolutely honest, I was angry for a while. But I don't think losing my parents in that way means I have abandonment issues."

"No?" He raised an eyebrow. "Then you won't have a problem if we get married."

"Dammit, Dmitri!" she shouted, standing up. "You aren't listening to me!"

"I am, you know," he said calmly, his mind forming a list of things that would have to be done. One, he'd have to warn the concierge not to allow anyone up to his apartment except those on an approved visitors' list. He'd have to get a marriage license for himself, a legal one, unlike the one Thyra had. He'd have to convince her that a legality wasn't going to mean that he, like all the others she had trusted, would leave her alone.

He didn't know when he'd come to that decision, but he accepted it just as he accepted the fact that she had irrevocably changed his life.

"I'm going to go back to the hotel and talk to Giorgi, who is unemployed and wants to go to England, where women will fawn on him because he's cute and has a nice accent, too," she said, striding to the door, her chin tilted up in what he assumed she thought was a noble, martyred manner.

Gods, she was delightful. Everything about her called to him, just as if she had been made in that fashion to most perfectly fit his desires. He couldn't imagine how he'd once thought that he would prefer anyone but his delectable princess, but she was his now, and the sooner she realized that, the happier they'd both be.

"I'll be back as soon as I tell Giorgi that I'll marry him, and that I'm a tiny bit in love with you, and I want to be with you rather than him. Please tell me you understand."

"Not in the least," he said, rising and pulling on his pants. "But I'm not going to let that stop me from marrying you."

"Gah!" she yelled, and left his room, slamming the door.

He padded barefoot after her, his phone in one hand while he looked up the marriage requirements between a citizen of Greece and a foreigner, glancing up when she slammed his front door, too. He smiled. Could she be any more contrary?

The knock came sooner than he expected. He opened the door, leaning on the doorframe, his arms crossed over his chest.

She glared at him, her gaze pausing for a long, long time on his bare chest before she cleared her throat. "I forgot my cat."

"Princess, you forgot a lot more than that." Before she could spout any more ridiculous reasons why she was going to marry some twit named Giorgi, he pulled her into his arms, and kissed her until he was out of breath. "You are going to marry me, Thyra. No, don't say it. It won't ruin our relationship. I don't particularly care about being married, and neither do you. Thus, since it will protect you, we are the perfect people to be bound together legally."

"Giorgi—"

"May well want to get married someday, and it wouldn't be fair to him to have to get divorced first, would it?"

She frowned, her fingers absently stroking his shoulders. He wondered how long he'd be able to last if she kept moving her hips restlessly against his dick. He estimated he had about thirty seconds before he'd have to pick her up, carry her back to his bed, and make love to her until she admitted that his idea was the sensible one.

"What happens if you want to get married someday?" she asked, biting her lower lip.

He gave in to temptation, and sucked her lip into his mouth, swiping his tongue over it before releasing it to say, "Then you will give me a divorce. Likewise if you wish to marry someone else. But until that time, we will be legally married, and I can make as much sweaty bunny love to you as you can stand. Starting right now."

"But—"

"No buts." He lifted her in his arms, very much aware of just how well her curved, soft parts felt against him. "I'll apply for a license in the morning. Now, do you want me to pick up where I was when you suddenly remembered asking me to marry you, or should I start over?"

She looked like she was going to argue, but after he set her down next to the bed and quickly removed her clothing, as well as his own pants, she gave a little sigh and climbed onto the bed before adopting an alluring pose that was all soft curves, and breasts, and legs, and her enticing belly. "Neither. Would you mind going to the main course? I'm kind of no longer in the mood for appetizers. I just want to feel you inside me."

Her words made him harder than he remembered being in a very long time. "Never let it be said that I did not give a princess exactly what she wanted." He slid into bed next to her, unable to keep from running his hands along her hips until they reached her breasts, those wonderful, plump breasts that he could have sworn were made to his exact desire. Her mouth was hot and sweet, and he smiled into it when she tried to pull him over onto the temptation that was her body.

"Dmitri!" she said, her frown turning to a slight squint when he carefully removed her glasses and set them on the nightstand.

"Yes, my demanding one?" He nuzzled her behind her ear, one hand sweeping down to slide a finger into her. Despite her insistence that she wanted to forgo any further foreplay, he wanted to make sure she was ready for him.

"What part of 'I want to feel you inside me' have you misunderstood? Wait, do you not like to be on top? I don't mind doing the cowgirl thing for you, although it's all I ever got to do with ... well, now is not the time to talk about just how controlling Kardom was."

He was about to take one pert little nipple in his mouth when her words penetrated the passion and desire and nipple-related thoughts that currently filled his brain. "Kardom?" he said, feeling that if he had been a dog who had hackles, they would at that moment be standing on end. "Your bastard cousin who tried to drug you into marrying him? You slept with him?"

"Years ago. Didn't I tell you?" She made a face, and slid her hands along his chest, making him bite back a groan of pleasure. "I was twenty and incredibly stupid, and I fell for his story. My brother just about had kittens, but since I was old enough—" She stopped, frowning. "Why the hell are we talking about that ass when we could be sweaty bunnying?"

He thought about that a moment, almost admitted that a spike of jealousy had stung him, and decided that he didn't want her thinking he was a caveman when it came to being able to control his emotions. "It just took me by surprise, but you're quite right. You have a lot of sweating to do, and I plan on seeing to it that you do it."

"Oooh," she said, her eyes misty with passion, sliding her leg up alongside his. "Do you want to be top or bottom?"

"I'm fine with either—"

"Oh good, because I really like to be on the bottom. He who shall not be named never let me, and there's something about having a man on top that just makes me feel … mrowr," she said, pulling him over her again, and this time, he allowed it, his body tight with the desire to just plunge into her. But he was a gentleman, and a thoughtful lover, and he did not simply pounce on a woman, no matter how much his erection was demanding that he do just that.

He dipped his head to kiss her, but she growled into his mouth, actually growled, wrapped her legs around his thighs, and grabbed his hips at the same time she thrust up to meet him.

"Princess," he said, unable to keep from chuckling when she swore at the resulting nonconnection. "I like that you aren't shy about letting me know what you want, but there are times when I need a little help. Now, if you would move just one of your arms, I could reach between us—"

"You are the most irritating man I've ever started to fall in love with!" she almost shouted, and, reaching down, found him, moaning when she rubbed the tip of him into her intimate parts. "If you have any mercy in your soul, now, Dmitri, now!"

He started to slide into her, had a very unwelcome thought, and burst into laughter when her expression went from the beginnings of bliss to fury. "No, do not say it—I fully intend on proceeding, but first, I feel it only right to ask if you are on a form of birth control?"

"Oh." The anger faded, and she flexed her hips, taking a little more of him into her depths. Gods, but she was hot. "Yes. There's nothing to worry about there. I assume you don't have any—"

"None. I believe we can proceed, then," he said, grinning when the irritated look was back.

"You're doing that on purpose," she said, writhing beneath him, trying to pull his hips forward. "Stop doing that, Dmitri!"

"Stop what?" he asked, withdrawing the head of his penis.

"Argh! You're going to kill me if you keep teasing me like that!"

He kissed her soundly, and slid into her a few inches, his eyes almost crossing at the grip her inner muscles had. "I'm on top, Princess. Therefore, I get to be the one to set the pace—"

She growled again, and tightened her muscles around him. He rose back on his hands, looking down at her for a second, fighting desperately for control, then gave up the battle and slid his arms under her legs, and dove into her, his mind unable to do anything but process the sensations of her body around his, of her scent—a citrus smell that reminded him of a lemon grove on a warm summer's afternoon—and of her heat. Dear Gods, the heat of her. He wondered idly if she had some sort of a residual fever from the drugging, decided he couldn't put the thought into actual words to ask her, and concentrated instead on making her as wild for him as he was for her.

It took only three minutes before Thyra, moaning nonstop and dragging her fingernails down his back, arched up beneath him. He was about to tell her he couldn't last much longer, but she tightened around him even more, pushing him past the point where he could do anything but thrust hard into her repeatedly, his shout of completing mingling with her cry of happiness.

His heart beat wildly in his ears while he kissed her neck, then her lower lip, then her mouth properly, but it wasn't a lengthy kiss. He simply didn't have the strength—or breath—to do more than to wordlessly tell her just how wonderful the experience was for him.

"That was—hoo! That was just about the most amazing thing I've ever experienced," she said, kissing his neck when he released her legs, unable to pull himself from her welcoming depths. "I mean, I seriously want to thank all your past lovers, because if they helped make you what you are today, they deserve it. Maybe even give them some money. I really wish Beck would see their way to making me the crown princess, because then I could give all your past lovers titles in recognition for their contribution to your abilities."

He laughed. He couldn't help it—she was just so utterly unique. He managed to gather enough strength to rise up on one elbow, looking down at her flushed face, the sting of sweat on his back telling him just how much she'd lost control. That thought pleased him greatly. "Most women would be jealous of past lovers, you know."

"I know," she said, gently biting the tip of his nose. "But I'm not most women, and you certainly aren't like anyone else I've ever met."

He kissed her again, managed to pull himself from her, and rolled to his side, scooting her over a little before pulling her up close so that her legs tangled with his.

"Did you just move me off the wet spot?" she asked into his collarbone, one of her hands caressing his ribs and chest.

"Yes."

"That is the most thoughtful thing ever," she said, stifling a yawn, which just made him yawn, as well. "Do you mind if I spend the night? I assume you don't, since you had my things brought from the hotel, but I figured it's better if I checked, first."

"My intention is for you to stay here as long as you like," he told the top of her head, nuzzling his face into her glossy hair, breathing deeply of the scent of her, and of their joined bodies. He was mildly surprised by the fact that he didn't even have a twinge of concern over whether inviting her into his life was best for them both—sometime in the past few days, she'd managed to not only infiltrate his life; she'd made a place for herself in his heart, as well.

Dammit, he'd have to admit to Iakovos that it was all too apparent he was a Papaioannou. He wouldn't hear the end of that for a long time, but somehow … he pulled Thyra a little closer, one arm protectively over her. Somehow, nothing seemed to be as important as making Thyra happy.

And keeping her safe. No one was going to touch his princess so long as he had a breath left in his body.

EIGHT

"Ms. Martin? Hello, it's Thyra Beck." I bit my lower lip, trying to work out what I was going to say on Harry's phone, attempting to make the call as fast as possible while yet still being polite. "I was wondering if there's been any word of … well, happenings."

"Your Serene Highness, what a pleasure to hear from you." The woman's voice in my ear was genuinely warm, with a slight German accent. "There are no happenings to report, I am sorry to say. The council is still set to meet in seven weeks to make a final decision about the royal family, and nothing more has been said on the subject. Except …"

I stopped myself in midsigh, hope bursting to life inside me despite the knowledge that the Beck government had been thus far tainted by Kardom's lies. "Oh? Something good?"

The silence that followed my question said it all. "No, I'm afraid not." Danielle Martin, one of the twelve ministers who sat on the council to organize the new Beck government, was one of the few people who'd give me any official encouragement, and I clung to her like a lifeline. "Just the opposite. Mr. Kardom has … well, effectively bought Minister Ross and Minister Bergen."

My heart fell at her words, the newly born hope dying and shriveling away to nothing. "That means Kardom has a majority of ministers who support him over me," I said, my throat suddenly painful with unshed tears.

"Yes. It is now seven to three in Mr. Kardom's favor. But do not lose hope, Princess. We just need a miracle, and I have confidence that you will find one."

"I don't know how I'm going to do that—" A thought struck me, one that I almost hated to put into words. "Er … would my marriage to a successful businessman be considered a miracle?"

Silence once again was the response to my question. "That would depend on the man in question," Danielle answered slowly. "I do not wish to tell you what to do with your life, but you must be very careful with actions that could be perceived in a way you do not intend. I take it you are going to be married?"

"Yes," I said, my feelings so tangled I wasn't sure I could ever unravel them. "To a very successful Greek man named Dmitri."

"Ah. Successful is good. What line of work is he in, if you do not mind me inquiring?"

"Real estate development," I said slowly, knowing how it sounded. "But they're green buildings, and mostly in areas of the world that need housing for underrepresented people. It's not like he'd use my connection to Beck to buy up land and develop the hell out of it."

"Just the fact that you recognize that is a possibility concerns me," she said gently. "Naturally, I know you have no ulterior motives, and I'm equally sure any man you marry will likewise not have plans to exploit your relationship with our government, or your position in society, but unfortunately, Mr. Kardom …" She let the sentence trail off.

"Kardom would use it as proof that Dmitri and I are up to no good, yes, I know." I sighed heavily. "Thank you anyway, Ms. Martin."

"I will let you know if anything else happens," she said with forced cheerfulness that was awful to hear. "Do not let your spirits get down. We still have seven weeks to convince the other ministers that you are ideal for the job."

I thanked her and rang off, my stomach knotted with worry until I reminded myself that would do no one any good.

A half hour later I pushed aside the concerns of Beck to focus on the matter at hand.

"Panoush has kind of a thick accent that makes it a wee bit hard to understand him, but he's a very nice man, and he was set to help me with our prenup, but then Iakovos went all bossy on me and refused to have one." Harry smiled at me, one hand resting on her belly. "But I'm sure he'll be a great help for you."

"I feel awful about this," I said glumly despite the fact that we were being driven through the busy traffic of Athens by Harry's own private chauffeur. "I don't like being beholden to people. It goes against everything my father taught me. He's probably rolling in his grave over the idea of me accepting help from you when it's not a matter of life or death, but I just don't see any other way around it."

"We're going to be family," Harry said, giving me a little nudge with her elbow.

"Still, it's going to cost a lot for a lawyer, and I was raised to not accept favors because ... well, because of the way people are—not that you are doing this with an ulterior motive—and it's hard to break the habit of a lifetime. I will pay you back, though."

"Bah. I wouldn't hear of you repaying me for a couple of hours of lawyer time."

"Our deal was that I let you front the money only if you let me pay you back," I reminded her. "Mind you, it might be a few weeks. I'll need a couple of interviews with the Noblesse magazine, but assuming they like the one with Dmitri, that shouldn't be a problem."

"You are not paying me for this. Consider it my wedding gift to you," she answered.

"This isn't a real marriage," I reminded her, rubbing my temple. Dmitri and I had decided to tell his cousin and Harry about the situation, in case they could see a way out of my predicament without having to go to such lengths, but they agreed that a marriage—even a temporary one—would stop Kardom in his tracks.

"A wedding!" Harry had said earlier when we broke the news to them that morning. We'd dropped in to let them know what was going on, which they appreciated, Harry looking particularly pleased. "I'm not big on them, myself, but I'm happy to help you plan."

"This is not even remotely a wedding situation that requires any sort of plans," I told her. "They kind of weird me out, to be honest. All those people standing there staring at you while you spout all sorts of personal, private stuff ... ugh. No, since we have to do this, we're doing it as minimal as possible. Dmitri looked it all up."

"I applied for a license first thing this morning," he said, nodding. "It will take three days before it becomes valid."

"But what about Thyra?" Harry had asked. "Isn't her license fake?"

"We assume so, since she doesn't recall any other time that she was drugged and could have been made to sign a license application without being aware of it," Dmitri answered.

"That's why I applied for a proper Greek one, as well," I said, taking a scrap of paper from Valentino. He was biting it viciously, tearing off little shreds and spitting them out.

Iakovos eyed me for a second before sliding his gaze over to look at Dmitri. I had a feeling he wanted to say a few things to his cousin privately, no doubt warning him about the folly of marrying me, and since I agreed with him, I made an excuse and took Valentino to the bathroom with me for a few minutes.

By the time I returned, Dmitri and Iakovos were arguing. Loudly.

"I understand that, but I'm not some idiot who doesn't know how to handle his own affairs," Dmitri said with a frown at his cousin.

Iakovos frowned right back at him. "I don't think you're an idiot. I wouldn't trust you with my business if I thought that. I just want you protected—"

He stopped at the sight of me, looking vaguely uncomfortable.

"Uh-oh, did I interrupt a discussion where you were telling Dmitri that he needs a really strict prenuptial agreement so that I don't take him for every cent he has?"

Both men looked away.

Harry sighed, and awkwardly got to her feet. "Bathroom break again. I swear, my bladder gets smaller with each baby. It's a good thing this is the last one, or I wouldn't be able to hold more than a teaspoon of pee at a time. Yes, Thyra, that's what they were talking about, not that any of us really thinks you are going to do that, but Dmitri is a very dear friend, and Yacky wants to make sure he hasn't gone insane with the thought of marrying an actual princess. No one say anything good until I get back."

She toddled off to the bathroom. I set down Valentino, who jumped up onto an end table and fixed his wicked yellow eyes on Iakovos, much to the latter's discomfort. "As it happens, I was going to bring up the subject myself. I don't want any of Dmitri's money, Iakovos. I haven't secretly tricked him into marriage just so I can benefit financially—I simply want to stop Kardom, and if you know of someone else who I could blight with a marriage to me—"

"No," Dmitri said, pulling me close to his side, making me feel warm and fuzzy despite the fact that I knew I should protest such a blatantly possessive demonstration. "You're not marrying anyone else. You'll blight me, and no one else."

"You romantic devil, you," I told him, unable to keep from flashing him a little smile in hopes he let his almost dimples go wild.

He did, and they did, and I melted into his side. "As to a prenup, I was, in fact, going to talk to Thyra about it, but not simply so as to protect Papaioannou Green. Thyra needs to be protected, as well."

"Me?" I laughed a jaded laugh. "I have all of fifty-seven euros to my name. I doubt if we got divorced the day after we got married if you'd benefit much from that."

He gave me a long look with his pretty green eyes that made me want to kiss him all over his adorable face. And chest. And, hell, the rest of him, too. "Whether or not you like the fact, you are royalty. I don't know what claims your spouse would have on Beck, or any hereditary rights and privileges granted to you, but you need protection, as well."

"There's not a lot of ways you could benefit from marrying me, so far as that goes," I said thoughtfully. "Unless I'm recognized as crown princess, then you might have access to whatever funds the government granted me. And I could grant you a title, but I don't know that it would benefit you financially, or, rather, hurt me should you marry me so that you could be Grand Duke Dmitri."

"Holy shit," Harry said, returning from the bathroom. "Dmitri could be a duke?"

"A margrave, actually. It's roughly the equivalent to a duke, and is one of the traditional titles for a male consort, assuming I'm remembering my family history correctly." I looked at Dmitri.

He pinched my butt. "I told my lawyer to start working on a prenup agreement this morning, but I think perhaps you should have your own lawyer to make sure that any agreement between us wasn't skewed to my benefit."

Which is why two hours later Harry and I were in the car, on the way to see her former lawyer Panoush. He did, in fact, have a thick accent, one that took every ounce of my attention to keep up with, but in the end, he agreed that he would have no problem representing my interests in the agreement, and after he insisted on a selfie with me so that he could show his wife he'd met a real princess, Harry and I returned to her apartment.

"You're welcome to stay as long as you like," she told me when we rode up in the elevator. "Iakovos said he has several meetings today, and some of them were with Dmitri, so I expect they won't be back until evening. Unless, of course, you want to go somewhere else, although if your cousin is out there looking for you, it might be better to stay where you know he can't get to you."

"Thank you, I wouldn't mind staying for a bit so long as I'm not in your way." I felt mildly guilty about infringing on her privacy, but she had assured me in the car that she was taking a break before writing her next book, and was going a little stir-crazy, since she wasn't supposed to be too active. "Although I don't think Kardom is running around Athens planning on snatching me on the street. He's much too controlling for that. He likes to lay plans, and then gets annoyed when people don't fall in with them."

"What a jerk. Well, you'll be safe with us. Iakovos already told the concierge team to not let anyone up to see us unless we clear it first. Hello, Mrs. Avrabos. I think we'll be ready for lunch in a few. At least, I hope Thyra is, because I'm famished."

The housekeeper greeted us, giving Harry a warm smile. "I am happy to feed you whenever you like, Kyria, but Miss Patricia is here with a friend, and she says she must see you urgently."

"Oh?" Harry frowned and dumped her purse on a console table next to the front door. "I wonder what she wants. You might as well come and meet the bane of the Papaioannou brothers, Thyra. Oooh, can I lay your title on her? She'll hate that I'm chummy with a princess who she doesn't know."

I giggled while I followed her into the living room, very interested to see this Patricia who had set Dmitri up with an old friend.

Two women were standing at the floor-to-ceiling windows, each of them holding a glass of wine, laughing about something as they turned and saw us.

"Harry, darling," drawled a petite blond woman who set down her wine and approached us, giving air kisses to Harry. "You're even bigger than you were the last time. Are you having quadruplets this time?"

"Thyra, this is Patricia," Harry told me with a long, martyred sigh. "She may seem like an obnoxiously predatory woman who will attempt to steal any man she desires regardless of whether or not that man is in a relationship or even married, but she's not. Most of the time."

I fought back a laugh, figuring that the two women had a complicated relationship. "Hello, Patricia," I said, offering a hand. She gave it a perfunctory shake, raking me over with a visual examination that ended almost before it began. She was clearly not impressed with what she saw.

"You know Audrey, don't you?" she asked Harry. My eyes widened at the name. This was Dmitri's date of the other evening?

I gave her a long, thorough visual examination, noting that she was about as different from me as could be humanly possible. Where I was short, had black hair, and was round everywhere, Audrey was tall and slim, with an elegant way of walking that reminded me of a model on the runway, with a touch of ballerina about her graceful hands. Hadn't Harry said something about the women the Papaioannou men preferred all looking like they were underwear models? That description fit Audrey to a tee. Not only did she have the willowy form of a model; she had shoulder-length red hair, and the sort of face that men swooned over.

She glided over to shake Harry's hand while Patricia added, "She's back in Greece now that all the legalities with her late husband's estate have been settled."

"Never marry a man with adult children," Audrey said, giving me a polite little nod before she turned back to Harry and added, "They cause you endless grief when it comes to proving a will is valid when they don't benefit by it. It's a pleasure to meet you, Harry. Patricia has told me so much about you."

"Audrey is in town for the bachelor auction," Patricia said, taking Harry by the arm and hauling her over to the couch. Harry shot me a look over her shoulder, the light of merriment evident in her eyes.

I bit my lip to keep from laughing, and followed Audrey, picking up Valentino to sit on the chair where he'd been curled up, snoozing. Audrey claimed the other chair, angling away from me and leaning forward. If I hadn't been an introvert, and more than happy to be on the fringes of a conversation, I'd have been offended by the way both women had excluded me.

"Oh, the auction!" Harry made a face. "I forgot all about it what with … well, family things. It's … let's see … tomorrow night, yes?"

"That's right," Patricia gave her a little frown. "You are still going to be able to MC it, aren't you? We can get you a barstool to park your bulk on, but if you don't think you're going to be up to it—"

"I'll be there," Harry said quickly. "Iakovos and I always support the children's hospital, and this seems more personal than just giving them money, which of course we do anyway. I was actually asking about the date because I wanted to make sure that Dmitri would be free to do it."

Patricia's frown grew darker. "Why wouldn't he be? He's in town. Audrey said they had quite the time together the other night."

"We did," Audrey said, brushing a nonexistent wrinkle on her dress. "We got along together very well."

The emphasis she put on the word "very" didn't escape me. And judging from the way Harry's eyes widened, she also heard the implication with which Audrey was all but beating us over the head.

For a moment, my stomach seemed to turn over, a sick feeling making clammy little tendrils grip it. Dmitri didn't say what he'd done that night other than spent it thinking about me … but what if he was exaggerating? I didn't think he was the sort of man who'd outright lie to a woman any more than I thought he'd engage in sexual acts with a woman one night and a different woman the following, but at the same time, what if he had a nicer time with Audrey than he had wanted me to know?

"Oh?" Harry asked, her eyes sparkling as she glanced at me. "You guys had an instant rapport?"

"Very much so." Audrey looked smug now, sharing a smile with her friend. "We have a lot in common, and clicked on a number of levels. He's such an interesting man. Very romantic, too," she said with a throaty laugh that I could never achieve without smoking six packs a day.

"Is he?" Harry asked before turning to me. "I had no idea. I mean, I've known him for more than ten years, but I had no idea he was Mr. Smooth. Would you say that was true, Thyra?"

I shot her a quick look of both reprimand and amusement. "He's definitely interesting. But as to romantic?" I thought about it for a minute. "I guess so."

"Do you know Dmitri?" Patricia asked, her gaze sharp on me as she gave me another once-over. She relaxed as soon as she'd done so, no doubt mentally comparing me with Audrey, and clearly marking her friend the winner in looks and personality.

"As a matter of fact, I do." I didn't say any more because I didn't think it was any of their business, and also, I refused to play the "Dmitri is mine" game that Audrey clearly enjoyed.

Harry covered up a laugh with a cough.

"Then you will know that he is the sort of man who makes the sort of little gestures that say so much," Audrey said in a tone that implied she didn't believe a word I was saying. "I find that infinitely more gratifying than a man who talks the talk without following through."

I just smiled but said nothing, refusing to be baited.

"Weren't you going out with him tonight?" Patricia prompted her friend, obviously hoping to score some points against me by showing me that Dmitri was far more interested in Audrey than me.

I thought of asking Dmitri if that was true, but remembered how he'd woken me up that morning, his hands and mouth and various other body parts making sure we both started the day with silly grins plastered all over our respective faces.

He couldn't do that if he was pining for the redheaded underwear model.

Audrey gave a little moue. "We were, but he had to cancel. I'll be seeing him tomorrow, though, before the auction."

"It's a good thing your husband's estate is settled, since I'm sure there will be quite a few people bidding for him at the auction," Patricia told her with a smug smile. "But I have a feeling you won't let anyone outbid you."

"Speaking of that," Harry interrupted with a bright smile. "When I asked about the bachelor auction being tomorrow, I wasn't checking just to see if Dmitri would have time for the event." Harry pinned me back with an unasked question, clearly asking permission. Although I hadn't intended on telling anyone what Dmitri and I were going to do, since it wasn't going to be a real marriage, for some reason that I refused to look at too closely, I itched to take that smug look off Audrey's face.

I gave Harry a little nod. She beamed.

"Oh?" Patricia shot a suspicious glance from Harry to me. "What do you mean?"

Harry's smile grew even wider. She clearly took a whole lot of pleasure in saying, "I wanted to make sure that Dmitri would still be a bachelor then. But it won't be until Thursday that you guys are getting married, right, Thyra?"

"Married?" Audrey squawked, staring at me in abject shock and no little amount of disbelief.

Patricia narrowed her eyes at Harry. "What's this? Since when is Dmitri getting married? I haven't heard anything about it, or about"—she gestured toward me—"her."

"The princess, you mean?"

"What princess?" Patricia asked, now in a full-fledged glare at Harry.

Audrey looked stunned for another few seconds; then her eyes also narrowed, but I was the target of her ire.

Harry adopted an astonished expression that had me

biting back laughter. There was a wicked sense to her humor that made me feel like we would be good friends. "Oh, that's right, I didn't introduce you properly. Ladies, may I present Her Serene Highness Princess Juliane of Sonderburg-Beck, although she prefers to be called Thyra. Dmitri and Thyra are going to be married on Thursday."

"But ... Dmitri ..." Audrey went from a confused stammer to anger. "I see. Naturally, you will understand that I'm more than a little startled by this news, given our date the other night, and how well we got along, and the things he said. ..." She let the inference hang in the air.

Once again a little doubt spiked me, but I quelled it. She was just trying to save face. Dmitri wasn't the sort of man to two-time anyone.

"They haven't made the engagement known," Harry said blithely, and at her words, a chill gripped me.

"No, we haven't, and I'd appreciate it if you didn't mention it," I said quickly, the sudden image of Kardom making my blood turn cold. If he knew I was going to be married in three days, he'd redouble his plans, going to who knew what lengths to stop it. I had a horrible image of him attacking Dmitri, my stomach turning over again at the thought of him being harmed. Or worse.

"Why?" Patricia asked, her expression hard with suspicion. "Why don't you want it known?"

I stared at her, unable to answer her, my mind too filled with thoughts of Kardom kidnapping me again.

"Because she's a princess, of course," Harry said after a very long few seconds. "Do you think the press would let her wedding to a local man go without a big hullabaloo? They want their wedding to sail under the radar of press and society until it's a done deal."

I shot her a grateful glance. "Yes, it's important to us both that we have a simple wedding, with just a few friends and family."

"How very ... quaint," Patricia said with a meaningful look at her friend.

I sat uncomfortably for the next ten minutes while Patricia, ignoring me, went over Harry's role at the charity auction the following evening. "It's too bad we lost Theo to that American, but I'm sure Dmitri will fetch a large sum," she said before rising. "I know Audrey plans on bidding for his services."

"Services?" I couldn't help but ask, wondering just what sort of an auction this was.

Audrey smiled at me, showing what I thought was more teeth than necessary. "All the bachelors have volunteered to donate twenty-four hours of their time to whoever wins the auction for them, the time to be put to whatever use the winner chooses. I have some amusing things for Dmitri and me to do for the entire twenty-four hours."

Harry slid me a questioning look, clearly wondering how I was going to react to such a blatant statement.

I stood up, as well, and laughed so loudly I woke up Valentino from where he was snoozing in a patch of sun on the carpet. "You . . ." I was so amused at the thought of the look on Dmitri's face when she asked him to do something sexy, like prance around wearing nothing, that tears leaked out of the corners of my eyes. Mindful of how rude I was being, I made an effort and got a grip on myself, wiping my weeping eyes when I straightened up and faced Audrey. "You can sure try," I finally managed to get out, but not without my lips twitching a few times.

She snarled something quite rude in French, then excused herself, telling Patricia that she'd wait for her downstairs.

"I'm so sorry," I called after her, still wiping my eyes. "No offense intended! You kind of hit my funny bone with that comment."

She said nothing, just marched out of the apartment, all righteous indignation.

"Well," Patricia said, giving me a scathing look. "You may be a princess—if, in fact, you are, since I've never heard of a place called Sonderburg-Beck—but you certainly have the manners of a pig."

"You're absolutely right," I said, sniffing back the running nose that inevitably accompanied tears, even those of hilarity. "I didn't mean to laugh quite so hard at your friend, and for that, I apologize. Although, hoo boy, I haven't laughed that way in a long time."

"I know all the royalty in the area, and I've never heard of you," she continued, narrowing her eyes.

"That's because Beck is a poor little country that's just getting back onto its feet after getting their independence, isn't it, Thyra?" Harry said.

I nodded. "It's located near Poland, so I'm not surprised if you haven't heard of it."

"Poor?" Patricia pounced on the word. "So, you've found yourself a sugar daddy to latch on to, have you?"

I stared at her in openmouthed horror.

She turned to Harry to add, "I'd say I was surprised you allowed such a gold digger into the family, but that's nothing new to the Papaioannou clan, is it?"

I felt sick, physically sick, my stomach turning over at the accusation. I wanted to protest that I wasn't like that, but knew she wouldn't believe me. It was suddenly all too clear that people would think I was marrying Dmitri for the monetary advantages it brought me. Worse, the Beck ministers were sure to think the same thing, no doubt assuming I picked him as a way to make myself look solvent and worthy in their eyes.

"For God's sake, Patricia—" Harry's frown was a thing of beauty to behold, but Patricia cut her off before she could really get going.

"I will see you tomorrow," she told Harry, her eyes all but shooting daggers at me as she stomped past me. "I hope that you and Iakovos will come without any unexpected … guests."

"I'm so sorry about that, Thyra," Harry apologized. "That was seriously uncalled-for, and I think it's about time we instigate another six-month Patricia ban."

"It's OK," I said, trying not to let her see how devastated

I felt. It wasn't her problem, and I'd be damned before I burdened her with my issues. "I'm sorry I ran them off, though."

"Don't be—although Patricia and I have worked out a relationship where we mostly don't hate each other, she is far from someone with whom I wish to spend time, and her friend seems to be just like her. What Patricia said was just over the line, though." Harry put an arm around me when I made an embarrassed face. "I can't imagine what she was thinking."

"Probably that there was no way a short, round woman with glasses and horrible social skills could interest Dmitri in any way, shape, or form."

"But you do," Harry said, watching me carefully.

"Evidently. I can't explain it, but I'm not going to question it too much. He's a pretty awesome man, and I'm counting my blessings that he gave me a second look."

"Don't be so hard on yourself. You're charming. You have the loveliest eyes, and the most beautiful hair I've ever seen. It lies so smooth and straight. Mine is always a wild tangle, and I'd give anything to have hair like yours. Dmitri is a smart man, and he knows what he's about. Like Yacky and Theo, he has the ability to look past the glamorous but incredibly shallow women who flit in and out of his life, and recognizes substance when he sees it."

I was flattered by her words despite making a little noise of protest, and quickly turned the subject to how she and Iakovos had met. By the time she'd told me about that, and how her brother-in-law had met his wife, we'd eaten lunch, sat outside in the shade until it got too hot, and then both had a little rest.

Mrs. Avrabos showed me into a guest room into which she'd placed a new litter box and a bowl of water. Before I could do more than take off my shoes, she was back with a little plate of tuna.

"Is for the kitty," she said, offering the treat to Valentino. "He keeps me company while you were gone. He is a very nice kitty."

He head bonked her leg before rubbing himself around her ankle, his shepherd's crook tail caressing her leg for a second before he ambled over to the plate.

"He is that. Thank you for putting up with him while Harry and I were gone."

"You bring him the next time you visit," she said, running a hand down his back, causing him to go into elevator-butt mode.

I lay back on the bed, not overly tired, but definitely needing some quiet time to recharge my batteries; however, before I could snort a couple of times over Audrey's comment—which still struck me as hilarious—I must have dozed off, because I woke up almost two hours later with Valentino lying on my chest, purring as he stared at me.

Dmitri was in the living room, looking just as he had that morning—adorable, sexy, handsome as sin, and extremely businesslike in a tailored suit. Iakovos was sitting with Harry cuddled into him, but he'd taken off his tie and suit jacket, looking much more relaxed.

"Hello," I said when Dmitri, who had been standing at the floor-to-ceiling glass wall looking out at the city, turned to greet me. "I hope you haven't been waiting long. I must have been a lot more tired than I thought."

"I looked in on you a little bit ago, but you were sound asleep with your protector on you. The look he gave me made it quite clear I wasn't to disturb you," he answered, and bent to pick up Valentino, who had come over to head bonk his shoes a couple of times.

"You'll get cat hair all over you," I warned him, frowning.

Dmitri shrugged. "That's what a cleaner is for. Harry has been telling me about your adventures today."

I slid a glance toward Harry. She gave me a little headshake, which I think Iakovos caught, because he pinched her thigh, making her giggle and whisper something into his ear.

"We went to her lawyer, yes. He said that he will make up a provision that under no circumstances will you benefit from my ancestry unless I should wish it. Assuming your lawyer does something similar to protect your assets, then I think we're good."

"He has, and will draw up a final agreement for us to sign tomorrow," Dmitri said. "He also suggested revising my will. I don't suppose you have one?"

I nodded. "I do, actually. My brother made me get one even though neither one of us has any money. Just so you know, if I drop dead tomorrow, Chris will inherit my vast fortune of fifty-seven euros. But I suppose I should change it to reflect being married to you."

"It's a good idea to update a will in such cases," Iakovos said, giving Harry a long look when she bit his earlobe. "Er ... would you both excuse us for a few minutes? Harry needs ... er ..."

"You're damned right I do," she said, using his arm to hoist herself up. "Bathroom first, then ... yes."

"Oh, Harry," I said, stopping her when she was toddling out of the room. "Do you ... since I'm in debt to you already, Papa really can't complain. ... Could I use your phone again? I'd like to call my brother in Scotland."

She looked at me in amazement for a moment, then slid a look past me to Dmitri. "Er ... I think the battery is low. Let me charge it for a bit first, OK?"

Iakovos more or less pulled her out of the room, down the hall to their suite. I frowned. "That was odd," I said, turning back to Dmitri. "I wonder why she—whoa. What's the matter?"

"Why," he asked, his expression as black as night, "did you ask to use her phone?"

"Because I want to call my brother and tell him we're getting married. Just in case for some weird reason he heard about it from someone else. Why are you so angry?"

"I am the man you are about to marry," he said, marching over to me, gripping me firmly on the arms. I had an idea he wanted to shake me but was restraining himself. "You agreed to live with me. You said you were falling in love with me. Dammit, I let you frolic on my body this morning in a manner that no other woman has frolicked. Why wouldn't you ask to use my phone instead of Harry's?"

Oh dear. I'd hurt his feelings. "I'm sorry. I didn't mean to make you feel like you weren't worthy of a phone borrow, but since I'm in debt to Harry—"

"You are not."

"I am. She's fronting the lawyer's fee until I get paid by the magazine."

He took a deep, deep breath, which I would have enjoyed much more if he didn't have a suit and shirt on hiding his glorious chest from me. "I will pay for the lawyer. It was my idea; thus it's only right that I pay."

"Oh, no," I said, sliding out of his grip. Now I was annoyed. "I thought we had this out already. Dmitri, I might have asked you to marry me, but I don't intend to take advantage of you—"

"It's not taking advantage to ask me to use my damned phone!" he thundered.

"No, and I'm sorry about that. I see now that you feel slighted that I'd ask to use Harry's phone and not yours, but I just figured that since I owed her already, an additional expense in the form of a phone call wouldn't hurt. But the phone situation aside—although I really would like to call my brother, so if you don't mind if I used your phone, I'd like to do that—the matter of a lawyer's fees is entirely different. It's my responsibility, and as you know because I've told you this at least a half dozen times, my parents taught me to always pay my debts."

He ran one hand through his hair for a moment, his green eyes blazing with a light I'd never seen. "I used to think Jake exaggerated the aggravation he had with Harry, but I see now I underestimated just what he went through. Well, I'm not going to have it, do you hear me? I'm not going to let you live like a pauper just because you are too stubborn to let me be proud of you."

I straightened my shoulders. "I am not stubborn! I simply don't like being used because of who I am, and I would never dream of doing the same to you. And as for help, of course I accept help! I'm letting you help me by marrying me, and I don't see how I could do any more than that."

"You won't even use my phone because you think it leaves you beholden to me, for Christ's sake," he almost yelled. "Thyra, I understand that you don't want to live like a parasite, but if we are to stand any chance of having a relationship that doesn't crash and burn immediately, you're going to have to accept a few things about me. One of which is how I treat my lovers. It gives me pleasure to give them things like jewelry or clothing or little trinkets and things like that. And before you say what I know you want to say, this isn't about self-sufficiency, and you taking pride in making your own way. I'm all for that. I've lived that. This is about trust."

I stared at him, unsure of why he was so angry. "I thought we had this out already. I trust you, Dmitri. And I don't mind little love gifts. Those are fine. I want to make things for you that I think you'll like. But you come from a different world, one where people take advantage of you because you are rich as sin—"

"I'm not," he said quickly, but the tight muscle in his jaw loosened enough that he gave a half smile. "Iakovos is rich as sin. I'm just rich as a minor misdemeanor."

I put my hand on his chest and gently bit his chin. Really, could the man be any more adorable? "You remember that I told you how my dad raised Chris and I to be responsible for ourselves?"

"Considering you've mentioned that at least once a day, including just a few minutes ago, yes," he said with a twist to his lips.

"If I'm hitting you over the head with it, it's only because you don't seem to understand how important it is to me. My dad instilled the importance of self-reliance because people equated our heritage with money. I can't tell you the number of times people assumed I was rich, and tried to use me for their benefit. Later, when I had enough smarts to make it clear that I did not inherit anything but an empty title, they wanted to use me to make themselves feel more important. So I very much know what it's like to have people use you for what you have instead of who you are, and I refuse to be one of them. You may be only moderately rich, but it's still rich, and I won't be like the others who expect material goods from you."

He tensed up again. "Do you expect to set a monetary limit of any gifts I want to give you?"

"No. Well, maybe just a rough guideline," I said lamely, confused by the anger I could feel inside him. I wanted to do whatever it took to make him happy again, but at the same time, I wasn't willing to simply cast off everything I'd been raised to believe was right. "I don't expect you to give me a house or something like that."

"I hadn't planned on giving you a house," he answered, his gorgeous eyes glittering. "But if I wanted to, I would expect you to accept it, just as you accept everything that goes along with living with me. Or did you plan to chip in on my electricity bill?"

I gasped in horror, my back stiffening. "No, I didn't. I'm not that stupid, Dmitri. I know you can afford to live in your apartment without me contributing to it, although I do think that perhaps we could work up some sort of plan with regards to cat supplies, but I was going to leave that discussion for another day. However!" I held up my hand to stop him when he started growling at me. A little tremor of excitement ran through me. Dear God, he was magnificent, even when he was irrationally angry. I just wanted to tear that suit right off him, and lick every inch of his glorious body. "However, I am not a gold digger, even if that's what people think about me. I want to be with you because I like you. A lot. I like talking to you, and touching you, and kissing you, and doing all that frolicking that you let me do this morning, but nowhere in the list of things I like about you is the plan to milk you for all the presents I can get. I'd rather die, first."

"And therein is the problem. Thyra, I want you to let me treat you like the princess you are."

"And I appreciate that, but your friend Patricia already called me a gold digger, and—"

"I don't give a damn what she thinks," he argued. "This isn't about anyone else. It's about you and me."

I was silent for a moment. "And what about Beck?" I finally asked.

"What about them?"

"You said you wanted me to fight for them. What will they think if gossip from people like Patricia gets around that I'm benefiting financially by marrying you? Just one person calling me a gold digger isn't a big deal, but if enough people say it, the ministers of Beck may think I really am the type of person who would take advantage of you like that. And I couldn't blame them at all for not wanting me to represent their country."

He stared at me for a few seconds, then released my arms. "I won't let such a smear campaign happen."

"You know what the Internet is like. Once a whisper hits it, it turns into a tidal wave," I pointed out.

"And that's where being minor-misdemeanor rich will help. Money can squash such waves before they get started."

"Which would make me feel hideously guilty that you had to spend your misdemeanor money just because of me. And on something so worthless!" I slapped my hands on my thighs, frustration mingling with a warm glow of appreciation for the fact that he wanted to protect me. No one had ever wanted to protect me. At least, not since I had become an adult.

Dmitri ran his hand through his hair again, disturbing the curls and making my fingers want to comb through them. "I just am at a loss with you. I swear, I just can't make you understand."

"I understand," I told him, giving in to my desire and gently finger-combing his hair back the way it should be. "You want to give me presents because it makes you feel good, and you want to protect me because you are a naturally chivalrous man. I'm willing to accept a little of both. Just not all of everything, if you know what I mean."

"It's not just presents—" He stopped for the count of eight, looking thoughtful. "You're not ... your objection is that you feel like you're using me if we live together as a couple, is that right?"

"Only if you give me a bunch of things. Expensive things. If you want to give me a car or something like that, and expect me to take money from you, then yes, that's going to make me feel like I'm using you. Like I'm the gold digger that Patricia says I am."

A slow smile curled up the corners of his mouth. "Then the solution is to have you work for me."

"Huh? Work how?" I asked, having vague, horrified thoughts of sex for hire.

"You can be my personal assistant," he said, his smile growing. "Yes, that will do nicely, I think."

"Personal assistant like office things? I can type, but I'm not superfast at it. My Google-fu is strong, though, so if you need something researched, I could do that." I had to admit, I liked this idea. I'd been an assistant before, and was perfectly able to fetch coffee, make photocopies, file, and so forth. If Dmitri really needed that sort of help, I was more than able to give it. "But what about Alexis? Isn't he your assistant?"

"I intended on moving him into doing more organizational work with the business, and less personal work." His smile got a bit cheeky. "Whereas I would much prefer to keep you entirely personal."

"Well ... so long as it didn't interfere with any work the magazine wants me to do, and of course if Beck comes through—but even then, that's likely to be just a part-time job, one that would leave me free to help you out, too."

"Yes, I think this will work very well," he said in a satisfied voice. "You will assist me, and I will pay you a salary for that work. That way, I can give you things, and it won't tweak your pride, or make you feel like you're taking advantage of me."

I had been about to kiss him, but I pulled back, my eyes narrowing. "Oh, hell no!"

"Pardon?"

I poked him in the chest. "You're going to try to give me a big salary, aren't you? I won't take it! I will look up what a normal PA makes, and you can pay me that."

"We will naturally negotiate a rate that allows me to not feel like I'm a slave driver, and yet will include periodic gifts to you as I see fit."

"Negotiate," I said slowly. "That sounds like a good idea. I can have Harry's lawyer draw up a list of my demands, as well as a list of deductions that I will expect to contribute if I am drawing a salary. Such as food for Valentino, since he's my dependent, vet bills, and litter, and treats and such."

He stared at me for a good half minute, the muscles in his jaw working again; then he pulled out his cell phone and handed it to me, saying as he walked away, "Call your brother. I am going to beat the hell out of Jake's punching bag for ten minutes. Possibly longer if I start thinking about what sorts of things you're going to tell the lawyer to include in your list of demands."

"Don't think I'm going to give in to you just because you're quirkily adorable, and I want badly to lick you," I called after him when he disappeared down a hallway, smiling to myself for a few minutes while I thought about how wonderful he was. Really, he couldn't be more perfect if he tried. I dialed Chris's number, thinking about how just the touch of Dmitri's hands had made me melt all over him. "And really, if he can do that to me while I was frolicking on him, just how am I going to survive when he really unleashes all that sexy … er … Chris?"

"Hullo. I was wondering if you were going to remember that you had called me. Who is unleashing his sexiness on you?"

"Of course I remembered I called you. It was only a few seconds ago that I dialed, and you know full well that I talk to myself. Mr. Sexy is Dmitri."

"Ah. Sounds Greek."

"He is Greek."

"I take it your trip to Athens is a success, then?"

"On so many levels. I have a cat now. His name is Valentino, and he likes to go for walks. How are you? Have you heard anything from Kardom? Or Maggie, for that matter?"

"I'm well, and no on both fronts. Why? Is he bothering you again?"

"You could say that." I debated telling Chris about the drugging, but decided that it would make his policeman's soul extremely unhappy, and since there was nothing I could do (or even prove) about it, I decided to withhold that information for a bit. "I wanted to let you know that I'm getting married in three days."

Silence filled my ear for a good fifteen seconds. "Dmitri?" my brother finally asked.

"Yes. He's a very nice man. I think you'll like him. And he knows about us, and doesn't care."

"What's his name?"

"I told you, Dmitri."

"Full name."

I sighed. "Chris, you don't need to do a background check on him. He's the man I was sent to interview, as a matter of fact, so not only does he make me laugh, and he doesn't mind that I'm overly curvy; he's a very successful businessman."

"Full name. Do you happen to know his date of birth?"

I knew well that I wasn't going to be able to get by without giving Chris the bare minimum of info on Dmitri, so I didn't fight it. "Christos Dmitri Papaioannou. Yes, I know it because I saw him fill in the marriage license application, and no, I'm not going to tell you. He's not a weirdo. He's not trying to use me. He doesn't give a damn about Beck. And for the record, I asked him to marry me."

In hindsight, that might not have been the smartest thing to say. Chris had an awful lot of suspicion about people, and if he thought that I was being slighted or used in any way, he'd take umbrage. A big, burly six-foot-two sort of umbrage.

"He must be the Christos Papaioannou who is thirty-eight, born in some town with an unpronounceable name in Greece … what did you say? Why didn't this man who is so awesome propose to you?"

"Because neither of us believes in marriage. You know how I feel about that. It's just a state-sanctioned legality, nothing more."

"And yet you saw fit to ask this man to marry you, rather than him doing the asking? How long have you known each other?"

Hell. I really didn't want to get into that. "Long enough to know that I want to live with him."

"Allowing him to do all sorts of things to you, evidently." I could hear Chris breathing heavily through his nose, as well as the faint tapping of computer keys. "What's going on, Tee?"

"Nothing other than I'm marrying a perfectly nice, very successful man, and I thought you would like to know so you can be happy for me. I didn't know you were going to give me the third degree!"

"Where are you now? Is this your phone?"

"I'm in the apartment of Dmitri's cousin and his wife, both of whom are also nice, although I have to admit that Iakovos intimidates me. But Harry is nice. She's going to have her fifth child in a few weeks." I added that last bit of trivia in because I wanted Chris to understand just how normal everything was here.

If you could call my life normal. Which I certainly didn't.

"I still want to get to the bottom of the reason this man didn't ask you to marry him."

"Really, Chris! It's not important!"

"Most men would think it was. Aren't Greek men supposed to be very macho? What sort of man lets a woman ask him?"

"One who is extremely secure in his masculinity," I snapped in return. "For God's sake, Chris, I didn't call to argue—I just wanted to tell you what I was doing. Oh, and before you ask, Dmitri is signing a prenuptial agreement that says he doesn't benefit in any way from Beck or our family."

"Christ, I didn't think of that. You'll need a new will to exclude him from all that. He's probably figured out that you're an easy mark, and he has some way to gain from marrying you."

"Gah!" I yelled into the phone. "It's like you don't even know me!"

"Of course I know you. I'm simply trying to establish why you feel it necessary to ask a man to marry you when you, yourself, just stated that the legality of marriage has no meaning for you. Did you promise to get this man a residency card?"

"No, of course not. His mom was Irish, so he probably could live in the UK if he wanted. And no, marriage doesn't matter, but Dmitri does. I like him a lot. I think I could very easily fall—" I stopped, swearing to myself.

"Fall in love with him? You're not in love with the man who you're marrying, and who does things to you, sexual things, that make you wonder how you are going to survive?" I had to hold the phone away from my ear. Chris was always a shouter when he got angry. I mused that Dmitri held on to his temper better, although he, too, evidently had limits.

"I'm going to have to go now," I told my brother, ignoring his sputtered protests and demands that I answer his questions and tell him just what the hell I was really up to. "I'm borrowing Dmitri's phone, and just in case he doesn't have free international calling, I don't want to rack up too big of a bill. I'll talk to you after the wedding, OK? Big kiss. Love you."

"Thyra, I forbid you to hang up your ph—" I tapped the phone symbol, ending the call despite what I knew would be Chris's dire threats.

"My brother can be a boob at times, but he really is a love," I told Valentino, who had been sitting and watching me with an unblinking gaze. He rose, crooked his tail, and marched down the hallway in the direction Dmitri had disappeared. I followed, not wanting to open doors to find him, since I didn't know which were family rooms, and which weren't, but I needn't have worried. Valentino stopped in front of a door. I tapped on it and opened it just enough to peek in.

It was clearly some sort of a home gym, with the standard elliptical machine, a weight bench, and in the corner a big punching bag. Dmitri had his back to me, his suit jacket and tie hanging over the bars of a stationary bike, his shirt clinging to his back as he punched the bag, moving in an oddly graceful rhythm. I watched for a few minutes, then opened the door wide enough for Valentino and me to enter.

That's when I realized Dmitri was muttering under his breath as he danced around the bag, jabbing at it, then suddenly unleashing a flurry of blows that, I had to admit, looked pretty damned impressive. "No wonder your biceps make me weak at the knees. Do you box?"

He stopped, glancing over his shoulder at me, little curls clinging to his damp forehead. "I used to. Why? Don't tell me—you are the premiere female boxer in England, and you'd like to challenge me to a fight. Well, I won't do it. I've learned from Jake and Theo."

I gave a little laugh and shook my head. "I don't know anything about boxing other than I've always assumed it was a sanctioned way for men to beat the crap out of each other, and that most boxers end up with some sort of brain damage. Were you, by any chance, swearing at me in Greek?"

"Not you, the man who drugged you." He was out of breath, his face rosy with exertion, his big chest heaving. I admired the way the shirt caressed the planes of his chest before I moved over to help him with the boxing gloves he wore. He waved away my help, peeling them off and tossing them onto a chair. "Did you make your call?"

"Yes," I said slowly, feeling like I should warn him. "If someone with a Scottish accent calls your office, don't be startled. My brother is most likely doing a background check on you."

"I'll tell Alexis not to dismiss such calls," he said, grabbing a small towel and wiping his face.

"You're not … annoyed?" I asked, a little surprised.

"About your brother checking me out?" He shook his head. "I'd do the same for a sister if I had one. No, hang on to my phone for a few minutes. I'm going to grab a quick shower. I had a lot more frustration to work out than I thought."

"Won't your cousin mind you just … you know … taking a shower?" I asked, Valentino and I trailing after him when he headed for the side of the apartment. He stopped at one of the rooms.

"No. This is Theo's room. I'm sure he's left some clothing behind. I won't be but a few minutes."

I pursed my lips when he entered the bedroom and went through to an attached bathroom. I looked down at Valentino. He gazed through the door, then looked up at me.

"Yeah, we'd be crazy to let that opportunity escape us," I told the cat, and started to enter the room, but Valentino clearly had the same idea. I stood back to let him go first, and he led me straight to the bathroom, where I perched myself on the counter, watching as Dmitri's slightly blurred shape took a shower.

He emerged from it looking momentarily startled at having an audience.

"We have tallied up your shower scores," I said, applauding lightly. "I give you a seven point five for that shower. Valentino is a kinder judge. He gives you a nine point one."

"Damn," Dmitri said, reaching for a towel. He eyed me with a speculative look while I let my gaze crawl all over his wet, steamy body. I damn near salivated looking at all those muscles and long, sleek stretches of flesh that I knew were like velvet over steel. "I was hoping I'd score enough for a silver medal, but it sounds like bronze again."

"You're going to have to work harder at your enticing shower moves," I told him, making a little face of disappointment when he started drying himself. "For instance, there wasn't enough flexing of your butt muscles, not to mention hardly any stroking of your hands down your chest and belly until you got to your penis. There needs to be a whole lot more stroking if you want the gold medal sorts of scores, Dmitri."

"I was rather hoping you would do the stroking," he said with a little waggle of his eyebrows that, for some reason, charmed me to the tips of my toes.

"Any time, any day, for as long as you want," I said, moving around behind him, snagging another towel in the process. "As a good personal assistant, I believe I'll start my duties by drying your back and your spectacular butt. Wow. It's really … it's even better than when you're lying down, and it's pretty magnificent then. You've got those indentions on your cheeks that drive me a little wild."

I spread my fingers across his butt cheeks, moaning softly when my fingers mapped out the contours.

"Thyra," he said, having stopped drying himself the moment I began touching his butt.

"I mean, really magnificent. If there was a coffee table book of butts, yours would be in the first chapter. It's like a classical statue's butt, which I guess makes sense since you are Greek … hmm?"

"If you don't stop touching my ass in the next three seconds, I am going to put Theo's bed to a use that he'd probably object to."

Reluctantly, I released his cheek. "All right, but I get to do this later, at your place."

"It's my turn next, since I let you have the morning romping," he told me, and finished drying himself before he strolled into Theo's bedroom and dug out of a chest of drawers a pair of jeans and a T-shirt.

"Yes, but you took over before I was done romping on you, so that means you have to share your time tonight, and I'm going to want to do a lot of butt fondling during my part of the evening. You're phone's there." I pointed to where I'd put it on the dresser top. Dmitri donned his shoes, taking his wallet and keys, and leaving his clothing in the bathroom. "Are we going to your apartment now?" I asked when he collected his phone and herded Valentino and me toward the door.

"Jake asked us to stay to dinner. Harry has taken quite a liking to you, it seems. If you wanted to go home right away, I'll make our excuses, but if you have no urgent reason—other than giving me my turn at driving you wild, and no, you do not get part of my time being in charge, since you willingly gave up control this morning—then I'd prefer to stay. I'm very fond of both Jake and Harry, and with the baby due soon, I know she's going a little crazy having to rest so much. Did she tell you about the auction tomorrow?"

"Yes," I said after a moment's thought. "I don't mind staying for dinner. I like Harry, too."

"Good." He smiled down at me, his lips warm and sweet and so seductive when he kissed me. "I'm glad you like them. They're my closest family, and mean a lot to me."

I was warmed, not only by the look in his eyes, but by the way he valued family. "Chris and I just have each other."

"Now you have me," he whispered in my ear before turning and answering Iakovos, who had emerged from the living room to ask if we were staying for dinner. "We would be happy to, although you have to take us as we are."

I cherished the feeling of belonging when Dmitri escorted me to the dining room, his hand warm and solid on my back. I wasn't sure where things with us were going, but I was beginning to think that in Dmitri, I'd found not just a respite from the threat Kardom posed, but paradise itself.

NINE

Dmitri woke to the sensation that he was being watched. He opened his eyes and found that indeed he was. Thyra was on her side, propped up on an elbow, watching him with eyes that were as pure as the clearest amber, while the cat Valentino sat on his belly, his orange front feet tucked under his chest. The look he gave Dmitri was one of intense speculation.

"Either someone let you in, or you've learned how to open doors, and if the latter is the case, I'll be getting new cat-proof locks," he told the animal.

"I let him in when I got up to use the bathroom. He was sticking his paw under the door, which I assumed meant he was lonely, and since I know he's probably still upset about being rehomed, I figured he could cuddle up with us."

"I am not opposed to cats in a general sense, and will agree that this one seems to be very little trouble," Dmitri said, sliding out from under Valentino, lifting him up and plopping him down on a low sea-green chaise that sat in the corner. "But I do object to them being on the bed with us when we're indulging in carnal acts."

"Are we going to have carnal acts?" she asked, sliding a hand along his arm when he climbed back into the warmth of the bed. "I sure hope so, because I believe it's my turn to be bossy."

"On the contrary," he said, rolling her over onto her back, and settling himself between her thighs. "I'm claiming the right to take the lead, because you drove me insane last night and I didn't get to do all the things that I wanted to do." He dipped his head to possess her mouth, thoroughly tasting her, teasing her tongue until she started teasing him back, a fact that delighted him.

For someone who talked a lot about wanting to be the one in charge, she was relatively submissive when it came to lovemaking. He knew she liked him kissing her, but most of the time she waited until he initiated the contact. He put it down to her innate shyness, which made it all that much more pleasing when he could drive her so wild with desire that she took control.

Not that he minded having the dominant role, he mused as she moaned when he moved his kisses over to her neck and shoulders. With all other lovers, he preferred that situation, but there was something about Thyra that made him encourage her wild side, praising her and telling her how much she pleased him when she did so. With time, he decided when she dug her fingers into his shoulders, wordlessly urging him with soft little cries and the restless movement of her legs alongside his, with time she would be so comfortable with him that she would be able to do all the things she told him she wanted to do.

"Dmitri, you're making me flat-out insane," she said in short, panting breaths. "And you're not letting me touch you at all."

He was about to tell her that she would have to wait when he changed his mind. "All right, but that just means I get a whole week of being in charge," he told her, rolling off her to lie on his back.

She looked surprised for a moment, then disconcerted. "Oh. Uh ... wait, a week? Are you insane? I'm not making that sort of a deal! If you're going to be that way, you can just finish what you started, and I'll have my turn the next time you want to do the sheet tango."

She wasn't quite ready to open her wings and fly, he noted, and proceeded to make sure that she was driven wild with need before he sank into the warm, welcoming depths of her. She bit his shoulder, she drew shapes on his back with her nails, and she wrapped her legs around him in a grip that would have done a boa constrictor proud, and by the time she arched up beneath him, her face flushed, and her eyes all but glowing with pleasure, he knew that the feeling of being in over his head wasn't going to fade away any time soon.

He poured himself into her, the feeling going beyond one of mere sexual satisfaction. There was something about Thyra herself that seemed to bind him with a thousand silken threads connecting them together in an unbreakable bond.

He knew, in the cautious part of his mind, that such feelings were unrealistic given the short time they'd been acquainted. But the fact remained that ever since he'd first seen her, she'd wrapped herself around him in ways he couldn't have imagined.

And he had absolutely zero problems with the thought of her in his life. He wanted her arguing with him, as she had the night before, making him so insane with frustration that he had to take out his pent-up emotions on Jake's punching bag. He wanted her looking at him as if he were the sexiest person alive, as she had in Theo's bathroom. He wanted her presence in his apartment, which, while pleasant, had never seemed to have the same warmth that Harry and Iakovos's homes had.

Thyra changed that.

As he rolled over to his side, aware again of a sting on his back telling him just how much Thyra had lost control in the heat of lovemaking, he smiled to himself at the memory of what had met him when they'd returned home the previous evening. Cat toys were scattered across the atrium that served as his living space, while in the kitchen, several cans of cat food sat alongside a plastic container of kibble. A few pieces of Thyra's clothing had been draped over the couch, and he had stumbled over a pair of her shoes that she'd left in the hall.

She had not only settled herself and her cat into his life; she'd made his place a home.

"Dmitri?"

"Hmm?"

"You OK?"

He opened his eyes to see Thyra looking concernedly at him, her own eyes crossing slightly when she tried to focus on his face from where she was still wrapped in his arms. He kissed the tip of her nose, his body so sated, he felt like he was made of soggy tissue. "I'm very OK, Princess. You have worn me out with your lustful demands, as usual. Would you do me a favor?"

"Sure."

"Look over my shoulder and tell me if that cat is staring at my ass. I feel like he is."

She laughed, and snuggled closer to him, tucking her head under his chin, her body soft and welcoming. "He is, but it's an admiring look, one that says while he personally doesn't find your butt anything but functional, if he were human, he would ogle it. Frequently. And ask if you minded this."

She shifted slightly, spreading her fingers and sliding one hand down his uppermost ass cheek before cupping his testicles.

He bucked at the feeling of her fingernails dragging gently along his flesh. "Dear God, woman, you can't possibly want to do it again so soon."

"No, but I wanted to do that earlier, and you wouldn't let me."

"I will let you do anything you want," he corrected her. "Within reason. I'm not, for instance, interested in having you poking around looking for my prostate, but anything else you wish to do is fine with me."

"I'm glad to hear both of those things, because the former isn't anything I'm interested in, either, but the latter I very much am. Do you have any massage oil?"

"No." He looked speculatively at her. "Do you want some?"

"Well, remember last night when I said I wanted to lick you all over, but then once we got going, you were all bossy and I couldn't?"

He thought of pointing out that she had started strong the previous evening but quickly got overwhelmed, leaving him to take over, but decided that wouldn't help her gain confidence. "I am a brute. I promise that I will let you have your womanly way with me, all right?"

"Not right now," she said, looking scandalized, and glancing at the clock. "Tonight, maybe. If we have some massage oil. The kind that gets hot when you blow on it."

"Oh, you're going to be very hot when I blow on you," he growled, smiling when she giggled and tweaked one of his nipples.

"I assume you have to go to work today?" she asked when he gave her one last kiss, then stretched, and swung his legs off the bed, checking messages on his phone. Luckily, there was nothing important scheduled that couldn't be moved. "Or do you have to get ready for your date?"

He frowned at a message from a supplier in Indonesia. He'd set Alexis onto reasoning with them, convincing the company that it really was in their best interest to honor the bid they'd given—as her words penetrated those thoughts, he looked over his shoulder at her. "What date?"

"The one Audrey says you have with her."

An icy chill touched his spine, and it had nothing to do with the air conditioner kicking on. "You know Audrey?"

"I met her yesterday at Harry's."

Dmitri tried to read her expression but was confused, because there was a certain amount of mirth in her eyes, but her lips were thinned and not at all happy. "I see. At the risk of seeming immodest, is it safe to assume I was the subject of some of the conversation?"

"Oh, you were very much the bulk of it," she answered, trailing a finger down his thigh to his knee when he turned so he could better see her. "Audrey likes you. A lot. She seemed to think you guys had a great time together the other night."

"We didn't," he said quickly, wondering if he was going to be called on to deal with a jealous lover. He'd never liked it when his women suspected him of flirting with others, an act that he took care to avoid. Was Thyra, unconventional as she was, going to fall into the same mold as the other women in his life? "I told you that I spent the night wishing I was with you."

"Oh, I know that." Her eyebrows rose, but the humor in her eyes caused little laugh lines to form. "And I believe you. We may not have been together very long, but I'm a pretty good judge of character—my fling with Kardom aside—and I know you're not the type of man to keep one woman dangling while you were getting it on with another. So, although we both know that there's nothing between Audrey and you, she doesn't seem to be in that same place."

He sighed. "I thought I'd made it clear that I wasn't interested in pursuing a further relationship—"

"Other than the date you had today, you mean?"

He frowned. "I don't recall making arrangements to see her today … ah. Perhaps she assumed that when we were discussing Agistri."

"Who's that?"

"What, not who. It's the island I want to take you to." He glanced at his phone. "And I still can if you can be ready to go in half an hour."

"An island?" she asked, sliding out of bed. He tried hard not to ogle her breasts and hips and thighs, because he didn't want Thyra to think that he wanted her only for that tantalizing body, but failed sadly. "Is that where we were going two days ago, before Kardom went batshit crazy?"

"Yes, I think you'll enjoy it. It's a favorite of mine, and there are some nice coves for swimming and snorkeling, although we'll only have a few hours to spend there, since

I have to be back for the charity auction this evening." A thought struck him, an unpleasant thought. "Er ... at the risk of starting yet another argument about how you don't want to take advantage of me, do you have a dress suitable for tonight? If not, I would be happy to advance you some wages—"

"Excuse me?" She frowned, just as he knew she would, and, to his sadness, hid her enticing body behind an oversized T-shirt, which she pulled on before marching over to stand in front of him, her hands on her hips, and a look in her eye that had him making a mental note that he should probably set up one of the spare bedrooms as a home gym. At the very least, he should get a punching bag, so he could teach Thyra to release some of the anger that she was clearly about to pour on his head. "One, I have a dress. I have my mom's dress. You should know—you've seen it. Twice. Two, I am not taking money from you, because I haven't started working for you. And I won't do that until we come to an employment agreement, and to do that, I have to get Harry's lawyer Panoush to make a list of rules."

"And yet," he said, striking a thoughtful pose as he rose from the bed. He wasn't so thoughtful that he didn't enjoy the way her eyes widened, and her breath caught as she caressed him with a gaze that left him wondering if he couldn't, perhaps, pleasure her a second time that morning. "And yet, I distinctly recall last night in Theo's bathroom when you mentioned helping dry me since you were a personal assistant."

"Oh, that wasn't real personal assisting," she scoffed. "It was just an excuse to touch you, and you know it."

He waggled his eyebrows at her, growing more and more delighted by her with every passing minute.

She took a deep breath, which caused him to focus on her ample breasts, and said, "And three, I haven't been invited to this charity thing where you're being auctioned off like the hunky slab of man flesh that you are. And while we're on that subject, are there limits to what people who buy you can ask you to do? Because Audrey made it pretty damned clear that what she has planned for you will run the gauntlet from lascivious to outright smutty."

"Yes, your dress is very charming, but I thought that since you have worn it twice in as many days, you might like to wear something different tonight."

"Why would I want to do that when I have a perfectly good dress?" she asked, and he realized with a start that she was genuinely confused by the statement.

He thought of Harry and Kiera, and couldn't stop himself from asking, "Do you, by any chance, dislike shopping?"

"For what?"

He made a noncommittal gesture. "Let's say clothing."

"No, I don't dislike it," she said, and he breathed a sigh of relief. He'd heard from both Iakovos and Theo about the fact that their respective wives disliked the act of shopping to the point where they would wear out clothing before replacing it. He spent a moment in smug pleasure that his wife would have no such issues, then realized that he was thinking of Thyra as if she would be truly his wife, a life partner. He considered her standing before him, and wondered why he shouldn't think of her in that way. She was, after all, almost perfectly suited to him.

"Mind you," she continued, making a face, "I don't get to go shopping for clothes often, but I do try to stop by the local thrift store fairly frequently to grab anything good that comes in."

"Have you always—" He stopped the sentence before it could continue, realizing that there was no way he could ask what he wanted without insulting her.

"Have I always what?"

"Nothing." In order to distract her, he lifted her up, and carried her into the bathroom. "You, Princess, are dirty. Very dirty. You need a shower."

"And you're just the rich Greek bachelor to give it to me?" she said, brushing her hand along his jaw. For some reason he didn't question, she loved his jaw when he hadn't shaved. She'd told him just the night before that it made her legs weak just looking at it.

"I am." He set her down and whipped her sleeping shirt over her head, tickling her adorable ass when she turned to open the shower door.

He didn't actually end up making love to her in the shower, but it was a near thing, and he wouldn't be honest with himself if he didn't feel a certain amount of pride when, as he held still behind her, assisting her washing her breasts ... over and over and over again ... she wiggled her ass against him and said, "Glorioski, Dmitri, you can't possibly be ready to go around again so soon after we just grabbed the brass ring."

"If I am, it is simply because I have a temptress wet and naked in my arms."

"Yes, well, this temptress would like to go see this fabulous island you mentioned, and there's no way I can do that if I can't walk because you've stripped all the strength from my legs."

He let her go after that, since he really did want to show her the island, shaving and dressing quickly so he would have a little time to give Alexis a few tasks to be accomplished.

"Before I forget," he said as he ate the last of a bagel. Alexis sat at the long counter in the kitchen, a plate of eggs, bacon, and potatoes piled high. Dmitri tried to remember the last time he had the metabolism to eat that much food in one sitting, and decided the less he dwelled on the fact that he'd be forty in a few years, the better his own breakfast would sit. "I want you to get those investigators we used last year for the contractor who ran off with our deposit."

Alexis consulted his tablet, writing a quick note to himself with the computer pen. "What are they looking into?"

Dmitri cast a glance to the short hallway where he could hear the hair dryer running in his bedroom. "A man named Friederich Wilhelm Kardom." He handed over the paper that Thyra had managed to take when she escaped her kidnapping. "He's probably still in Athens, possibly in the company of Thyra's cousin Maggie. Margaret … er … Colton, I think."

"You just want to know this man's whereabouts?" Alexis asked.

"That, and any information they can find. Are you ready to go after you eat?" The last was asked of Thyra when she entered the kitchen, her hair wrapped around her head in a braid. She was followed by the cat, who sat at his feet and stared at him until he handed over a plate of cat food.

"Sure. I can grab a couple of pieces of toast and eat them on the way. Good morning, Alexis. Oooh, that looks yummy."

Alexis paused in the middle of shoving a forkful of food into his mouth. "Would you like me to make you some?"

"Lord no!" Thyra gave him a bright smile. "I'd explode if I ate all that. Dmitri, do you … er … are you going to eat that yogurt?"

With a smile that Dmitri kept to himself, he moved the carton of yogurt over to her, replied to an e-mail regarding a land use study, answered a couple of Alexis's questions regarding a possible plot of land in Panama, then frowned at a text that just pinged.

FROM: Patricia

Darling, is it true what Harry says? Thyra is really your personal assistant?

Quickly he texted back an answer.

TO: Patricia

I don't know why it matters to you, but yes, we have that arrangement. Temporarily.

Almost immediately he received a reply.

FROM: Patricia

So suspicious! I just want to get to know her better, and Harry says she doesn't have a phone, but that she's going to be working with you, so you'll probably get her one. Until then, she said I should contact Thyra through you. Would you mind giving her the following message?

He handed the phone to Thyra. "We're going to have to

get you a mobile phone. For work purposes, naturally," he said quickly when her eyebrows pulled together, indicating a rising objection. "Patricia sent a text for you."

"She did?" Thyra took the phone, her eyebrows now raised. "She wants to go to lunch today in order to get to know me better. That's … singularly odd, don't you think?"

"Not really. You said she knows you're marrying me, and she does a lot of work for both Iakovos and Theo, and I would have no issue hiring her if I needed the type of interior work she specializes in. She's quite talented even if she's a bit …"

"Yeah, not going to fill in the blank there," Thyra answered. "I'll just tell her I'm going to Agistri, and we'll have to do lunch another day. Like … in a long, long time. I don't need to be told again how much of a gold digger I am."

Dmitri waited until she'd sent her text, then took back his phone and said, "We should be back by three, Alexis. You'll let me know anything turns up?"

"About—"

"Yes," he interrupted, casting a quick glance at Thyra, who had finished the yogurt and was now offering the cat water. He didn't think she'd be upset if he was investigating her cousin, but she might kick up a bit of a fuss at the cost of hiring a team of investigators to do that, no doubt feeling it was an obligation she owed, so it was just better for them all if she didn't know.

"Ah. Yes, I will," Alexis said with a conspiratorial wink.

Dmitri made a mental note that he really did have to move Alexis to a more executive position, and after a few last instructions, he got Thyra and Valentino out to the car.

"No Jeep?" she asked when they emerged from the front of the apartment building to find his car waiting, one of the concierge's assistants holding the door open for Thyra. She ignored it to put the cat in the backseat, snapping the seat belt through his harness.

"I have no need of it. This one was being repaired when I took you sightseeing. Now, shall I point out a few more of the sights on the way to Piraeus, or do you want to tell me exactly what Audrey said yesterday that has you looking alternately entertained and furious?"

"I'm not jealous," she said with a rapidity that he found amusing. "I know she was trying like hell to make me so, but like I said, I know enough about you to know you're not what Maggie calls a horn dawg."

"That, I think, is one of the nicest compliments I've had in a long time," he said, relieved once again that she wasn't going to raise a fuss about perceived causes of jealousy. If he needed any other sign that she was perfect for him, that was it. "Allow me to return the compliment and tell you that I appreciate you being not at all the sort of woman who indulges in useless emotional displays in order to garner attention."

"Oh, I can be as emotional as the next girl, hence the fact that I now have a cat, but my brother tells me I have a lot of oppositional defiance at weird things, and I'm afraid Audrey triggered that. I wasn't nice to her, Dmitri. Her attempt to bait me hit my funny bone hard, making me laugh until my nose ran, and I'm afraid she was offended. I tried to apologize, but she just flounced off all ruffled feathers and stompy feet."

"I'm sure she'll survive," he said, his admiration for her growing. He knew just how well-sharpened Patricia's claws could be, having witnessed her tear through both cousins, finally going head-to-head with Harry before they worked out some sort of an accord, and the short time he'd spent with Audrey left him with the idea that she was cut from the same cloth. One thought led to another, and he asked, "Are you sure you wouldn't like to do a little shopping for tonight? We could spare a half hour if you wanted to find something for the auction, and I'd even wait in the car to make sure Valentino didn't get overheated."

The look she shot him should have shriveled his balls, but he was evidently immune to her potent glares now. "If you are so offended by my mother's dress—which is quite nice even if it probably could use a little freshening up—

then I will get something later. And no, I don't need your money."

He knew better than to argue, so confined himself to a nod, and took a leisurely drive down to the marina in Piraeus where his boat was docked. "We could sail there, but it would take longer than the hour it would take using the motor," he told her when they parked, and he pulled out the cat life vest he'd had Alexis pick up the night before. "I hope this fits. He's a pretty big cat."

"Oh, I'm sure it will." Thyra examined the vest, reading the instructions while Dmitri shouldered the bag of items necessary for the trip. The port was busy, and they had to wind themselves through crowds of people on the overcrowded docks. "That was really thoughtful of you to get it for him. It'll make me feel a whole lot better about him being on—uh."

Dmitri had been looking at a text that Alexis had sent that said the investigators were on the job re Kardom when next to him, Thyra came to a halt. He glanced over at her, noted the less-than-joyful expression, and turned to see what was causing it.

"There you are!" Audrey smiled and strolled over to them. She had a large straw bag with her, and as she reached them, she pulled off her sunglasses and leaned in to kiss him. He moved just enough that she hit his cheek rather than his mouth, unable to keep from shooting Thyra a quick appraisal.

Her glorious amber eyes had been narrowed at the sight of Audrey, but they widened with the kiss, then went absolutely blank, as did the rest of her expression. He wondered for a moment if she was so angry she had shut down emotionally, but a little tremor of her delicious lower lip had him relieved.

"Good morning, Audrey. What an unexpected pleasure this is," he said, throwing as much emphasis on the important word as he could without seeming overly rude.

"Unexpected?" She gave a little laugh, and tucked her

arm into his. "Darling, don't you remember planning the excursion to Agistri the other evening? We talked about going out today." She flashed a toothy smile to Thyra. "As I told your assistant."

Dmitri heaved a mental sigh. Damn that Patricia. Of course she had to run straight to Audrey with the information that they were going out today.

"That's right," Thyra answered, the note of amusement rich in her voice. He relaxed even more, the urge to kiss her for being so understanding so overwhelming, he almost did just that. However, the last thing he wanted was a public scene, and the fact that Thyra seemed to want to avoid the same filled him with satisfaction. "She did say that you guys had a date planned for today."

"I hate to contradict Audrey, but although we discussed the possibility of going to Agistri, we did not come to an agreement on a date and time." He addressed himself to Thyra, but felt Audrey's hand tighten on his arm.

"I distinctly recall you mentioning something about sailing there today," she told him, giving him a look that was mostly seduction, but he noted a bit of ire creeping in.

"If so, it was in relation to taking Thyra out, which I had planned to do two days ago, but our trip was delayed."

"It was that," Thyra agreed with a placidity that was starting to make him feel nervous. Although he was grateful she wasn't a raving lunatic, frothing at the mouth with jealousy, she didn't seem to mind at all the fact that Audrey had shown up, not to mention latching on to him.

Was it natural for a woman to be that completely lacking in jealousy? Or was it that she truly didn't care? Had her declaration that she was falling in love with him been a calculated act?

He shook that thought away. Thyra wasn't manipulative like that.

Dammit, she could show a little bit of jealousy, though. Just a tiny bit, not enough to cause a scene, but enough to let him know that she was staking a claim to him.

Pushing aside the thought that he'd never before wanted any woman to do that, he remembered his manners and, in the name of keeping relations pleasant between the Papaioannous and Patricia, said, "If you wished to join us, you may do so, although we are making a fast visit, since I need to be back in time for the auction."

"Darling, I would love to go to Agistri with you. Er … and Thyra, of course. Oh, but I see she has her kitty with her, so perhaps she's just seeing you off?"

Thyra held up the cat's vest. "No, Valentino is coming with us. He is too traumatized by his loss of family to be left alone, and Dmitri bought him a safety vest so he could come with us."

"But … he's a cat," Audrey protested. "Cats don't sail."

"This one does," Thyra insisted. "At least, I think he does. If he seems to hate it, then …" She looked at him. "Do you have a cabin or somewhere enclosed he could stay until we are back?"

"Yes."

"Good. Problem solved, not that I think there will be any, because Valentino is a pretty chill cat."

They all looked at the big orange cat, who strolled a few feet in front of Thyra, his tail and head up as he looked around him with interest.

"I have had cats my entire life," Audrey said in a voice that Dmitri thought was louder than necessary. "I have three now, and I can tell you that cats do not like sailing. There's wind and water and unstable movement, three things that every cat I have known has disliked intensely. Furthermore, as a cat lover, I feel compelled to tell you that to drag that poor kitty onto a boat and expect him to survive a trip to Agistri and back without being distressed is downright mean. Probably borderline animal cruelty."

He heard Thyra's angry intake of breath and, before she could reply, said in what he hoped was a reasonable tone, "I can assure you that Thyra takes Valentino's welfare very seriously, and she would never knowingly put him in either danger or a distressing situation. I am equally as confident as she is that his temperament is such that he will enjoy the trip, but if he does not, we will simply turn around."

Thyra didn't say anything, but slid her hand into his, giving his fingers a squeeze, the smile that curled her lips for him alone.

He wanted badly to kiss her right where she stood, but a desire to just get through what he had a suspicion was going to be a stressful day was now uppermost in his mind.

"What's that you have there?" Audrey asked a few minutes later, her voice coy when she touched his hand with a little caress. He thought for one startled moment that she was nodding toward his groin, but realized almost immediately it was the bag of supplies. He had set it down to unlock the cabin. "Something delicious for lunch? Champagne? Pâté?"

"Not quite." He got the cabin open, and pulled open the cinch holding the duffel bag closed, and removed from the depths a small plastic pan and bag of litter. "Supplies for the cat."

Audrey shot him an annoyed look, which she quickly changed into a smile. "How thoughtful you are, thinking of everything ... for the kitty."

Behind him, Thyra sat on one of the bench seats and talked to the cat while she got him into his life jacket. "Let me just snap that. ... There you are—now you're safe and sound. And don't you look stylish in it! Go show Daddy just how adorable you are."

Dmitri had to pretend to cough in order to smother the laughter that rose from the Daddy comment, pretty sure that it was Thyra's way of poking a little fun at Audrey.

Valentino hopped off the seat and strolled past him, disappearing into the cabin, clearly going to check it out. He hurried after the cat, setting up the litter box in a corner of the cabin before returning above deck.

"So, darling, Thyra tells me you're going to be married. If I'd known that marrying the boss was an option, I'd have volunteered to be your assistant," Audrey said in a conversational tone of voice, but the look she gave Dmitri could have steamed broccoli.

He glanced with surprise to Thyra, who gave a little shrug. "It kind of came out yesterday."

"Tell me all about it," she cooed, moving over to Dmitri, raising her voice to be heard over the engine and wind when they set off. "How you met, how you fell for each other, why you decided to make her an employee, where the wedding will be held—much though I hate to angle for an invitation, you know I am dying to be there for the big event."

He glanced back at Thyra, but she was sitting on the low bench seat, her arms spread, her head tilted to the sky with a blissful expression on her face. "I don't know that any of that is very interesting, to be honest, Audrey. And as for the wedding itself—we're opting for a private affair, just a few family members. But we'll have a reception later, one for all our friends, and I'll be sure you receive an invitation to that." He congratulated himself for his deft handling of what he knew would be a highly awkward situation should Audrey show up at the wedding, such as it was.

"So thoughtful, taking into consideration Thyra's ... circumstances," Audrey said with a smile that Dmitri felt was almost entirely false. "Her poverty, that is. Patricia says she's skint, flat broke, and thus forced to take a job with you just to rub together a few coins. Odd that someone who claims to be a princess would find herself in that position, don't you think?"

"I don't see why," he said, badly wanting to end the conversation, but unable to think of a way to do so without being outright rude. So much for his deft handling of Audrey, he mused sourly. "Lots of royalty bankrupted themselves over the course of the last few centuries. Thyra's ancestors were no different, and it's hardly a judgment on her that her family inheritance didn't come with a large bank account."

"Still, it's sweet that you're willing to overlook the fact that she's so obviously desperate for a man to support her."

Audrey put a hand on his arm, stroking it down to his hand. "I just hate to think of you being hurt."

"It's a good thing, then, that I'm marrying Thyra, because I have full confidence that she will be an ideal wife." In a less-than-suave attempt to separate himself from Audrey, he put the ship on autopilot and picked up Valentino when he emerged from the cabin, before carrying him over to sit with Thyra. "Enjoying yourself, Princess?"

"Yes, completely. It's so beautiful here, although I have to say it reminds me of the trip I took with Chris to California."

"So, when is the wedding to be held?" Audrey asked, to his surprise sitting down next to Thyra, not, as he expected, overly close to him.

"Erm … in a couple of days," Thyra answered, shooting him a fast look. He gave an imperceptible shake of his head. She slumped back in relief. "But we're just having a quick civil ceremony without any fanfare."

"How very odd," Audrey drawled. "If I was a princess and was getting married to a very eligible, and entirely adorable, bachelor, then I would want the world to know about my marriage. And yet you both seem to want just the opposite. I can't help but wonder, why."

"It's like Harry told you yesterday," Thyra said with a somewhat brittle smile. "We don't want the press there. It's a private affair, just us and Dmitri's closest family."

"That doesn't sound in the least bit romantic, but naturally, you must do as you please," Audrey said, turning to gaze out at the passing scenery.

Dmitri relaxed, allowing his fingers to tangle into Thyra's hair, stroking the back of her neck, wishing like hell that he'd had her alone on the boat.

Almost two hours later, he shook the water from his eyes and picked up his phone, which he'd heard ringing while he was climbing up the ladder onto the boat.

A text message waited for him.

FROM: IAKOVOS

Harry would like to know if Thyra needs the loan of a dress. She volunteered to go through E's things if so.

"How bad is it?" Thyra asked, her expression tight and guarded. She was turning pink, from either anger or too much sun, and since he'd pressed a full bottle of sunscreen on her at the beginning of the trip, he assumed it was the former.

"The propeller shaft is bent, and one of the propellers has sheared off."

"There, you see?" Audrey almost crowed. "I told you to turn starboard, but you insisted on going port."

"I'm sorry I hurt your nice ship," Thyra said, her back stiffening. Every line of her body language screamed how uncomfortable she was. "I didn't mean to run into the sandbar, but Audrey told me to go left—"

"Port is left, darling," Audrey said in that sneering voice that grated on Dmitri's already raw nerves. "Starboard is right. I told you to go starboard. And this is a boat, not a ship. Honestly, I'd think you'd try to learn the things that are important to your employer, such as the fact that the boat he just bought less than a month before was his pride and joy."

He couldn't see Thyra's eyes, since she wore a pair of oversized sunglasses over her eyeglasses, but he was willing to bet they weren't happy. "I didn't ... your boat was new?"

"Yes," he said, deciding it didn't matter whether it was Thyra's inexperience or Audrey's deliberate attempt to mislead her—he never should have left Thyra driving the boat while he went down to relieve himself in the head.

Dammit, and she'd been enjoying herself so much, too, being thrilled with the power of the boat.

"Is it going to cost a lot to fix?"

"A fair bit. I'll see if we can hire a boat on Agistri to pick us up and take us back to Piraeus."

"Tsk," Audrey said, shaking her head, and leaning over to splash a little water onto her face. "What a shame. I wouldn't have had that happen for the world, but at least Thyra can work off the amount of the damage. It'll take years, no doubt, but still, it must be of some satisfaction to her that she can repay you for your misplaced trust that she wouldn't run your boat aground the first minute she could."

TO: IAKOVOS

I'll ask her just as soon as I find someone to haul my boat in for repair.

"That is so uncalled-for," Thyra said, a warning note in her voice that Dmitri decided would be best if he ignored. "And for the record, I've about had it with you needling me. I've put up with it for long enough."

"Oh, you have? Well, I've had enough of you blighting what was supposed to be a perfectly lovely day spent with Dmitri," Audrey snapped back.

"Blighting!" Thyra rose to her feet, her hands fisted. "He's my fiancé, if you would be so kind as to remember!"

FROM: IAKOVOS

What the hell? What happened?

"Are you so insecure and jealous that you can't stand for him to spend time apart from you?" Audrey asked. "And while we're on the subject of this wedding and why you don't want the press to know about it—could it be that perhaps you haven't been as factual as you've led Dmitri to believe? I looked up the name of the place of which you're supposed to be a princess. There is no such country as Sombleburg. I would have thought Dmitri had the common sense to verify your claims before he allowed you to force him into marriage, but evidently he had his reasons for not doing so. I'm happy to give you the information I found, Dmitri. Or rather, didn't find."

Dmitri ignored the comment, and responded, *Think Audrey directed Thyra to run my boat aground while Thyra was driving and I was taking a piss in the head. Going to have to replace the propeller shaft and propeller blades. Possibly more.*

"It's Sonderburg. Sonderburg-Beck, to be exact. The whole may not exist any longer, but the Beck part does." Thyra sounded downright irritated now.

The cat sauntered past him, paused to bat at the water

streaming down his legs to his feet, then headed into the cabin, no doubt to use his facilities.

FROM: IAKOVOS

Do you need me to do anything other than offer sympathy?

"If it does, I'm sure it's filled with annoying little gold diggers like you."

He heard the deep breath that Thyra made, and was just in time to see Thyra march over to where Audrey knelt on the seat, scooping up handfuls of water and patting it on her face and neck. "I am not a gold digger," Thyra said through ground teeth.

"Oh really? It sure didn't take you long to find a rich man into whom you could dig your chubby claws. If that's not the sign of a gold digger, then I don't know—"

A shriek and splash followed the trailed words.

TO: IAKOVOS

No, the water's not that deep, and Audrey knows how to swim. I'm sure she'll be spitting mad when I haul her back on board, though. I do want to kiss Thyra, but I suppose I shouldn't reward such behavior.

FROM: IAKOVOS

???

TO: IAKOVOS

Scratch that. Kissed her anyway. Just as Audrey climbed back on board. She's claiming she's going to file assault charges against Thyra. Oh wait, cat is involved now.

FROM: IAKOVOS

Thyra assaulted Audrey? Wait, let me guess—pushed her overboard?

TO: IAKOVOS

Now she's threatening to sue the cat, who just bit her on the thumb. Valentino seems to feel it's his duty to protect Thyra. I'll have to have a talk with him later and tell him to stand down. That's my job. Shit.

FROM: IAKOVOS

The cat just shit on Audrey?

TO: IAKOVOS

No, Audrey tried to hit Thyra on the head with the first aid box, which I brought out to bandage the bleeding thumb. Had to confine cat—hissing and about to attack—to one of the cabins, and separate the women. Thyra's gone to the bow. Audrey is prone in the aft, claiming she needs a doctor after the attack by both Thyra and the cat. Waiting for boat to come from Agistri.

FROM: IAKOVOS

I'll have bottle of whiskey waiting when you and Thyra arrive.

TO: IAKOVOS

You are the best of cousins. Damn. Just heard breaking glass from cabin. Think the cat has broken out and

FROM: IAKOVOS

What did the cat do?

FROM: IAKOVOS

You there?

FROM: HARRY

Dmitri? Are you all right? Iakovos isn't sure if his texts are getting through. Dammit, why didn't we get a duress word. Yacky says you've got a full-fledged girl fight going on. Why is Audrey there?

TO: HARRY, IAKOVOS

Sorry, was dealing with broken oil lantern. Valentino is fine. Audrey may end up with a black eye, but possibly not. She's floating facedown in the water now, for the swelling, since I have no ice. Rescue boat just arrived. Back in port in an hour.

FROM: IAKOVOS

Come early. We're going to want to hear all of it.

FROM: HARRY

Amen to that!

TEN

"Good evening, Mrs. Avrab—"

"There you are!" Harry appeared dramatically, her belly leading the way when she marched over to us, wearing a long navy-blue chiffon dress, beaded on the bodice with tiny white crystals that reminded me of the night sky. "What happened to you guys? Does Audrey have a black eye? Why did the cat break glass? Wait, is he wearing a bow tie?"

"—bos," I finished, giving the housekeeper a smile before letting Valentino greet Harry, rubbing his face on the bare toes that peeked out of her sandals. "Yes, Dmitri bought Valentino this bow tie collar. Isn't it cute?"

"Very," she said, waving a hand toward him. "I'd pet him, but that would mean bending over, and I can't do that without people holding on to me."

"I'm sure he understands. That's a gorgeous dress, Harry," I said, trying to keep the envy out of my voice. "I like the crystal bit. It's very galaxy."

"It's not green," Iakovos said when he strolled out to punch Dmitri in the arm, which—since Dmitri repeated the gesture—I gathered was their traditional method of greeting.

"Thank you, Thyra." She did a slow twirl. The dress seemed to flow around her big belly. "I thought it was particularly flattering, even if it isn't Yacky's favorite color. I can have the pleats over the tummy taken in once the baby is born, so I can wear it once I'm back to non-baby shape. Did Dmitri tell you that I raided the things Elena left behind?"

"I don't think so," I started to say, glancing at Dmitri, but he was talking quietly to Iakovos.

"Well," Harry said, taking my arm and leading me down the hallway to the family rooms, "I see you're in your pretty gold dress, but I thought you might want to have a peek at her things just in case there's something you'd like to borrow for tonight. I asked her if she minded, and she said not in the least, and you were to feel free to wear anything of hers that you liked. She's in Los Angeles for a few months, which is driving Iakovos nuts, because she's been dating some actor who he says looks like a gigolo and is clearly after her solely for her money, but you have an older brother, so I'm sure you know what a pain in the ass they can be."

"I heard that, Eglantine!" Iakovos called after us.

Harry giggled and opened a door, gesturing to the closet before sitting on the edge of the bed. "There's a gorgeous red dress in there that I thought would be perfect for you. It reminds me of one of those flamenco dresses, all sleek lines and flouncy bits. What did Audrey do to you?"

I had idly opened the closet and looked at the array of garments, but turned to face Harry. "Oh, God. I'm so embarrassed. It was a shit show, Harry, an actual shit show. Minus the—you know—literal shit. I didn't intend to give Audrey a black eye, even though she was being as obnoxious as she humanly could be, and then when Dmitri was showing me how to drive his ship … boat … he had to use the bathroom, and we were coming up to a sandbar, and stupid me, I listened to her when she said to go left. Or right. Now I can't remember which. And I broke his boat, Harry." Tears of frustration welled up in my eyes, which just made me angry. I hated crying over stupid things like a broken boat. "He just bought it, too. I asked him if it was expensive to fix, and he just clammed up and refused to talk about it, which means it'll cost a fortune to fix."

Harry nodded. "I know the one he bought, and those boats are expensive. Iakovos has a couple, and he only allows me to drive if he's with me. I'm so sorry this happened. You're sure Audrey did it on purpose? Not that I don't believe she would, because she's Patricia's friend, and Patricia is . . . well, we won't go into that. But you're sure?"

"Pretty sure, yes. We were coming head-on to the sandbar, so I wanted to turn to the left, and she said no, there was an arm of the sandbar there, and to go the other way, only that was where the arm was."

Harry made mean eyes, which, oddly, made me feel better. "That bitch."

"Yes, well, in the end, the responsibility was mine. Now I owe Dmitri a ton of money to have the boat fixed."

"Don't worry about that," she said, waving away the idea. "He has insurance. That will pay for the repairs."

"That's what he said before he clammed up, but I bet his rates go up because of it. I feel awful about it."

"So, did you push Audrey into the water? Is that how she ended up with a black eye?"

"Oh, God." I sat next to her on the bed, and simultaneously wanted to laugh and cry. The laughing won out. "No, that was afterward. She'd been making snarky comments about me since she forced herself on our trip, and I let most of it wash off me, because no matter how many times she touched Dmitri's arm, and the two times she brushed her hand against his thigh, I knew that he wasn't going to fall for her so-called charms. He's not that sort of man."

"No, he isn't, and he seems very much taken by you," she said with a little smile that I shared.

"Yes, well, our blossoming relationship aside, I let most of it go, but then she started in about me not being a real princess, and I kind of saw red."

"Oh?" Harry asked.

I made a vague gesture. "I don't much care about what people think about me, or whether I have the title … but my family did nothing wrong. They treated the people of Beck well. They were good to the country, and even handed over a lot of power to the government in the nineteenth century. They simply weren't strong enough to stand up to the German Empire. So when she started slagging off the title, and then called me a gold digger on top, implying I was with Dmitri just for his money, I … oy … I kind of lost it. And I shoved her overboard. I figured she needed cooling off. Literally."

"And of course, it had the opposite effect."

"Of course it did. I was stupid to give in to my emotions, and I did apologize afterward, but she was livid, and told Dmitri she wanted to file assault charges. Then Valentino took exception to her shoving me, and bit her hand, and she tried to bean me with the first aid box, and that was all she wrote. So to speak."

"Jeezumcrow." Harry thought about that for a minute. "There's more, though, right?"

"Sadly, yes."

"Dmitri put Valentino in the cabin?"

I nodded. "I went up to the front of the ship—"

"Bow of the boat."

"—to the bow of the boat to cool off, figuring Audrey would be happier moaning and groaning to Dmitri if I wasn't there, and all of a sudden, there was a crash. Valentino had pushed the screen out of the cabin window and, in doing so, knocked over one of the emergency oil lanterns. I got to the back of the sh—boat just in time to see him walking on the deck above where Audrey was lying down, talking on the phone and waving a cloth that Dmitri had used to wipe up the blood on her hand. Valentino did that squatty, wiggle-butt sort of move that cats make before they pounce, and I knew he was going to jump at the cloth that she was waving around while she was being dramatic on the phone, and so I yelled for him to stop, at which point Audrey looked up and screamed just as he jumped. She threw her hand up in reaction and knocked him to the side."

"Oh my God! Was he hurt?"

"No, thank the stars, but he did go flying over the edge of the boat into the water, so of course, I ran the few feet to where he went in, but Audrey was trying to get up at the same time—I honestly don't think she meant for him to go overboard; she says she loves cats, and she was really horrified—so I slammed into her just as I was jumping over the side. I didn't know that Dmitri was already in the water, having been looking again at the damage, and he had Valentino."

"Bless Dmitri for being in the right place at the right time," Harry said, patting my hand.

"And for buying Valentino the water vest. It kept him above the water, so his head barely got wet. Anyway, I dived in only to come up and find Valentino sitting on Dmitri's shoulders while he climbed back onto the ship, and then when I got aboard, Audrey was sitting on the floor bitching that I'd kicked her in the face when I jumped in."

"Wow." Harry and I sat silent for a few minutes while we thought about the events of the day. My thoughts were tinged heavily with guilt and regret. "That was some outing. Well, it's over, and we have the fun of the auction ahead of us. So, what about that red dress?"

"I'm fine in this dress," I said, nonetheless looking when she pulled a dress out of the closet. I had to admit, it was gorgeous.

"I even found a couple of pairs of shoes that might fit, assuming you aren't weirded out about wearing someone else's stuff."

I laughed. "Other than this dress, which was my mother's, and underwear—which I get new—I shop exclusively at thrift and consignment stores. So no, I don't have a problem wearing used things. But that's not the point. I like this dress. I don't see the need to wear something else just because people have seen it before."

"And so you shouldn't," Harry agreed. "I just wanted to let you know there were options available other than buying a new dress."

We returned to where the men were sitting on the patio, sipping whiskey. Dmitri, who had been a bit quiet since we'd returned from the ill-fated trip, offered me a glass, but I shook my head.

"If you would prefer something else—" he said softly in my ear while Iakovos got Harry comfy in a deep chair.

A little skitter of heat went down my back at the brush of his breath on my skin.

"No, I don't drink much. I don't really see the purpose in it, to be honest."

A little line appeared between his eyes. "Are you in recovery?"

"No, I'm not an alcoholic. I just don't like liquor. Sometimes, if I'm feeling wild and crazy, I'll have a lager and lime, but otherwise, alcohol doesn't really appeal to me."

"Does it bother you if I indulge occasionally?"

"No. Why are you so serious all of a sudden? Are you still mad at me?"

"I'm not mad at you, Princess," he said with a thinning of his lips that told me that he might not be angry, but he was annoyed. "I wasn't mad earlier, which I told you three times while we were dressing."

"And each time you sounded angrier and angrier."

"Because you wouldn't believe me when I told you I wasn't angry over what happened!" He looked downright exasperated now, his voice rising to the point where, out of the corner of my eye, I could see Harry and Iakovos turn to look at us.

"I feel horrible about what happened," I told Dmitri, wanting to calm him down, but unsure how to do so. "I'm so sorry. So very sorry that I ruined your nice boat. And I will—"

"Don't say it!" he thundered, the line between his brows now a full-scale frown.

"But I really am sorry—hey! You don't get to tell me what I can and can't say," I said, guilt at the damage I'd done to his boat mingling with annoyance that he thought he could dictate to me. "You can't stop me from apologizing and saying I would take responsibility for the damage."

"Like hell I can't." The words came out a growl. Valentino, giving Dmitri a long look, hopped up onto what remained of Harry's lap, and started purring.

"I will pay you for the—"

"That's it! I've had more than I can bear!" Dmitri slammed down the glass and bent, hoisting me onto his shoulder before striding toward the interior of the apartment.

I stared in shock at his upside-down ass for a moment before I slapped my hands on his back. "How dare you pick me up this way! Let me down!"

"You dared me to stop you from saying you'll pay me back, and I'm going to do just that," he snapped, pausing when Iakovos called from where he was standing next to a laughing Harry. "What?"

"We have to leave in twenty minutes. Also, speaking as a man who knows the ways of wives, I would encourage you not to wrinkle Thyra's dress."

"Fine!" Dmitri all but spat the word out, and carried me into the house and straight to his cousin Theo's room, where he set me down, then—before I could recover from all the blood that had rushed to my head—spun me around and pulled down the zipper on my dress, whipping it off over my head and laying it on a chair.

"Dmitri, you can't possibly—" He was on me before I could even protest. I had a few seconds of being scandalized that he had carried me off in a manner that made it very clear to his cousin and Harry just what he had planned, but evidently, that didn't matter to Dmitri.

He simply pressed me against the wall, his mouth hot and urgent on mine, his hands trying to find their way through the petticoat needed to give the skirt shape. "What the hell is this tortuous thing?" he almost snarled while he kept trying to find a way through all the ruffled layers.

"It's my mother's petticoat," I said, the warm pool of desire that immediately started up at his touch making me feel restless and needy despite the situation. "It has layers. Dmitri, you can't do this!"

"I can! I'll simply take the blasted thing off you."

"No, not the petticoat." I moaned into his mouth when he kissed me again, his tongue bossy and demanding and so sensual when it touched mine, I damn near went up in flames. "We can't do this now. Harry and Iakovos will know what we're doing!"

"So? Jake does this all the time."

"Well, they have several children, so I assume so."

"No, the second he sees Harry all dressed up, he takes her off and makes love to her. I can't tell you the number of times they've been late to functions. For the love of God, help me find the end of this petticoat thing!"

"But you're dressed! And I'm still wearing—" He growled something in Greek, bending down until he could slide his hands up from my knees, under the petticoat, at which point he dragged my underwear down, one hand dipping down my public bone until it found very sensitive flesh. "Oh, dear God, yes! To hell with still being dressed and your cousin knowing exactly what we're—just a smidgen to the left—hoobah!—doing in here."

It was just that fast. One moment I was interested but hesitant, and the next, my body went up like dry kindling on a bonfire. He hoisted me up, pulling my legs around his hips, pressing me against the wall with his body while he fumbled at his fly, the whole time his mouth continued to torment mine. I jerked my glasses off, since they were getting in the way of me kissing everything I wanted to kiss, clutching them at the same time I clung desperately to his shoulders.

"This is so … mmrowr!" I said in between panting.

"It is definitely that, and so much—dear God, woman, are you hiding your parts? Where is your—"

I snuck my free hand down the froth of my petticoat and his tuxedo, tilted my hips, and placed him right where he needed to be. His eyes seemed to bore into mine for a second while he hesitated, the desire in them making the skitter of sexual tension inside me coil even tighter. "Tell me you want this, Thyra. Tell me you want me."

"Are you deranged? I'm almost coming unglued because I want you so much."

"All of me?" he asked, a strange note of intensity in his voice that I didn't want to acknowledge. "You want all of me, everything in my life, everything that's part of me?"

"Yes," I said without hesitation, part of my brain cheering, the other part wondering what I thought I was doing. "I want you, Dmitri. All of you. Every last irritating, incredibly sexy, wonderful bit of you. I want you now, I want you tomorrow, and I will want you for the rest of my days. Which aren't going to be many if you're not inside of me in the next three seconds."

He smiled a wicked, steamy smile and hoisted me up a few inches, then sank with exquisite slowness into me. I didn't want slowness, however. I tightened my legs around him, and urged him on. "Such a demanding princess," he murmured, gently biting my bare shoulder. "Such a warm, tantalizing woman. No, don't do that. Thyra, if you do that, I'm not going to be able to—"

I tightened around him again, the tension inside of me about to release. I rocked my hips, tightening and releasing until he was groaning my name nonstop, and when I arched back, my body clenching with the power of the orgasm, he pushed roughly into me, giving short, hard little thrusts that made my girl parts damn near sing with happiness.

Ten minutes later, having had a quick wash in Theo's bathroom, and with my dress on once again, and the petticoat fluffed out properly, we sashayed out to where Harry and Iakovos were chatting with two giggling girls via video on a tablet propped up on Harry's belly.

They said good-bye almost immediately, at which point they both turned to look at us.

"We did not just have sex," I informed them.

Harry grinned. Iakovos didn't smile, although I swore his lips twitched and one of his eyebrows rose.

"Yes we did. And it was damn good," Dmitri said, his hand warm on my back.

"No, we didn't." I kept my gaze firmly on the two people in front of us, ignoring the sexiest man in the world next to me. "Because if we did, I would not be able to face Harry and Iakovos due to embarrassment, and would, in fact, have to go back to your apartment, where I would become a hermit. I would never be able to face anyone again and would probably become the sort of a recluse who saves her own fingernails and bottles of urine."

"Ah." Dmitri was silent a moment; then from the corner of my eye, I could see him nodding. "In that case, we did not just have damned good sex."

"Thank you," I said, turning so that I could smile at him. "Are we ready to go? I should probably walk Valentino in case he needs to go potty."

Harry grunted a little as she let Iakovos get her to her feet. "Not that I have ever heard of a cat who will do that on a leash, but you don't need to. Iakovos put him in that big planter on the side while you and Dmitri were not having sex, and Valentino evidently did a little excavating in the dirt before he did his business there."

"You're going to be cleaning that up later," Iakovos told Dmitri, who just laughed.

ELEVEN

The charity function was not being held at a hotel, as I imagined. Instead, it took up the entire upper-floor ballroom of a building in the heart of Athens, which was evidently used for important social events. The other floors were off-limits to the attendees, with the bank of four elevators running only from the ground floor up to the top. Security, I couldn't help but notice as we passed through a metal detector, was pretty tight. I wondered if it was simply a reflection of the times, or if there was an expected threat. There certainly were enough security guards milling around the lobby, checking everyone's invitations and waving wands up and down those folks whose keys or accessories set off the metal detector.

We made it through the security, and upstairs, garnering only a few odd looks when people spotted Valentino in my arms.

"Don't give him anything salty to eat, since I didn't bring a water bowl for him," I told Dmitri when he showed the invitation a second time to two men who were guarding the double doors that led into the ballroom.

"We can probably find a bowl for him."

"He'll just have to pee if he drinks. He should be fine for a few hours, since he just went, but I don't want him loading up his bladder until we get home."

To my relief, the room wasn't packed, although the people who were there were in full evening dress, the men all in tuxes of various designs and colors, while the women were dressed to the nines, sequins and beads sparkling everywhere I looked. I won't say I stood out like a sore thumb, but for a moment, I wished I'd given in to Harry's urging and had borrowed one of her sister-in-law's formal dresses.

"I'll have to leave you midway through the proceedings," Dmitri said, when we went to what was apparently an assigned table with Harry, Iakovos, and two other couples.

"I figured they probably wanted to round up you bachelors into a corral or something, just in case one of you barged out and got married on a whim," I answered, sitting down at the table and setting Valentino on Harry's seat, since she was making herself comfortable on a barstool that sat behind a podium next to a stage.

"One of them is, but I'd hardly call marrying you a whim," he answered, brushing his hand across the back of my neck in a caress that had me shivering. Someone called his name, and he lifted a hand in acknowledgment. "Will you be all right here if I leave you for a few minutes? I see a business contact that Jake wants to sweeten, and I might be able to help."

"I'm an introvert, not agoraphobic, Dmitri. I'll be fine by myself, not that I'm alone when I have Valentino to protect me," I said, smiling up at him. His almost dimples flashed, and he leaned down to give me a swift kiss.

"Just remember that you're my princess," he answered, somewhat cryptically, I thought, and then he moved off through the sea of tuxedos and sequins.

I watched him talk to an older man and woman, noting to myself how graceful he was, hugging the secret knowledge of what he looked like under that tuxedo. My mind touched for a moment on the episode in Theo's bedroom, but I shied away from the declaration I'd made. I knew I was going to have to address it, both with myself and with Dmitri, but I didn't want to do it here, surrounded by people.

"Besides," I told Valentino in a whisper as the cat sat and watched the people around him with interest. "I may be his princess, but he's our hunky Greek heartthrob, and we're not going to let him get away."

Valentino slid me a yellow-eyed gaze before turning his head to look at Iakovos, who sat in the seat next to his. Iakovos gave him almost exactly the same sort of measuring look, then straightened the bow tie portion of the collar, which had been knocked askew when I had carried him in. Once that was done, Iakovos slid his gaze up to me, one of his eyebrows cocked. And it was at that moment that I ceased to be intimidated by him, and accepted him as Dmitri's much-loved cousin. "Dmitri tells me you don't care for crowds. If this becomes too much for you, feel free to step out. There's a balcony to the right of the doors where people go to have cigarettes, if you need a breath of air that isn't polluted by too many women wearing too much perfume."

"Thanks," I told him. "I'll remember that."

He got up when Harry frantically waved at him, returning almost immediately. "Harry wants to know if you'd mind the cat sitting up with her. She feels like he would be a good mascot, and that people will bid more if he's helping her."

"It's fine with me. Let's see how Valentino feels about it." I walked him over to where Harry sat, now accompanied by Patricia.

The tiny little blonde shot me one very hard look, but for the most part, she pretended not to see me. "Once the women are done, we'll have a half-hour break so the desserts can be brought in, and then we'll start with the men. Are you sure you're going to be able to do this?"

"Perfectly," Harry said with dignity, squaring her shoulders. She stacked the cards in front of her, tidying them into an ordered pile. "Oh, there he is. Thyra, you don't mind if I borrow him, do you? He looks so dashing with his bow tie on, and who doesn't love a cat?"

"I don't. I'm allergic to them," Patricia said. "I'll be backstage, but we should be ready to start in five minutes."

"Oh good, time for one last potty break," Harry said. Then she hurried off, giving Iakovos a little kiss on his jaw on her way to the restrooms.

"You have some lipstick there," I told him, nodding toward the mark while I pulled a tissue out of my cleavage.

"I'm sure I do. Harry likes to mark me whenever Patricia is around. No, I can't remove it yet. She'll just do it again until Patricia sees it." The look on his face was martyred resignation, but it had me making a mental note to get myself a tube of bright red lipstick just in case I needed it with Dmitri.

Since Valentino seemed quite happy to sit on a light blue woolen shawl that Harry had carried with her, looking like some exotic orange feline potentate examining his minions, I returned to my table with Iakovos. He lasted a minute before he, too, saw someone he wanted to talk to.

I didn't mind sitting by myself. I smiled when the two other couples assigned to the table periodically returned, only to see another acquaintance who needed to be greeted. I just sat and watched everyone, trying to pick Dmitri out of the crowd, but there were more people here than at the previous party, the ballroom about half-full. A catwalk extended from the stage, with big placards on easels on either side announcing the charity auction, one of which had a picture of Harry and a mention that she was a famous author.

Dmitri returned just as the lights flashed a few times, warning people that the shindig was about to begin, giving me a quick glance. "Everything OK?" he asked when he took the seat next to me.

"Sure. Was your schmoozing successful?" I asked.

"I hope so. Jake used to send Theo out to deal with people he wanted to influence, and I'm afraid I don't have his charm."

"Oh, I don't know," I said, pulling my tissue out again, and leaning across him to wipe the far edge of his mouth, where a smear of maroon remained. "Looks to me like you made at least one woman happy."

He eyed me with a hesitant air.

I smiled and leaned in to whisper in his ear, "Don't look so wary. I know you're not going to run around kissing other women. I assume that was a friendly little greeting from Audrey."

"You are a paragon amongst women," he said, lifting my hand, and kissing my fingers. "And yes, it was. She nailed me before I could move an appropriate distance away."

"She's going to bid for you, you know," I said with a sigh that I couldn't help. Music blared at the same time Patricia walked out to the center of the stage, welcoming everyone to the event, and listing details about the charity itself (a children's hospital). I leaned closer to Dmitri so I could be heard over Patricia. "And I just bet she's going to ask you to do all sorts of immoral things once she buys you."

A muscle in his jaw twitched. I'd chosen my words carefully, knowing he wouldn't like the reference to being bought. "She can ask me to do whatever she wants. What I will do is another matter," was all he said.

I settled back, and we sat through almost an hour of various women—young twenty-somethings all the way up to a very bent old lady of eight-two (who got an astonishing bid from an equally bent and white-haired old man)—parading up and down the catwalk, while Harry gave the volunteers' names, a few interesting biographical details, and then some witty banter that had the crowd loosening up, and bidding freely.

Dmitri had been given a cardboard paddle with a number on it when we entered, and when they were about two-thirds of the way through the bachelorettes, he leaned over and asked me, "You know, if you wanted to borrow some money against your salary, I would have no problem writing a check for whatever amount you needed."

I looked from the young woman on the stage to him,

frowning. "You want me to bid on one of these girls? I admit this one is pretty, but I don't really swing that way."

"I meant in case you wanted to bid on someone male."

I stared at him, wondering if he meant himself, or another man. "Er … I don't need another man, either."

"Me!" he said loudly, causing Iakovos to shoot him a warning look. Dmitri leaned in closer. "I thought you might want to try to outbid Audrey. I just wanted you to know that since the money goes to charity, I would be happy to loan you whatever amount you needed to do so."

I thought about it, I really did. The idea of seeing Audrey's face when I bid some obscene amount of money and got Dmitri out from under her nose was enticing, but in the end, sanity prevailed. "Thank you, but although I'd be happy to donate to the charity, I think I'd rather work for it in some other way."

"I just wanted to make sure you know that option is available," he told me.

The intermission allowed everyone to get up and stretch their legs, as well as hit a glorious display of dessert items.

"Do you mind if I keep Valentino for the second half?" Harry asked around a mouthful of the most deliciously sinful chocolate gâteau. "Several people have told me how cute he is."

"Sure, so long as he doesn't mind." I looked down to where Valentino was on the floor, doing a spot of intimate grooming. "That's right, get that out of your system. You have to be handsome and charm all the ladies into bidding like crazy."

I saw Audrey twice during the break, but neither time did she do more than shoot me potent glares. I was happy to see that she didn't have a black eye, although I did narrow my eyes a bit when, as Dmitri returned from a visit to the men's room, she snagged him by the arm and dragged him over to a group of women, all of whom cooed over him.

"You'll get used to that," Harry said, standing up.

I glanced up at her, handing her Valentino's leash. "Really?"

She made a face. "No. But you'll learn how to deal with it better. Dammit, Yacky got that lipstick off. He knows better. Time to reapply it …"

She went to retake her seat, Iakovos coming to help her. I caught him hiding her evening bag when she was looking for it, which made me smile until I saw that Dmitri was still in the clutches of Audrey.

"Right," I said to no one in particular, "I may not have lipstick that will show up, but I think I can do a little something to let Audrey and her gang know he's very taken."

I started to stroll over to him, but just then Harry announced that the bachelor part of the evening's auction was about to start, and would all participants please go to the backstage area.

Dmitri gave me a little wave as he headed off with about thirty other men, none of whom were as handsome as he was. I caught a look of triumph in Audrey's eyes when she glanced toward me, but I didn't let it bother me. She could pretend to herself all she wanted; I knew the truth.

When I was about to return to my seat, one of the men who guarded the door came up to me, a slip of paper in his hand. "You are Thyra Beck?" he asked, mentioning the surname that Chris and I used when we needed to provide one.

"Yes."

"I have a message for you. It came in to the desk downstairs," he said, glancing at the note. "It asks that you call a Christian Beck immediately."

A cold chill hit my gut. Chris! Something must be horribly wrong if he had called me. "Oh, lord. Uh … I don't have a phone." I spun around to look for Harry and Iakovos, but she was in full swing describing the first bachelor, and Iakovos was nowhere to be seen.

"There is a phone in the ladies' room," the man told me, opening the door. "Down the hall, turn right, first door on the left."

"Thank you," I told him, dashing from the room. The door clicked closed behind me, cutting off the noise of the music and Harry, leaving me with only the sound of my heart beating wildly in my ears.

It took a few tries before I managed to get an operator who would accept my emergency-use-only credit card to make a call to Chris, but at last, I heard his sleepy voice.

"What's wrong?" I asked, clutching the pay phone. "Are you hurt? Did you get shot? You got shot, didn't you! I knew that one day you'd get shot."

"Thyra? What in the blazes are you babbling about? What time is it?" I heard a click. "For God's sake, it's half after nine. I just went to bed half an hour ago."

"It's not that late—"

"Not if you haven't been involved in preserving a fragile crime scene for the last twenty-seven hours without a break. I have to be up in six hours, Thyra. What is so important that you are depriving me of sleep that I desperately need?"

I stared at the fancy tile wall, not understanding. "What ... you called me."

"I did not. I was asleep." He yawned loudly. "For all of a half hour."

"But—I got a message saying to call you."

"Someone's yanking your chain. Probably Maggie or Kardom."

"Oh, God. I can't imagine Maggie doing it, but Kardom ..." I spun around, expecting to see him loom up in the doorway, but it was empty of anyone. "You're sure you're OK."

"Yes. And I have to be up early so I can clear a few cases in order to—"

"Thank God," I interrupted, feeling more than a little twitchy at being away from everyone. "Sorry for waking you, Chris. Go back to sleep. Night."

He murmured something, but I didn't wait to hear him complain about being woken again. I hurried out of the bathroom, and tried to open the door to the ballroom, still looking behind me every few seconds, but there was no one lurking menacingly in the hallway.

The door refused to budge. I knocked on it, and a man pushed it open, peering out at me. "Hi," I said, and tried to sidle inside it. He blocked me with an arm across the door.

"Do you have a ticket?" he asked.

"No, my ... er ... fiancé has it." I pointed into the room. "He's in there. If I could just go in—"

"No one is allowed in without tickets," he said, starting to close the door.

"Hey, wait a minute," I said, unable to believe what was happening. "I just left here to go to the bathroom. You must have seen me."

The man shook his head. "We just came on duty."

"Great. What timing. Where's the guy who brought me a message a few minutes ago? He'll vouch for me."

"What man?"

"Tall, dark hair, little goatee."

The man shook his head. "There is only Stavros and me on duty, and neither of us has a goatee. Please remove yourself from the door, or I will be forced to call security."

"Oh, for the love of all that's good on this earth—fine. Iakovos Papaioannou. You know him, right? He's at the table I was at. If you go ask him, he'll tell you I'm with his wife and him."

"I thought you said you were with a fiancé?" the annoying doorman said, giving me a bit of a sneering look.

"I am! Iakovos is his cousin. Just go ask him!"

Once again, the man shook his head. "I am not allowed to disturb the patrons."

"It won't be disturbing him—"

"Is there a problem?"

A familiar voice burbled out the door to me. The man who stood blocking the entrance with his body shifted slightly until I could see Patricia.

"No problem, Mrs. Perry. This woman claims to have been inside, but she has no ticket, and neither Stavros or I saw her leave."

I swallowed my anger, and kept a pleasant expression on my face. "Patricia, would you mind telling these two that I am with Dmitri, and that he has our tickets?"

"I'm sorry," Patricia said, her eyes alight with enjoyment. "But I'm afraid these gentlemen are correct. You must have a ticket in order to be allowed entrance. We have to keep a tight control over who gets in, you know. If you don't have a ticket, then you'll have to leave."

I stared at her in utter disbelief for a minute before my ire rose. "You may think kicking me out will help your treacherous friend, but all it's going to do is piss off Dmitri even more than he already is pissed off."

"Call security if she doesn't leave in the next seconds," Patricia said, turning away with a smile on her lips, which I badly wanted to slap right off her face.

I started forward, but the two men shoved me back, slamming shut the doors. I banged on them a couple of times, but they didn't open them again.

Fury rose inside me. I spun around on my heel just as the elevator pinged and two of the security men exited, each of them taking me by an arm. "You don't have to do that—I'm leaving," I snarled, fuming in silence while we rode down to the lobby. I kept my tongue behind my teeth until I got to the reception desk, when I stopped and said loudly, "I need to use your phone. It's an emergency."

"I'm sorry, the phone is not available," the woman who sat there said coolly.

"It's right there," I said, pointing at it where it sat two feet away from me. Next to it were a couple of paper cups of lattes, a paperback book, and a magazine with a bare-breasted woman featured on the cover. Evidently the guards had a wide variety of reading materials. "I can see that it's not in use. I just want to make a local call to my fiancé. He's upstairs."

"The phone is not available," the woman repeated, and with studied indifference turned to address one of the other security people.

"Oh, for God's sake—" I started to lean across to grab the receiver, but the guard behind me evidently interpreted the move as a potential attack, because he slammed me forward into the curved reception desk, scattering latte cups, magazines, and the paperback.

Above me, the guard spoke harshly in Greek.

"I don't understand Greek," I said, a bit breathless with the attack. Worse, I felt wetness soak into my chest. I prayed it was coffee, and not blood.

The second guard pulled me upright while the woman at the desk made a face, said something that I was sure was quite cutting in Greek, and mopped up the latte that dripped down onto the lower part of the reception desk.

Thirty seconds later, the guards dumped me outside with a warning that they would call the police if I returned. I looked down at my front. My lovely gold lace dress was soaked brown from my cleavage down to my groin.

For a second or two, I felt like I was going to sit right down on the curb and cry, but Dmitri and Valentino were inside that blighted building, and by God, I was going to get in there, and read Patricia the riot act.

A sudden flash to the side had me pausing in my act of vowing revenge. I turned and, to my horror, saw five people who had been lounging around on motorbikes suddenly charge toward me; two women were holding digital video cameras, while the other three had cameras hung around their neck, the kind with the big, phallic lenses.

"Princess Juliane! What do you have to say about marrying one of Greece's richest bachelors!" one of them called out as they formed a semicircle in front of me, the cameras snapping away wildly.

"What?" How the hell had they found out about the wedding? I spun around and dashed to the lobby entrance of the building, but the guards stood at the door, scowling, obviously not about to let me return. "I don't know what you're talking about," I said hastily, ignoring the bright, blinding flashes as I tried to push my way through the paparazzi.

"When's the wedding?" one of the women asked.

"Who's dressing you for it?" another called.

I turned in a circle, desperate to find my way out of the hellish nightmare. Someone shoved a small pocket recorder in my face, which I batted away.

"Can you tell us how you met Dmitri Papaioannou?"

"Have you cleared the marriage with the government of Beck?"

"Let's get a shot of you and Dmitri together—"

I shoved past one of the women and ran down the street, mindless of the voices calling after me. I heard the roar of motorcycle engines and knew they were chasing me. I leaped across an intersection, the light against me, and almost got run down, the driver of the car leaning out of the window to lambaste me in Greek.

The paparazzi were stuck in traffic at the intersection, but just as I dashed across yet another street, drawn to what looked to be a pedestrian zone, I saw one of them pull up onto the sidewalk and zip after me.

I flung myself around a corner and, hesitating for just a second, raced into the open doorway of a restaurant, flattening myself against the wall when the light of the motorcycle grew on the pavement.

Several people shouted at the driver as he slowly made his way down the red-tiled area, but he hadn't looked into the restaurant where I'd taken refuge.

Behind me, a man said something that I didn't understand.

"Hi. I'm so sorry to disturb your patrons," I said, smiling at everyone who had glanced up from their meals. I hurried over the to the small reception desk, saying, "Do you have a phone I can use? I'll pay for the call, and I swear it's a local one, but it's an emergency, and I really do need to make it."

In the end, I had to hand over half of my entire bankroll just to use the phone. I called Dmitri's number, but it went straight to voice mail, no doubt because he was gearing up to parade down the catwalk.

"Allowing all the women of Athens to ogle him, dammit. Well, Audrey will not win," I spat out, dialing Harry's number. I had almost given up hope that it would be answered, but a man's voice said something abrupt in Greek.

"Iakovos? It's me, Thyra. I've been kicked out of the building."

"You've what?" He sighed, and I could have sworn I heard him say, "It's Harry all over again—no, love, I wasn't calling you. It's Thyra."

Before I could ask him what was going on, Harry's voice was there. "Thyra? What happened? Was it the light board going wonky? If that freaked you out, it's safe to come back. They turned off the strobe lights, and one of the tech guys has the computer fired up again so that we can continue the auction."

"No, I don't know anything about that. Patricia got me kicked out."

"She what? Yacky, stop it, I'm fine. No, you go watch Valentino and make sure he doesn't try to bite anyone. He doesn't seem to like Audrey. I'll deal with Thyra's situation."

"I'm sorry to saddle you with a situation," I said, my adrenaline starting to fade, leaving me weary, and told her quickly what had happened.

"Paparazzi and everything. How did they know you were there?"

"I can give you one guess, but I assume you won't need it," I said sourly.

"You're probably right. I can't believe … oh, crap, they're ready to start again. Where are you?"

I gave her the address of the restaurant.

"Stay there. I'll send Mikos to pick you up. Your dress is ruined?"

"Yes." I looked down. The whole front of it was covered in brown latte. "If I knew where I was in relationship to your apartment—"

"No, don't go out. The paps are probably still out there.

I'll have Mikos swing you by the apartment, and you can grab Elena's red dress."

I opened my mouth to object, but the vision rose in my mind of Patricia's smug face. "That would be lovely. Harry, can you do me a big favor? Well, another one on top of everything else you've done."

"I'll be there in two secs," I heard her yell before she returned to the phone. "Sure, what?"

"Put Dmitri on last. I'm going to bid for him, and I don't have a lot of money."

Harry laughed. "Don't worry. I'll make sure you get him."

"Thanks, Harry. I'm going to like having you as a cousin-in-law."

"Likewise! OK, OK, I'm coming."

She clicked off, and I gave the manager, who was standing protectively in front of me, his phone.

What happened in the following half hour was kind of a blur. Ten minutes after I hung up, a man pulled up to where I was hiding behind a collection of signs advertising shops, saying with a smile, "Hullo again, Thyra."

"Hi, Mikos." Relief filled me at the sight of him.

"Harry says you are in desperate need of a ride."

"I need that, and a lot more," I said, sliding into the seat next to him, looking around for the photographers.

"They're two blocks over. Saw them as I came in. Hold on, I'm going to run that light."

Six minutes later, I was in the apartment, Mrs. Avrabos waiting for me. "Come, come, I have the dress ready. Tsk, such pretty lace, too. I clean for you, all right?"

"You don't have to," I said, yanking off my dress before I was even fully in the bedroom.

Mrs. Avrabos fussed around while I tried on first the dress Harry had picked out, but it was too long. I went for a different dress, one that was two-piece sky blue, with a full skirt, and a top that was heavily embroidered on the front all the way up to a choker collar, leaving the back exposed.

"I won't be able to wear a bra with this, but what the hell. People will just have to live with the girls being free-range for one evening," I said, sucking in my breath when Mrs. Avrabos hooked the skirt closed. Luckily, it had a couple of hooks along the waistband, allowing it to fit my more substantial self than the slimmer form of its owner.

"Your hair?" Mrs. Avrabos asked, glancing at my ponytail.

I thought for a minute, then twisted it around itself, using a few bobby pins to turn it into a quick updo.

"That's going to have to do," I said, hurrying out, wearing the same shoes that I had on, because I didn't want to take time to find a pair that went with the dress.

"I texted Iakovos," Mikos said when we were on the road again. I felt a driving sense of urgency, a need to get my revenge. More, I wanted to be there when Dmitri took the stage. He was mine, dammit, and I wanted everyone to know it. "He will make sure you get in."

"Thank you for all your help," I told him. "I'm sure you had something else you wanted to do tonight."

He flashed me a grin right before he pulled to a stop in front of the building in question. I won't say he broke actual laws getting there, but if he didn't, it was a near thing. "It's OK. Dmitri, he is a good friend. I'm glad to know you will be keeping him happy."

I pressed a kiss to his cheek before leaping out of the car. True to his word, Iakovos was at the door, the security guards suitably cowed behind him. The look on his face was grim as he gestured toward the elevators.

I hurried past the guards, not bothering to give them so much as a glance. "I'm not too late, am I?"

"No. Harry was stalling. But I don't know how long she can do that, and I've been here for five minutes."

We were both silent during the ride up, but I noticed Iakovos had pulled out his phone and sent a text message before we made it to the top floor.

The doors to the ballroom were open. I glared at the

man who had previously refused to let me in, took a deep breath, and sailed into the ballroom, my head up.

"—will be seeing the last bachelor in just a minute, but before we do, I wanted to thank you all for your contributions to the Children in Crisis fund. Oh, look!" Harry pointed to where I was marching across the floor, fire in my blood giving me courage where I would normally have none. "It's Her Serene Highness Princess Juliane of Sonderburg-Beck. What a honor it is to have you, Your Serene Highness. And with that, I believe we can bring out our last bachelor, Dmitri Papaioannou. I'm sure I don't need to tell you all about Dmitri."

Dmitri appeared at the back of the stage, casting a curious glance at Harry before strolling forward.

People at the tables nearest the end of the catwalk scooted their chairs out of their way as I stalked forward, my eyes firmly affixed to the man who had so completely captured my heart. I saw him hesitate for a moment when he caught sight of me, a little frown of confusion pulling his brows together, but when I reached the end of the catwalk, I waved the wad of money I'd been holding.

"Bidding is now open for Dmitri Papaioannou," Harry said, watching me.

"I bid twenty-seven euros," I yelled, slapping down onto the stage all the money I had left to my name.

"Sold to Her Serene Highness!" Harry called, banging down a gavel.

Around us, there was the murmur of people who were not happy. A squawk from the left preceded a flurry of movement. I stared up at Dmitri, and smiled.

He looked startled for a moment; then a slow answering smile curled his lips. He leaped off the catwalk, and pulled me into his arms. "And here I thought you didn't want me enough to bid for me," he murmured against my lips.

Behind me, I could hear Audrey shouting to Harry that she hadn't given them time to bid. Patricia's voice joined the protest, but I didn't pay any attention to anything but the man pressed against me.

"I love you," I told him, then nipped his bottom lip, and kissed the breath right out of his lungs.

TWELVE

"I have to give it to Harry," I told Dmitri an hour and a half later, when I peeled Valentino's harness off his body and gave him a scratch on all the spots that I knew were itchy. He head bonked my ankle twice, then strolled off to visit his facilities and food bowl. "She sure didn't wilt under Patricia's onslaught."

"Harry is an old hand dealing with her," Dmitri agreed, checking his phone. "Ah, I see Alexis will be away tonight. Just in case you had any ideas about running naked through the atrium."

I turned to look at the atrium. Dmitri's apartment was laid out with his bedroom, bathroom, and a small dressing room to the south side, while a kitchen opened into an atrium that spread over two floors. The upper part of it led out to a patio with stunning views of Athens and the Acropolis, and even had an infinity pool, which I hadn't yet had time to try. Back on the main floor, the north side of the apartment was taken up with three more bedrooms (one of which Alexis used) and assorted utility rooms. Since Dmitri didn't have a live-in housekeeper, I considered the idea of doing some form of a striptease for him, but in the end, I decided to simply pounce on him once he'd taken off his tux, and I'd gotten out of Elena's dress without damaging it.

"Now, let's see what sorts of things I'm going to want you, my official charity slave, to do," I said a short while later when we were both naked, and I was straddling his thighs. I spread my hands on his belly, enjoying the way his eyes glowed green with passion, and his breath hitched.

"I am wholly and completely yours to do with as you will," he said, his hands next to him. I wondered for a moment at that. Usually, he liked to touch me. I wondered if something was wrong.

That's when it hit me, a question that slammed into me with the force of a truck. Had Dmitri been embarrassed at the tiny amount of money that he'd been "sold" for? I froze for a moment while I thought that through in horrified realization: all the other bachelors had gone for thousands of euros, some in the tens of thousands.

But not Dmitri. He raised all of twenty-seven euros.

Worry, guilt, and shame made a hard little knot in my belly. I debated apologizing, but decided that since he was clearly anticipating me giving him pleasure tonight, that was the least I could do. "I guess we'll use some of this massage oil you got," I said, pouring a little into my hands, and rubbing them together to warm it up before I took his penis into my hands.

"That would be … oh, Christ, yes." His head fell back, his hands clutching the sheets convulsively as I oiled up all the pertinent parts. He moaned when I worked up a rhythm that he liked, his hips moving along with my hands. And when I bent to take him in my mouth, he started speaking in Greek.

I swirled my tongue, I stroked long, intricate patterns into him, and I did my damnedest to give him even a tiny fraction of the joy he always brought me, but after about fifteen minutes without him blasting off, I stopped. "Am I doing something wrong?" I asked, the horrible emotions in my belly holding me in an iron grip. Had my stupidity damaged our relationship? I couldn't bear that. "You don't seem to be enjoying this."

"I am, but I was actually going to ask the same thing of you. If you're tired, we can do this another time."

Oh, God, I had ruined it. I'd broken our relationship. Normally when I touched him, he went up like flash paper, but now …

"I'm sorry if I've … if I'm … I'll just go wash this oil off my hands." I was off him and into the bathroom before he could say anything. I bent over the sink, my hands on either side of it, staring down at the gray marble through blurring eyes. Dammit, I swore to myself, I would not cry. He'd notice if I did.

"I have the feeling I've done something to upset you, but I'm not sure what it is. Please tell me, Princess."

Big, fat tears fell into the sink. "You haven't done anything, Dmitri. I have. I'm so ashamed of myself, of my stupid need to prove to Audrey that she couldn't have you. I didn't think how … how embarrassing that would be to you. All those people who saw me march in and win you for twenty-seven euros … people you work with, and want to work with, and I let my damned pride get the better of me. I'm sorry. I'm so, so sorry. I've never been ashamed of who I was before, but I am now. All those people know that my damned Serene Highness self only valued you to the tune of twenty-seven euros."

He stood behind me, not touching me, which made me feel a thousand times worse. I couldn't even bring myself to look up from the sink, afraid of the pity or worse that I'd see in his eyes.

"Your pride is definitely a thorn in my side," he said, and I bit back a sob of anguish. Then his hands were on my arms, turning me around to face him, his thumb brushing away the tears. "But only because it won't allow me to give you the sun and moon and stars, as I want to do."

I'd been staring at his Adam's apple, but looked up to his eyes at the words. "But … I shamed you—"

"You did nothing of the kind. You gave me the highest compliment I've ever had."

"By making a fool of myself and dishonoring you?" I shook my head. "Everyone else raised so much money—"

"And you bid everything you had. Every last euro. I know how hard your life has been, how even twenty-seven euros matters to you. The fact that you didn't keep any of it back for yourself, or Valentino, but you gave it all makes me feel like I'm the luckiest man in the world to be marrying you in two days."

Could he be serious? My heart wanted so desperately to believe his words. "It's just a fake marriage—"

"It's a very real marriage, even if the reason for us doing it is to keep you safe at my side."

I stared at him in confusion, wanting to believe his beautiful words, but worried that he was trying to make me feel better simply because he was such a nice man. "But everyone else saw what I did, Dmitri. Hell, I made a big show of it. What they must think—"

"What they think doesn't matter," he said, handing me a box of tissues when I started to sniff back my runny nose. He waited for me to blow it, then pulled me up against his body, his warmth and understanding making me leak hot tears all over his shoulder. Could any man be more perfect? "Only you matter, Princess. And if you don't know that by now, then I'm going to have to redouble my efforts to make you understand just what you mean to me."

I stopped watering his shoulder, wiped my eyes and blew my nose again, and said somewhat stuffily, "You wouldn't happen to be falling in love with me, too?"

"Perhaps," he said, smiling with a soft, warm light in his eyes that made my heart sing. "Or perhaps I'm already so head over heels in love with you that I can't remember a time when you weren't in my life, driving me mad with desire, and filling my life with happiness, and making me want to shake you with irritation."

I laughed at that. "You're the only man who can make being irritated at me sound like a compliment."

"It is, my adorable one. I know it's just your way of keeping me on my toes, and I'm grateful to know that with you doing so, my life will never be boring. Now, shall we return to bed and give that massage oil another try?"

"All right," I said, letting him lead me back into the bedroom. "But if I don't drive you crazy in five minutes flat, then I'm going to know you're secretly angry with me."

He lasted all of three minutes.

"Cove is back today," Dmitri said the following morning. We were in the kitchen, my body humming with the aftereffects of the method in which he'd woken me up. At my feet, Valentino graciously accepted a plate of food, while, sitting across the island, Alexis scarfed down enough food for three grown men. I caught Dmitri watching him with a fascinated sort of horror, which made me giggle to myself and make a mental promise that just as soon as I could arrange for my laptop to be sent to me, I'd study some videos on how to cook. Dmitri wasn't skinny by any sense of the word, but he was a bit too thin for my liking. What he needed was home-cooked meals, and although I hadn't ever had success at that endeavor in the past, now I had good motivation to learn.

"Who's Cove?" I asked, realizing my mental musings had almost caused me to miss what he had said.

"My driver. He'll be available to take you anywhere you like after he drops Alexis and me at the office."

"You have a driver?" It didn't strike me as odd that Iakovos should have a driver, but I'd never imagined Dmitri had one, too. It made him seem once again out of my class.

"I do. He's been on vacation the last two weeks, but he's back, and I've told him to make himself useful to you, should you need a ride somewhere. Ah. And speaking of that, Alexis has something for you."

"Thankfully, yes." Alexis stopped shoveling in a mountain of eggs and potatoes that he'd placed on top of a piece of toast and, wiping his hands, bent down to hand me a battered green canvas bag. "It is with much gratitude and no little sense of relief that I officially pass to you the ceremonial messenger bag used through the ages by personal assistants of Dmitri Papaioannou. Use it with my blessings, and in good health."

He made a dramatic bow that had me laughing. "I take it you've been promoted?" I asked, knowing full well that Dmitri had intended on doing just that. I felt a moment of pride that he truly intended on me being his assistant. I'd never had such an exciting job, and I very much looked forward to helping him with his work.

"I have. As of this morning, I am officially an associate broker in Papaioannou Green."

"And to fill your new ceremonial messenger bag—really, Alexis, you couldn't have found something a bit nicer for her?—I have your official phone," Dmitri added, handing me a cell phone.

"I like this bag," I said, pulling it close to me. "It looks like it's been through a war or two."

"I found it at a military-memorabilia shop," Alexis told me with a wink. "So it has."

"This is a nice phone," I murmured, quickly flipping through screens. "Latest version of Android, nice amount of memory, and the fastest network. Is it a hot spot, too?" I asked Dmitri.

"I believe so. It has access to an unlimited data plan, so you can do what you like with it."

I glanced at him. "For work," I pointed out.

He nodded. "For work. Speaking of that, do you have your list of employment demands?"

"They aren't demands as much as just sensible ground rules."

Dmitri gave me a jaded look. I giggled in return, and added, "No, but I'll call—or text—Panoush today and have him send that over, along with the prenuptial stuff that he said he'd have by now."

"Good." Dmitri looked at his phone, quickly swiping through a few messages just as Alexis was doing the same thing.

I eyed my new phone, feeling very professional. "When do I start?"

"The job?" Dmitri considered the question. "I thought next week, if you are willing. That gives us this week to get married and for you to get settled here, as well as get your things brought over from England. Assuming you want them."

"Oh, yes, please. I'm tired of living in the same four outfits."

He nodded. "If you prefer to stay here, I can have your things packed and shipped out to you."

"I should let my roommates know that my room will be available, but since I'm paid up through the end of the month, I don't think they'll kick up too big of a fuss," I mused. "So long as you bill me for the cost of bringing my things out, I would be grateful not to have to go back to London."

"I'll mark it down under moving expenses," he said, flashing his almost dimples at me. "Were you planning to see Harry today?"

"I thought I would. She asked me to stop by because she says it's boring having to sit around so much without her kids to entertain her, but if you needed me—"

"Every second of every hour of every day," he said, kissing the tip of my nose, which just made me want to melt into a big puddle of goo. "But I'm willing to lend you to Harry so you can keep her spirits up. And you may get to meet Theo and Kiera if they get in today as Jake said they planned. You ready?"

The last question was aimed at Alexis, who nodded, shoved several orange slices into his mouth, then waved at me as he hurried off to get his jacket and laptop bag.

Dmitri kissed me, his lips warm and sweet and infinitely wonderful. He brushed a strand of hair off my cheek. "Call me if you need me, Princess. Cove should be back in half an hour. His number is in your phone already. Just let him know when you want him, and he'll be at the front entrance."

"Thank you," I told him, nibbling on his earlobe. "For everything, but most especially for being the sexiest almost-list-making Greek bachelor."

"Only for one more day," he said, pinching my behind. Then he was gone, leaving me sighing with happiness.

An hour later, I emerged from the apartment building, and smiled at the man who leaned against a familiar dark blue car. "Hi, you must be Cove."

"That I am. And you're a real princess!" The man who greeted me had a wild mop of curls, dark skin that hinted of African ancestry, and small gold barbells pierced through both eyebrows. The hand that he held out to shake was covered in tattoos, and he had a wiry physique that reminded me of my brother. He also had what I thought of as a California surfer accent, his words coming out a little slow, like there was no need to hurry. I liked him instantly. "I almost dropped my dentures when Dmitri told me he was marrying royalty. Not that the Papaioannous aren't almost tantamount to that here, but still, you're, like, really a princess. Dude!"

"I might be, but I prefer to be called Thyra—" I paused when a man who was passing stopped and stared at me. Immediately uncomfortable, I got into the front seat, glancing over my shoulder when Cove started up the car and pulled out into traffic.

"So, where to?" he asked.

The man stood on the sidewalk, holding up a phone like he was taking a picture of us. He couldn't be a paparazzo, because he'd have a proper camera. Which meant … "Kardom," I said, a cold hand gripping my innards at the thought of him.

"Where's that? I've been driving Dmitri around for two years now, but I don't think I know of it. Is it a town up the coast?"

"No, Kardom is a who, not a what. He's my cousin."

"Oh, is he the dude who roofied you and tried to do the legal with you?" Cove shook his head. "Bad juju, that. Seriously bad juju."

"Amen to that. Er ..." I thought for a minute about where I was going. "I have to go to the post office. One of my roomies sent me a present for Dmitri. My wedding present to him, that is."

"What's that, or can't you tell me?" Cove asked.

I shook away the worry that Kardom had tracked me down. I knew Dmitri had talked to the concierge, and there was no way Kardom would be allowed up to the penthouse. "I don't mind telling you, so long as you don't let Dmitri know. I found out yesterday that he's as big a gamer as I am, and he loves an RPG series that I play. It so happens that one of my roommates works on his favorite game, and she offered to send me an alpha copy of it. I know Dmitri will be beside himself to play it before everyone else can."

"Sounds like a righteous choice, Your Highness."

"Thyra, please," I said, laughing at his surfer intonation. I half expected him to call me "brah" at any minute, but to my surprise, he was quite knowledgeable about Athens and Greece, and he pointed out various favorite cafés and shops as we went to the post office so I could pick up the package I'd had my roomie send me.

On the way to Harry's apartment, I texted Dmitri.

TO: DMITRI

A man outside the apartment stopped and stared at me, and I think took a picture of your car.

A few minutes later, the response came.

FROM: DMITRI

Well, if I didn't know you and I saw you, I'd take a picture, too.

TO: DMITRI

I just bet you it's Kardom.

FROM: DMITRI

Doubtful. Information I have says he flew to Rome yesterday.

TO: DMITRI

Information? What information? Why would he go to Rome? Dammit, I'm going to have to call Maggie, and I've been trying to avoid doing that because the things I have to say to her aren't nice.

FROM: DMITRI

You don't have to do anything you don't want to do, although if you have news of your cousin Kardom, please let me know.

"He's entirely too unconcerned," I said aloud after reading his last text.

"Dmitri? Dude's chill," Cove said, nodding.

"He's just a little too chill about this, when he should be concerned. That tells me he's done something to keep tabs on Kardom, like having people watch him. Dammit, that costs money." I bit my lower lip, wondering if I should raise a fuss about it, but knowing I wouldn't.

I would, however, have to confront Maggie. "Would you mind parking for a few minutes at the National Garden?" I asked Cove. "I need to make a phone call, and it's not going to be pleasant."

"Sure thing," he answered, and a few minutes later, he dropped me off at the entrance, promising to pick me up in ten minutes. I claimed one of the scattered benches and, after a moment of steeling my nerves, dialed Maggie's number.

"Who is this?" her voice answered.

"Your cousin. The one you helped drug and kidnap."

"You have a lot of nerve calling me. I assume it's to apologize?"

A stab of pain went through me at the coldness in her voice.

"What on earth do I have to apologize for?" I asked, annoyed despite the pain. "I'm the victim here, Maggie."

She snorted in disgust. "Oh, right, you're always the victim. Poor little Thyra who got all the breaks. How about thinking about someone other than yourself for a change?"

I stared at the pavement beneath my feet, my mind whirling as it tried to cope with the words coming out of her mouth. Maggie, my friend and cousin, whom I had trusted. "Why did you do it, Mags? Did Kardom offer to pay you? Was it revenge, or just the money?"

"Money is never just anything. Not when you don't have it. But then, you wouldn't know that, would you?"

I rubbed my forehead, feeling a headache coming on. "You know full well that I'm flat broke."

"I know nothing of the kind. You know what Kardom told me? He said that you and Chris have oodles of money, only you want everyone to think you're dirt poor. I trusted you, Thyra, and believed you, and then I found out the truth about you."

"The only reason that Chris is slightly less broke than me is because he has a good job," I argued.

"Whatever, Thyra. I know the truth now. And I can't believe that I fell for your sob story for so many years."

"Kardom really told you a tale, huh?" Anger filled me now, not anger that he could be so devious, but that my own cousin would believe him over me. "I hope someday you realize how manipulative he is. Until that time, I think it's better if we don't see each other."

"Oh, you're going to see me. You owe me too much," she said, her voice as hard as nails.

I was gripped with an alienating sense that I was talking to a stranger. Maggie couldn't say such things to me, could she? Not the cousin I'd grown up with my whole life. "What, exactly, do I owe you?"

"Compensation," she snapped; then before I could say more, she hung up on me. I thought of calling her back but didn't think there was any use in doing so. I'd just end up arguing with her, and she clearly was not in the mood to believe anything I said.

I sighed to myself and tucked the phone away in my bag, then got to my feet and started toward the parking area where Cove was due to pick me up. A flash of sunlight on metal caught my eye, causing me to turn to the left.

A man on a motorcycle held a camera up, aimed in my direction. A woman emerged from a car beyond him, also holding a camera, but she called out to me. "Princess Juliane! Rumor has it that your cousin has come to an agreement with the Beck government to be recognized as crown prince. What's Dmitri think of that? Is he going to bankroll your run at the title? Where's Prince Christian? Is he coming out for your wedding?"

"Dammit," I snarled, and ran out to the street, praying I could get to Cove before the paparazzi did.

I didn't, but by the time I flung myself in next to Cove, he had seen the two people.

I slammed the car door behind me, locking it and slumping down in the seat, thanking Dmitri for the foresight in having a car with tinted windows.

"Looks like someone spotted you. Should I lose them, or don't you care?" Cove asked, watching in his side mirror as the man tried to pull alongside us. Luckily, oncoming traffic limited that ability.

"Lose him, please. So very much lose him."

It took fifteen minutes, but he did the job. I slumped back with Valentino, my hand absently stroking him, my heart sick.

Had Beck really made a deal with Kardom? And more important, how on earth was I going to convince them that he was all wrong for them, and that they needed to give me a chance?

THIRTEEN

A half hour after my unsettling call to Maggie, I sat in the lobby of Harry and Iakovos's building and held my phone, trying to psych myself up for the second unpleasant call of the day.

"It's not easy," I told Valentino where he sat on a plush white leather bench next to me. I ignored the concierge, a woman I'd seen before, and who knew I was allowed up to the penthouse. "But after what the paparazzi said … well, I think I have to do it. OK. Here goes. Wish me buckets and buckets of luck."

Valentino put a paw on my leg that I interpreted as his good wishes … until he used that to leverage his body into a personal-parts grooming pretzel.

"Ja?" a man answered in German.

"Hello," I said slowly in English, in case he wasn't well versed in that language. As one of the two undecided ministers, he was a stranger to me, but I'd decided that I had to do something to try to sway him over onto my side. "I am Juliane of Beck. Is this Minister Hans Sauber?"

"Ah, Princess Juliane, yes, it is I." The man's voice had an unreadable note to it that I desperately wished I could interpret. "What may I help you with?"

"I wanted to know if any further progress has been made with regards to the proposal I made to represent Beck. As you know, I am a direct descendant of the last crown prince, and although my brother, Christian, technically holds that title now, he is willing to cede it to me."

"My dear Princess Juliane, surely you cannot be under any delusion that Beck would be interested in being represented by a woman of no means, with no way to support herself, and a dubious claim on the illustrious title of crown princess," Hans interrupted, his voice now clipped, each word being uttered as if it were made of hard edges.

"Dubious claim?" I asked, outraged, lowering the volume of my voice when the concierge glanced over at me. I half turned on the bench, my back to the window in case any paparazzi were outside it. "What do you mean dubious claim? My great-grandfather was the last ruler of Sonderburg-Beck—"

"So you say, but we have yet to see any proof other than a family tree that, quite honestly, anyone could modify and print."

I stared in horror at the wall, trying to understand what the man was saying. "There's been some mistake, then, Minister, because I submitted full documentation as to my identity almost six months ago, including certified birth, marriage, and death certificates for not only myself but the last three generations of my ancestors. Ms. Martin has it all. She said she submitted it to the council."

"Indeed? Sadly, I can find no record of such documents." He was back to sounding oily.

I had to ask the question that I dreaded the most. "Would you, by any chance, have approved my cousin Friederich Kardom's petition for recognition?"

"I'm afraid I can't speak about that to the public," the annoying man said, and I'll be damned if I couldn't hear the smile in his voice. "Although I don't think it's breaking any confidences to say that we here in Beck have nothing but the greatest respect for Prince Friederich, and have, in fact, moved up the council vote on the subject of the royal family. It will take place in slightly less than two weeks."

"He's not a prince," I almost snarled, so frustrated I wanted to scream—or hit Iakovos's punching bag. Dammit, Kardom had gotten to this man, too. I had no doubt that by now he'd snagged the only other undecided minister, too. Why else would he convince them to move up the vote? "And if you believe he is, then you're just as deluded as he is—"

"I'm afraid I have work to do, Princess. You will naturally excuse me."

The phone clicked before I could respond. I sat and swore to myself for a good ten minutes before I managed to get my strident emotions under control.

"I'll have to deal with Herr Asshat later," I told Valentino while we rode the elevator to the top floor. "After I've talked to Dmitri to see what he thinks."

Less than five minutes after that, Valentino settled on Harry's lap with a contented, but wary, expression. I bent awkwardly and shook the pudgy hand of a toddler named Peter.

"He loves to shake hands, even though he doesn't quite grasp the concept of what the purpose is," his mother, Harry's sister-in-law Kiera, said. "He makes Theo shake hands with him every time he comes home from work."

"Puppy! Mine!" Peter said, pointing at Valentino.

"He's a kitty, Peter, not a puppy, and he lives with Thyra," Harry said, waggling her fingers at Peter at the same time I pulled Valentino off her lap.

I wasn't quite sure how the cat would react to a young child, and wanted to be able to remove him from the situation if he felt threatened.

"He started the 'mine' thing a month ago. We've pointed out the differences between cats and dogs, but he pretty much calls all animals puppy." Kiera smiled proudly at the boy, who headed straight for me when I sat down with Valentino.

"Do you know how to make a soft hand?" I asked him when he bounced to a stop at my knees, glancing back at his mom. Both women were watching me, and I had an uncomfortable feeling I was undergoing some sort of a test. I felt oddly excluded at that moment, a sensation that left me desperate to do whatever it was to be accepted. I liked Harry, and I wanted to like this tall woman with freckles. I realized with a sharp pang of longing that I wanted to be part of Dmitri's family.

"Mine," Peter said, pointing again at Valentino. "Puppy."

The cat sat on my lap in his standard loaf position, but his eyes were watchful.

"This is Valentino. He likes to be petted, but you have to use a soft hand on him. Here, hold your hand out open, and very gently pet the back of his neck." I held Valentino with one hand, while showing Peter how to pet. "See? Gentle pets. He likes it when you are soft with him."

"Soft puppy?" Peter asked, looking doubtful.

"That's right, the kitty is very soft. Aren't you good with words describing your surroundings?" Kiera watched her son with an indulgent eye, adding to Harry and me, "We haven't yet gotten a dog, but Peter does like the baby lambs on the island. Which, of course, he also calls puppy, but that's neither here nor there."

I was a whole lot more nervous about the child getting scratched, but Valentino didn't seem to mind being petted with awkward little pats and sticky-handed strokes.

Peter abandoned us once Kiera brought out a big tablet of paper and some crayons. Valentino went to the patio to sun himself. "So, here we all are," Harry said, beaming at us. "I'm so glad you got in early, Kiera, because I was going to surprise Thyra by taking her shopping for a dress for her wedding, but I'm feeling a bit worn out today, so you can do the honors."

"That's very thoughtful of you," I said quickly when Kiera, with a horrified look on her face that Harry laughed at, said she'd be happy to fill in, "but I have a dress. Mrs. Avrabos told me when I was putting Valentino's litter box in your laundry room that she had cleaned the coffee out of it. And thank you for that, by the way."

"For Mrs. Avrabos?" Harry nodded. "She's a wonder, isn't she? Worth her weight in gold, and absolutely adores the kids, which is amazing given how wild they are."

"She is, but I meant for letting me park a litter box here. It makes me feel better knowing Valentino doesn't have to hold anything in."

"I'm just happy you bring him with you. He's such a love. I'm going to have to start working on Yacky to let me include a cat in our menagerie."

"Speaking of your children, I'm surprised they aren't with you," Kiera said.

I sat feeling like an intruder, and wondered if I shouldn't make an excuse and leave.

But where would I go? Back to Dmitri's apartment? His cleaner would be there now, and while I didn't mind chatting with her, I felt a bit awkward having her clean when there was no reason I couldn't be mopping the floors and cleaning the toilets, too.

Except that Dmitri had made it quite clear that he preferred I not do the woman out of her job, especially since she was putting a daughter through college.

"Iakovos had to come to Athens for a week, and since he doesn't like to leave me this close to D-day, he insisted that I needed a break from the kids. And I admit, it is a lot more quiet, but I do miss the little rug rats. We're going back on Saturday. I hope you plan on staying with us for a bit while the house is being finished. Thyra, you will love Theo and Kiera's new place. It's about a half an hour south of our island. They've been having the house remodeled for the last four months—when it's done, it's going to have solid glass walls facing the sea. The view is breathtaking, since the house is right on the water. Iakovos is pea green with envy, and has already started making noises about doing some remodeling on our house."

I smiled, and nodded, and made polite noises while the two women talked about their children, and the houses, and what Kiera was doing in New Zealand, where I gathered they lived part of the year. I wondered if there would be a time when I felt comfortable with them both, or if my weird social anxieties meant I would forever feel like an outsider.

"So, what do you think?" Harry asked a half hour later when Kiera went to change Peter. Evidently they had started potty training, but it wasn't going too smoothly. "I hope you like Kiera. She's been through a lot in the last few years, but she and Theo are madly in love."

"She's very nice. Peter is adorable," I said politely.

Harry shot me an acute glance. "But you're not very comfortable with them?"

"I'm ... kind of weird that way," I said, hastily adding, "It's nothing to do with them. I'm sure your brother-in-law and Kiera are super nice. I don't want you feeling like I'm being judgmental or anything."

"Thyra," she said, hoisting herself over on the couch so she could give my hand a squeeze. "You're a friggin' princess. Kiera is intimidated to death by you. She almost begged me not to leave her alone with you because she was terrified she'd say the wrong thing to you."

I blinked a couple of times, not sure what to make of that. "She's intimidated by me? But you guys are good friends. You've known each other so much longer than I've known you. I'm the one who is the outsider intruding on your family group."

"Not anymore you aren't," Harry said with a pat on my shoulder. "Now you're a part of the sisterhood of Papamaumau wives."

"Really, Harry?" Kiera asked, returning with Peter on her hip. "You still can't say the name?"

Harry grinned. "I told Thyra you were terrified of her."

Kiera's eyes opened wide. "Oh, God, you didn't!" she said, then set down Peter and slumped to the floor next to him, covering her face. "A real princess knows I'm afraid of her. I shall now die of embarrassment."

"You won't be the only one," I said softly.

"Thyra has social anxieties," Harry told her. "She also seems to be pretty shy, which isn't, I would imagine, standard princess makeup. So really, you two are a whole lot more alike than you know."

I looked at Kiera. She looked at me. "I'll try not to be afraid of you, if you try not to be shy around me," she offered.

I thought about that, decided it was fair, and nodded. "Deal."

The rest of the day went better. I didn't relax fully, but by the time I returned to Dmitri's apartment, I felt like I had triumphed and beaten my feeling that I was an outsider.

I told Dmitri so when he came home and took a shower before we went out for dinner. "I can't imagine anyone being afraid of me. I mean, afraid! Of me! It's bizarre."

"You're royalty," Dmitri pointed out while he pulled on a pair of jeans and a T-shirt. "That's very intimidating. I can completely understand why Kiera was nervous meeting you. Hell, if I'd known who you were before I slammed the door into you, I'd have been nervous, as well."

I thought about telling him about my call to Beck, but decided not to ruin the evening with contemplation of that frustrating situation.

Valentino, who was lolling on the bed like he was a king, put out one big orange paw and patted at the tie Dmitri had peeled off with his suit, tossing it all on the bed. I picked up both items, shook them out, then hung them in the closet. "Oh, come on. You've met royalty before. Harry says Iakovos did work for some Saudi prince a while back."

He grimaced. "And swore afterward that he'd never repeat the experience. You couldn't be more different than that family if you were from another planet."

I gave a little eye roll, and put his shoes into the closet, as well, tossing his socks and underwear into the hamper. "I just don't get it. I was born with this. But people like you, who succeed because you work hard and don't allow the possibility of failing, you guys are the ones who are impressive. I can't imagine doing what you do every day, although I am very excited about helping out."

"We'll have to agree to have a mutual admiration society," he said, giving his hair a quick brush before patting Valentino on the head. "Are we leaving His Majesty home?"

"I thought we could. He didn't seem to mind Peter, but he also didn't head bonk him, and you know that's Valentino's standard rating of approval."

We told the cat to behave himself, and ran into Alexis as the latter was on his way out. I gathered from the comments made while we rode down in the elevator that Alexis was a bit of a ladies' man.

The two men paused to talk to the concierge, leaving me to emerge into the soft night air, the smog making my nose wrinkle a little. Cove got out of the car at the sight of me, and just as I started forward, a man appeared from behind a palm tree in a massive planter and, before I knew what he was doing, had one arm around my waist and hustled me down the street a good ten yards. He stopped, spun me around, and glared into my face, his hands hard on my upper arms.

"What the—what are you doing here?" I asked.

"Waiting for you to come out. Do you have any idea how hard it was to find you? I've been trying to get in to see you for the last two hours, and the blasted people there won't let me—"

A blue shape seemed to blur in front of me, and the next thing I knew, I was standing by myself while Dmitri held a man up by his throat against the wall of the building.

"What the hell do you think you are doing?" Dmitri snarled in a tone that I'd never heard him use. Behind him, Alexis menaced, while Cove took my arm and tried to hustle me into the car.

"If you think you're going to so much as touch Thyra—"

"Dmitri, stop! That's not Kardom!" I almost yelled,

twisting out of Cove's hold to run over to where Dmitri was glancing in surprise over his shoulder at me.

"It's not? Then who the hell is it?"

"My brother. He's turning bright red. Do you think you could let him have some air now?"

"Your …" Dmitri turned back to look at where Chris was, indeed, turning red. "Shit."

"That's what I was about to say," Chris wheezed when Dmitri stopped leaning on his windpipe. Both Alexis and he grabbed Chris when the latter's knees buckled for a few seconds. He coughed a couple of times, rubbing his throat, his eyes watering when they turned on me. To my complete surprise, he wasn't furious at the treatment, although when he spoke, his voice was a bit thin and hoarse. "I guess this answers my question about whether or not this man you're marrying will keep you safe."

"This is your brother," Dmitri repeated, looking more than a little stunned. "The one who is the Scottish cop?"

"Detective chief inspector, thank you very much," Chris said with dignity, straightening his shirt, which had been rumpled when Dmitri slammed him against the wall.

"You got the promotion!" I said, giving him a hug and a kiss to the cheek. "I'm so happy for you. When did you find out?"

"Two days ago. I would have told you when you called, but I figured since I was coming out here anyway, I'd just tell you then." He grinned and for a moment, I felt as blessed as anyone could be.

I took Dmitri's arm. "Dmitri, this is Chris. Chris, this is Dmitri. That's Alexis, Dmitri's new associate person, and over there is Cove, the driver."

Dmitri gave me a long look.

"No," I told him.

"You have to," he answered.

"I don't."

Chris eyed Dmitri for a few seconds, then gave me a half smile. "You do, I think. Go ahead, it won't kill you."

I sighed a dramatic, martyred sigh. "Why do you people make such a big fuss about this? Fine. Dmitri Papaioannou, may I present His Serene Highness Crown Prince Christian Leopold Friederich of Sonderburg-Beck, oldest living legitimate member of the house of Sonderburg-Beck, detective extraordinaire, and pain-in-the-ass brother who didn't bother to tell me that he was coming to Athens."

Chris laughed and gave me a squeeze before turning to face Dmitri, holding out his hand. "'Chris' will do nicely. I've been wanting to meet you ever since Thyra told me she was marrying you."

"Likewise," Dmitri said, looking oddly relieved. I wondered about that for a minute, and then I realized that both Alexis and Dmitri had been standing very straight until Chris held out his hand. I bit back a little giggle at the thought that they had been on the verge of bowing.

"We're just off to have dinner with Dmitri's cousins." I glanced at Dmitri. "Er ..."

"I'm sure Jake and Harry would be delighted to have you join us," he said smoothly, and after shooing away Alexis (who had announced he'd be willing to put off his date just so he could say he had dinner with a prince and princess), we headed out with Dmitri and Chris discussing such fascinating topics as Dmitri's ability to keep me in the style Chris wanted for me (that earned my brother a glare and a lecture on how I didn't need a man to support me), why Dmitri had an arrest record (another glare, another lecture, this one regarding invasion of other people's privacy, which was interrupted when I asked Dmitri just what he was arrested for—a political protest when he was a young man), and, finally, why he felt he was worthy of wedding a Sonderburg-Beck.

"Right, you are being the worst sort of obnoxious," I told Chris. "I hope you've worked all of your older-brother protective crap out of your system, because I'm tired of hearing it, and you're giving Dmitri the wrong impression about us."

"On the contrary, I have nothing but respect for your brother," Dmitri said with a little shrug. "He's protecting you. I would do the same for a sister, although I might not have the investigative resources that he does."

Chris just grinned.

We spent a pleasant evening with Dmitri's family, although I'm not sure that Chris knew what to think when Harry insisted taking a selfie with him. "I am sending this to Patricia right now," she said, tapping furiously on her phone, "with a message that reads I am having both a prince and princess to dinner, and what's she up to? Ha! Oh, she's going to froth at the mouth over this. Wait, Chris, do you mind if we do a picture where you're kissing my hand? I think that might just send her over the deep end."

Iakovos and Theo were off checking something to do with the air-conditioning unit when we arrived, which just sent Dmitri after them with a muttered comment that neither one of his cousins knew anything about changing filters. Chris chatted politely with Harry; I sat on a chair with Peter on my lap while he played with my braid.

Kiera sat next to me, sending Chris periodic startled glances until I leaned over and whispered, "He's not going to demand that someone cut off your head if you say the wrong thing, you know. We can't do that."

She gave a gulping laugh.

"Not any longer, that is," I added, keeping my lips from twitching.

She shot me a horrified look.

Chris told Harry—who evidently had a love of all things forensic—about some of his more interesting cases. Peter continued to chatter to himself while he played with my hair.

"He loves long hair," Kiera said just as the men returned. "He used to love to suck on mine, but we finally taught him that it wasn't polite to do that to other people—no! Peter, no! You are a very bad boy. I'm so sorry, Thyra. Here, let me get a wet towel."

"Peter? A bad boy? Never!" A man who was just a smidgen taller than Dmitri strolled out, his gaze going first to

Kiera as she dashed into the apartment, then to Peter, who had stuffed the tail of my braid into his mouth and was happily chewing on it. "Ah. I see. Peter, old man, we've had this talk several times now. It's not polite to chew other people's hair, especially those of royalty. You must be the princess that Dmitri managed to brainwash into marrying him. Please forgive my son. He's not really a cannibal."

"And just when I had decided I wasn't going to die of embarrassment in front of Thyra and her brother," Kiera said, hurrying forward with a small hand towel, and managing to get my braid out of Peter's mouth and hands. "Here, take this spawn of your loins while I try to wipe the slobber off of her hair."

Theo—who I decided was just as handsome as Iakovos, but still not close enough to Dmitri to give him a run for the title of handsomest Papaioannou—laughed and took his son, who immediately started telling Dmitri about the puppy.

"It's fine, I can do it," I said with a little warm glow when Dmitri, who was now squatting down to chat with Peter, gave me a questioning look that asked me if I was all right. The fact that he knew I would be uncomfortable meeting new people warmed me to the tips of my toes.

Chris rose to greet Dmitri's cousins, all of whom turned to look at me.

"No," I told them all, taking the towel Kiera was using on my hair, and heading into the apartment to rinse out the tail of my braid. "I did it once, and that was enough. If you want the formal introduction, Dmitri can do it."

"All right, but it's going to lack panache this way." Dmitri made a bow first to Chris, then turned to Iakovos and Theo and made bows to them, as well.

Harry laughed as her husband and brother-in-law, evidently getting into the spirit of things, returned the gesture. Dmitri then swept a hand toward Chris and said, "Cousins, may I present His Serene Highness Christian Something Something of Sonderburg-Beck."

I left them, shaking my head over Dmitri's silliness, which made me feel wonderfully happy.

"How did I get to be so lucky as to find Dmitri so that I could meet him and ask him to save me from Kardom?" I asked a short while later, while Harry, Kiera, and I were examining my gold lace dress. Mrs. Avrabos had been as good as her word, and the dress was back to its pristine state.

"I ask myself that question every day," Kiera answered, then made a face and added with a little laugh, "Well, not about you and Dmitri, although I'm happy you're joining the family. I never had any sisters, and even though you are a princess, and I feel like I should curtsy every time I see you, I'm looking forward to having friends nearby."

"I'm not the curtsying sort of princess," I told her.

"Oh, you are when you want to be. You should have seen her at the auction last night, Kiera. The way she marched into that room, I could almost hear fanfares. I thought Patricia was going to explode, and the look on Audrey's face! It was worth all the hell of stalling Dmitri's appearance."

Kiera looked confused, so Harry explained about the two women, and the events of the night before. I waited until Kiera was absent for a few minutes before asking Harry, "Dmitri says he wasn't at all upset or shamed by me only offering twenty-seven euros for him, but I thought I'd ask what Iakovos and you thought. I wouldn't want to insult the family, but that was all the money I had, and—"

"Oh, lord no, we weren't insulted! It was the best thing I'd seen in a long time. Plus, if I know Dmitri—and I do—he'll pony up a big donation to compensate. Not that you should feel bad. All of us, Dmitri included, would much rather have had you win him than Audrey."

I relaxed a little, ready to let go of the worry about shaming the Papaioannous, and instead focused on enjoying time with Dmitri's family.

"I'm so glad you got here in time for the wedding," Harry told Theo after dinner as we were preparing to leave.

I froze, and glanced at Dmitri, who was talking to Iakovos about something business-related. "What ... uh ... we're not having a wedding."

Harry shot me a puzzled look. "You're not? But you're getting married."

"Yes, in the registration office."

"Smart," Kiera said, nodding. "It's what we did. No fuss, no muss, just agree to be married, and sign some papers."

"I know you're having a civil ceremony—it's what Iakovos and I had—but I thought Dmitri said something about having it somewhere nice, like the National Garden, or up on Lycabettus Hill. There's a church up there—"

"No church," I said quickly. "Neither Dmitri or I are religious."

"I don't blame you at all for not wanting a big ceremony," Harry said. "But I think getting married on Lycabettus would be terribly romantic."

It was on the tip of my tongue to tell her that romance had nothing to do with our wedding, but the thought occurred to me that perhaps Dmitri hadn't told Kiera and Theo the real reason we were getting married, and although I had a twinge of guilt over that, I let it go. I loved Dmitri. He said he loved me. In the normal course of events, I'd be with him anyway, so what was a marriage but a legal confirmation that we were together? "I suppose something outdoors wouldn't be objectionable, but I didn't anticipate having an actual wedding, if you know what I mean."

"But your brother came all the way out here," she pointed out.

"Yes, well, he is my only sibling, not that I expected him to come, but he feels he has to do the family thing properly. Oy. Which means he brought ..." I stopped, feeling way too awkward to continue.

Luckily, Harry didn't seem to notice. She pursed her lips. "Small and intimate is nice. You can always have a party at a later date to celebrate with friends, if you want. You're going to let us come, right? Oh, man, that came out pushy. Let me try this again. Iakovos and I—and I assume Theo and Kiera—would be delighted if you allowed us to be there when you get married, no matter if it's in a registry office or out on the side of the mountain."

"That should be all right," I said, trying hard not to sound ungrateful or unwelcoming. I reminded myself that just because the actual marriage was nothing but a formality to me didn't mean others held the same belief. And then perhaps Dmitri wanted his cousins and friends there.

"Iakovos will have a hissy fit if I have to do too much walking, but eh. So long as I take it slow, I'll be fine. I still have almost two weeks to go, and none of the other babies were early. Hmm. I wonder if I have something appropriate to wear. I assume you don't want evening wear for the event. I have a dress I bought years ago in New York that I can have brought out from the house. …"

"Oh, good point on a dress for the wedding." Kiera looked thoughtful. "I have a nice sundress. If I wore a shrug over it, I don't think it would look too informal. We want nice, but not too nice, yes?"

"I think that would be best." Harry nodded, pulling out her phone. "I'll just call home and see if Rosalia can pull out my red dress and have it brought out here. I bought it when I was pregnant with the twins, and I always thought it was cute, but Iakovos doesn't like how much leg it shows."

The two women discussed what would and would not be suitable in their individual wardrobes. I looked down at my mother's dress, wondering if I shouldn't get something else to wear. Was Dmitri dressing up for this? I had a sudden panicked thought that I didn't know him, that he was a stranger, but the second that thought went through my head, I realized just how stupid that was. Of course I knew him. He was my Dmitri, the man who made me happy just thinking about him.

Except when he was trying to have a wedding that was more than a simple legal arrangement.

I left the two women still discussing the various merits of semidressy versus comfortable, and went out to find Dmitri.

He sat on the arm of the couch, a tall drink in his hand, chatting with Chris, Iakovos, and Theo, the last of which was on the floor playing with Peter while he colored.

I poked Dmitri on the arm. "Why didn't you tell me you wanted an actual wedding?" I asked when he looked up at me.

He looked surprised. "An event, you mean? A party?"

"A wedding where there are guests dressed up, and which is held at a scenic spot. Where people watch us get married." The meaning behind my words was crystal clear, or at least it should have been to Dmitri, but Theo and Iakovos were in a different situation.

"Why shouldn't people watch you get married?" Theo asked, looking up from where Peter was coloring on his sneakers.

"Er ..." Dmitri made a face. "You know how I feel."

"About getting married? Yes, but I assume that changed when you found Thyra," Iakovos said.

"How do you feel?" Chris asked, his eyes narrowing on Dmitri.

"Please do us all a favor and turn down your brotherly suspicions," I told him. "Dmitri isn't going to dump me at the altar. He simply feels the same way I do about marriages."

"Oh, that," Chris said with a little roll of his eyes. "Just so we all understand that I'll have his balls if he hurts you."

"You leave his balls alone—they're mine," I said a little crossly. I'd about had enough of Chris's overprotective brotherly concern.

All four men looked at me with raised eyebrows.

"So to speak," I said, patting Dmitri on the thigh.

"Dmitri's balls aside," Theo said, stopping his son from extending his show of artistic ability onto the rug. "I won't say I was looking to get married, but it's the best thing I've ever done. You'll see, Dmitri. It'll be the making of you."

"I don't dispute that Thyra has enriched my life in ways I never thought possible, but I don't believe that's in question. We don't particularly want a ceremony," Dmitri said, slanting a glance up at me. "I suggested Lycabettus because you liked the outdoors, and I thought you'd like to have the ceremony—such as it is—in a scenic spot, but if you prefer not to, then we'll simply have it at the registry office."

I felt like a heel. Here Dmitri went to the trouble of planning something nice, and I was making a big fuss about it. "Lycabettus would be fine. I just don't want to put anyone to trouble for what is going to be a five-minute thing."

"Harry shouldn't do much, if any, walking," Iakovos said, frowning. "She could go into labor at any minute. I don't want her out of the range of immediate medical care just so she can watch you get married."

"I don't care where we get married—"

"I understand your concern," Dmitri said to Iakovos, interrupting my mild objection. "I don't want Harry to be at risk, either, but this is, after all, our wedding, and if Thyra wants to get married on Lycabettus, then I'm going to see to it that we are married there."

"We could carry Harry up the path to the top of Lycabettus," Theo offered. "Or rent a wheelchair. Or one of those motorized scooters that old people use."

"I really don't need to be—" I started to say, but stopped when it was apparent that none of the men were listening to me.

"She'd still be on top of the mountain, and it would take some doing to get medical aid were she to go into labor," Iakovos pointed out.

"You could bring the midwife with you," Dmitri said, frowning as he puzzled out the situation.

"Do you have private ambulances here?" Chris asked, joining in the fun. "If so, you could arrange to have one present just in case it was needed."

"Or a helicopter," Theo said, nodding. "To airlift her out."

"Oh, for the love of ..." I went to find the women.

"There you are," Harry said when I stopped at the doorway of Elena's room, where the two women were still talking arrangements.

"I was out trying to talk sense into men."

"What were they saying that wasn't making sense?" Kiera asked.

"The last I heard, they were planning on putting Harry on a mobility scooter, and airlifting her out after the ceremony—which, again, is going to be as minimal as possible—is over. Via helicopter."

The two women stared at me; then to my surprise, Harry looked thoughtful. "A mobility scooter. That might not be a bad idea. I know Iakovos is going to be annoyed if I do much walking—"

I left them and went to sit in a chair next to the door. It seemed like the only sane place in the apartment.

Later that night, after we'd returned home (and argued with Chris until he agreed to stay with us rather than the hotel he'd checked into), and I had wrapped up the flash drive containing the game for Dmitri, I lay snuggled up against him, listening to him breathing into my hair. Our bodies were still slightly damp from the lovemaking session that had ended with me feeling like I'd exploded into a thousand bits of sheer bliss, but a tiny worry crawled around in my mind, ruining the sense of satisfaction and happiness.

What was I going to do about the lies that Kardom was obviously spreading in Beck? I could prove who I was well enough—and provide the government with another set of the documents that I suspect had been conveniently "lost"—but I had an uneasy feeling that a dark cloud of doom was hanging over my head. Kardom was planning something. I could feel it. I could feel him out there thinking things about me, making plans, wallowing in his perverse determination to have the position that I so badly wanted. I thought about what it would mean if he convinced the newly formed government of Beck to recognize him, and what I would do to ensure that never happened.

"I don't know if I can stop him," I whispered into Dmitri's collarbone. He murmured something unintelligible and tightened his arm around me. "But I will do everything I can to make sure they pick the right person for the job."

They'd just better realize that person was me.

FOURTEEN

Dmitri protested when Kiera and Theo arrived the following morning to take Thyra away.

"Hey, it's not like we made her spend the night elsewhere," Theo said, shooing Kiera and Thyra out of the door. "Harry thinks it would be nicer if you didn't get to see her until the actual wedding. More of a surprise and all that."

"Oh, it's going to be a surprise," Thyra said, shooting her brother a black look.

Chris smiled at her. "We have the family to think of, Tee."

Thyra said something very rude that had Dmitri secretly amused, but he kept his expression mild when Thyra was torn from his side three hours before the time they were due to show up at the church at the top of Lycabettus. Although they weren't going to be married inside the church, there was a very nice paved area outside that Dmitri decided would be scenic yet informal, and thankfully, Thyra had agreed to it.

Dammit, she was a princess. He couldn't condone the idea of her getting married at city hall.

"I wouldn't worry about dressing up," he told Chris when the latter picked up a small leather overnight bag, and started to follow the women out. "Your sister made it quite clear when we came home that I am not to get dressed in anything nicer than a suit. Just in case your bag contains a tuxedo, or a kilt, or whatever crown princes wear at formal events."

"That would be satin knee britches and a lace cravat, and I assure you that what I have in here is much, much more horrible than those," Chris said with a mischievous grin; then he, too, left.

"I feel obligated to ask you if you're sure you want to do this," Theo said once they were alone. "Oh, Jake sends his regards, and says he'd be here doing his duty as best man, but he has to stay back at the apartment and forcibly keep Harry from what he calls 'doing too much,' which I gather means anything beyond getting up to take a piss. They'll be at Lycabettus at eleven with Thyra in tow."

"I'm sure I want to marry Thyra, yes, and with all due respect to Jake, I'd much rather have you here than him. The last month of Harry's pregnancies are the worst. You were lucky in that you avoided the last two, but I was stuck by Jake's side, watching him glare at Harry if she so much as tried to lift a book."

Theo laughed. "You'd think he'd be used to it by now, but he told me he's concerned because she's forty now, and although the doctor says she's fine, he's convinced that only his vigilance in making her rest is keeping the baby from popping out early."

Dmitri shrugged. "Who knows? He may well be what keeps her healthy."

Theo looked thoughtful. "That's something to think about. Hmm."

"That sounds like a man contemplating having another child," Dmitri said, eyeing his cousin.

"We are, but we're not in any hurry. Peter is a handful, although Kiera couldn't be a better mother to him. And now he's into everything, but she takes it all in stride."

"You're a lucky man," Dmitri said, pleased that his scapegrace cousin had finally found someone who gave him a purpose in life.

"I am, as are you. Right, I know the tradition is to toast the bride with a little morning libation, but I'll have coffee, if you don't mind."

Dmitri didn't mind at all. He was thankful that Theo had remained sober after fighting so hard to overcome the addiction to alcohol, and he toasted Thyra with a latte before getting into the nicest suit he thought she'd tolerate without comment.

After that, he pulled from the small safe in his bedroom closet a velvet box. "I wasn't going to give this to her now, because I figured she'd give me absolute hell over it, but since Cove told me she'd picked up a wedding present for me, I figured it was only fair for me to give her one, too."

"You're taking your life into your own hands if she's anything like Kiera," Theo said, looking with interest when Dmitri opened the case. He whistled when he saw the contents. "Isn't that your mother's necklace?"

"Yes."

"It's worth a small fortune," Theo commented.

"It is." Worriedly, Dmitri studied the pearl, diamond, and amber necklace. "My grandfather bought it right after the Second World War. He said it belonged to some long-dead Russian princess. I thought it only fitting that Thyra should have it. Besides, the amber matches her eyes. You don't think she'll … er … refuse to take it? I thought of telling her the diamonds were rhinestones."

Theo raised an eyebrow. "Anyone with working eyes is going to be able to tell those are real diamonds. Damn. All I gave Kiera was the house in Parga, not that she knows I put the house in her name, so don't mention it or she'll give me hell, but regardless of that, I'm going to look like a cheapskate next to you."

"It's not a contest, Theo," Dmitri laughed, closing the case and tucking it his breast pocket. He hoped Thyra would like the design, aware it was very old-fashioned, but he felt the fact that she treasured her mother's dress meant she liked vintage and antique items. And with luck, she might feel like wearing the necklace to get married in. He felt sure his mother and grandfather would approve of that.

Almost three hours later, he stood outside the white-washed Church of St. George at the top of Lycabettus, and greeted his bride-to-be. The officiant, a man whose last-minute services had come at a price Dmitri fervently prayed Thyra never learned, murmured something pointed about hoping the ceremony wouldn't take long, since the day was getting hot.

Harry and Kiera had clearly been busy with Thyra, since part of her gloriously black hair was twisted up onto the back of her head, with the rest spilling down her back in long curls. Her glasses glinted in the sunlight, and behind them, her eyes smiled at him, their golden depths as clear as the amber stones he prayed she'd accept.

"You look like a goddess come down to earth," he told her, going in for a kiss, but, at a cleared throat from her brother, managed to divert the kiss to the tip of her nose. "I have a present for you, but before you even think about objecting, know that it didn't cost me anything. My mother gave it to me before she died. I thought you might want to wear it today."

He pulled the jeweler's box out of his pocket before she could do more than start to scowl, opening it and placing it in her hands. "I hope you like amber. It has a royal history, which I thought was fitting for you. Evidently it belonged to some Russian princess, but the son she left it to died without children, and he gave it to a cousin, and after that, it ended up on the market. My grandfather bought it shortly after 1945."

"Oh," she said, staring down at it for a moment, then to his utter surprise burst into laughter. "It's … it's gorgeous, Dmitri. I'm sure the Grand Duchess Victoria Feodorovna would be pleased, as well."

"Grand Duchess Victoria?" He must have looked confused, but when Thyra lifted the back of her hair and turned around, he slipped the necklace around her throat and fastened it, pleased that she liked his offering.

"Yes, that's who it originally belonged to."

It was on the tip of his tongue to ask her how she knew the history of the necklace, but almost immediately, he was distracted.

"Holy cheese balls, that's gorgeous," Kiera said, coming forward with Peter dressed in a little suit, complete with shorts, and shiny black shoes that were already covered with dirt and smudges. "Is that amber? Those pearls are massive! It's so pretty on you, and it goes perfectly with your dress."

"What does? Dammit, am I missing things? Yacky, let me off this thing."

"I will if you let me unbuckle the seat belt, Eglantine," Iakovos said sternly, but helped Harry off the motorized mobility scooter that had brought her up the side of the mountain. "I'm going to put a chair over here in the shade. If you get the least bit tired, I want you to sit. Here is some cold water."

"Honestly, you'd think we haven't done this three times before," Harry told them all.

"You had contractions this morning," Iakovos told her. "You could go into labor at any moment."

"Those were Braxton-Hicks, and you know it. Now. Where is this pretty thing—oooh, the necklace? That is absolutely beautiful! Nicely done, Dmitri."

"It was my mother's," he said, watching Harry worriedly for a few moments. She seemed a bit flushed despite the wide-brimmed hat, but he put that down to the excitement of the day. "I think in order to keep Jake from exploding with worry, we should get this wedding under way."

"Sorry, I got held up by a tourist who was lost," Chris said, hurrying up the last of the hill, pausing to wipe his face before approaching Thyra. "It's time, sister."

"It doesn't have to be," she said, turning toward him, one hand on the necklace. "Look what Dmitri gave me as a wedding present."

Dmitri thought his almost brother-in-law's eyes were going to fall out. He stared at it, then glanced up at Thyra, who made a face at him. "It's the necklace."

"Yes. Dmitri's grandfather bought it in 1945."

Chris looked thoughtful. "Princess Henry of Karne?"

"Probably."

"How do you know about this necklace?" Dmitri asked, more confused than ever.

Thyra sighed. "It's part of a set of jewels owned by the Grand Duchess Victoria Feodorovna, who died in the last quarter of the nineteenth century. She was related to my family, which is why Chris dragged this all the way out from Scotland."

"At no little cost, may I point out," Chris said, pulling a big square velvet box from his overnight bag. "I had to get special insurance for the week it's away from the bank, the cost of which will eat up all of the rise in salary I just received, so I hope you're grateful, sister mine."

"What—oh my God." Harry grabbed Iakovos's arm when Chris opened the box and removed a silk-wrapped object, pulling off the cloth to reveal a tiara that glittered brilliantly in the sun. "She has a crown!"

"Tiara, not crown," Thyra said. "We're not monarchs, so we only wear tiaras. Well, the ladies do. The princes in my family get stiffed in that regard."

Dmitri stared in amazement at the tiara, noting the linked circles set with diamonds; in the center of each, a large pearl hung, while above it, set on diamond-encrusted peaks between each circle, an inverted amber teardrop rose. The bottom of the tiara held a band of still more diamonds, followed by a line of perfectly matched pearls.

The gems in it looked to be incredibly pure. It had to be worth a fortune. No, more than a fortune … it was priceless. His princess, who had spent her last twenty-seven euros on him, had in her possession a priceless tiara the likes of which he'd never seen.

"This is the Feodorovna tiara," Chris said, placing it on Thyra's head. "All the women in our family wear it at special occasions, weddings included."

"I'm so sorry about this," Thyra told Dmitri, her eyes

searching his. "But Chris would make a fuss if I didn't wear it. He'll take it back just as soon as this is over."

"Damn straight I will. Bloody thing is worth more than your fiancé and his company," Chris murmured, pulling another item out of the tiara box.

It appeared to be a diamond royal order, the kind with a miniature in the center that Dmitri had seen various kings and queens wear at state affairs. This one had a diamond-edged background of blue beneath the diamond cross, topped by two laurel wreaths (also set with diamonds) that ended in three large vertical stones. Dmitri's mind staggered to a halt trying to figure out how much the order was worth.

"I think I need that chair," Harry said, blinking rapidly. "Holy moly, a princess with a crown is marrying our family. I am so writing this into a book. I'm just … wow. So very many wows."

Dmitri knew how Harry felt. He was feeling a bit stunned himself, which was why when Iakovos escorted her over to the chair in the shade, he didn't pay attention to Harry doubling over.

"So both the tiara and the necklace belonged to the same person?" Kiera asked, a horrified look on her face when Peter lunged forward, trying to grab the necklace that glittered in the sunlight.

"You guys are making too much about this," Thyra said, gesturing away the general sense of disbelief that clearly gripped everyone but the Sonderburg-Becks. "It's just a tiara. Yes, it's ironic that Dmitri gave me the necklace that goes along with it, but truly, it's nothing to—um. Do we know those people?"

A group of three men emerged from the path, which had been closed for the half hour necessary to conduct the ceremony, all of whom had big digital cameras slung around their respective necks.

"Paparazzi," Dmitri snarled, and started forward toward them. The bastards took one look at Thyra standing in a tiara, diamonds and pearls all but dripping off her, and their cameras started clicking.

Theo moved protectively in front of Kiera and Peter, but Alexis was at Dmitri's side as he stalked forward to the photographers, growling, "This is a private ceremony. You will leave now."

"Don't be that way. We were told that you were happy for us to take a few shots of you getting married," one of the men called, the camera held to his eye.

"Is that Prince Christian standing with Princess Juliane, Dmitri?" another photographer asked when Dmitri and Alexis tried to block their view. He glanced behind to see where Iakovos was, but he was squatting next to Harry, where she sat on the chair. In front of them, Thyra stood holding Valentino, who had been in Alexis's charge, while Theo looked torn between guarding his family and helping with the photographers.

"Go," Dmitri heard Kiera say as she pushed him forward. "We'll be fine. Get rid of those creeps."

"Finally getting married, are you, Dmitri?" another of the paparazzi called. "Does that mean the rumors are true that Papaioannou International is investing in Beck?"

"Are you going to be part of the Beck royal family?" a woman behind the photographer called out, holding out a digital recorder. "What title will you have?"

"How much are you investing in Beck?"

"How long have you known Princess Juliane, Dmitri?"

"Prince Christian, what do you think of the proposal to give your cousin Friederich your title?"

The questions came hard and fast, tumbling over one another in the press's determination to get some information from them. Dmitri was an old hand at handling them, having done so for years on Iakovos's behalf, but suddenly, he seemed to have lost his panache. "I have no statement other than you are intruding on a private event. If you don't leave now, I'll be happy to escort you down the path," he snarled, his voice filled with threat.

"Come on, just let us film the ceremony, and we'll let you be," the third said, glancing at the others. "Theo, you best man for your cousin?"

"That's enough out of all of you," Dmitri said, and started forward toward the photographers.

"We'll take care of them," Theo told him in a low voice, glancing behind at the interlopers. "Go marry the princess so she can take off that crown, and we can get out of here."

"What's going on with Iakovos and his wife? She sick?" a voice called out, followed immediately by, "Theo, you going to tell us the name of your wife?"

Dmitri debated shoving a couple of the photographers off the side of the mountain, but he decided in hindsight that it was better to do as Theo asked.

"I believe you have been asked to leave," Chris said, strolling toward them. "If you remain, you are liable for harassment charges."

"You give your official blessing to the marriage, Prince Christian?" one of the men called. "You happy to have your sister married off to a man who can pump millions into Beck?"

"Get the hell out of here," Chris thundered, and for a minute, Dmitri thought he might go after the men, but with a worried eye at Thyra, who stood close to Kiera, he decided to take care of the most pressing matter first.

"Keep them back," he said quietly to Chris, and quickly ran across the paved area to take Thyra by her hand. He stopped in front of the officiant, saying quickly in Greek, "We are ready to proceed. The press is here, and we wish to avoid further confrontation with them, so speed is appreciated."

The man nodded and started reciting the civil ceremony, which Dmitri translated in a low tone to Thyra. She set Valentino down, holding firmly to his leash with one hand, her other hand gripping Dmitri's so tight, he had to wiggle his fingers to bring blood back to them.

Suddenly, in the middle of it, Iakovos ran past them toward the path, shouting. "Get those bastards out of my way," he roared, almost shoving one of them off the path and into the steep slope of scrubby shrubs. "Harry's water broke, and she's gone into labor. I knew she would! I told her, but would anyone listen to me? Where the hell is the ambulance I hired?"

"Oh no! Should we—" Thyra started to pull her hand from Dmitri's, but he held tight to it.

"No. We're almost done. Finish it," he added to the officiant, who evidently knew enough English to understand that Harry was about to give birth. Kiera was at her side now, looking helpless. "Think of round things," Dmitri heard her tell Harry. "It'll help calm you."

"I'm very calm," Harry said, and he had to admit, she didn't look particularly distressed. "It's Iakovos who is going to burst a blood vessel if he doesn't stop saying 'I told you so,' which, as any woman in labor will tell you, is just way out of line. Oh, lord, I think a contraction is coming. No, don't hold my hand. Wheel the scooter over and let me hold on to it."

While Theo, Alexis, and Chris more or less shoved the photographers down the path to the barrier that closed it off during the ceremony, and Harry leaned on the scooter at an awkward angle, moaning and rocking as she worked her way through a contraction, Dmitri promised to take Thyra for his wife from that day forward.

By the time Iakovos returned with four men pushing a wheeled gurney, Harry was walking around in a small circle, Thyra holding one arm, while Kiera was on the other.

Harry was wearing the tiara, a fact that made Iakovos come to an abrupt halt in front of her, an indescribable look on his face.

"Thyra thought it would distract me," Harry said between pants. "It's pretty cool, you have to admit. I can tell our baby that while I was having her, I got to wear a real royal crown. You better take it back now, Thyra—I think I'm going to have another one."

Jake shot Dmitri a look just like it was his fault that Harry had chosen his wedding to go into labor, and by the time that they got her onto the gurney, and down the path to the ambulance that Iakovos had, indeed, hired just in case, Dmitri was starting to see the humor of the situation.

"Er ..." Kiera gave Thyra an odd look.

"You want to have a go, too?" Thyra asked, and placed the tiara on her head.

"Wow! Theo, get your phone. We have to get a couple of selfies."

Chris, who had been monitoring the lower path, returned, raising his eyebrows at the sight of Thyra taking pictures of Theo and Kiera. "I take it you're married all right?"

Dmitri held out the signed marriage certificate. "We are legal, yes."

"Hallelujah," Thyra said. "Now Kardom can't do a damned thing. Oh, thanks, but give it to Chris. He'll tuck it away safely."

"And back to the bank it goes tomorrow just as soon as I get back home," he said, wrapping the tiara and the glittering order before he placed them securely inside the bag.

"Just out of curiosity," Dmitri started to ask.

"Millions," Chris answered. "Which is why I'd prefer going back to your apartment as soon as possible."

"I think he was going to ask why we haven't sold them," Thyra said, taking Dmitri's arm when he picked up Valentino, tucking him under his other arm. "Naturally, he will understand that they don't really belong to us."

"They don't?" Dmitri asked.

Thyra shook her head. "We're just caretakers for them. It's our duty to preserve them so they can be passed on to the next generation."

His eyes widened when he realized that if Thyra and he decided to have children, they might be in line for a hell of an inheritance, and asked, "You do realize the irony of you spending your life in relative poverty, while possessing what is probably literally a king's ransom in jewels, yes?"

"Of course. But we could never sell them. They aren't ours to sell. We just get to wear them while we're alive. Do you think Harry is going to hang on until she makes it to the hospital?"

He shook away the idea of Thyra round with his child, and glared at the trio of persistent photographers who were now perched on motorbikes in the parking lot. Cove was waiting for them, though, and Dmitri got Thyra and Chris into the car before answering, waiting a moment for Alexis—who had gone to threaten the photographers one last time—to join them before breathing a sigh of relief.

"Dmitri?"

"Hmm?"

Thyra's hand was warm on his, but her eyes were warmer still, glowing with the same rich light as the amber droplets that rested on her chest. "Harry?"

"Oh, she'll hang on. Iakovos wouldn't let her give birth anywhere he didn't feel was suitable."

She laughed, and leaned into him, one hand rubbing Valentino's head, her hair brushing against his cheek.

A tight band that he hadn't known was across his chest seemed to ease as he relaxed into the seat. Thyra was his, legally his, and nothing could change that.

Now they could settle back and live the rest of their life in happiness.

It was just going to be that simple.

FIFTEEN

The dawn arrived at Athens on soft little winds accompanied by a few high clouds that turned the sky a delicate peach, long fingers of which stretched across the sky until they touched the retreating navy of night.

And a whole lot of screaming.

Fortunately, we missed most of it, although occasionally we could hear Harry from where we sat in the maternity waiting room. She definitely had some inventive things to say while she worked out her frustration over the labor being too far along for her to have an epidural.

I stood outside the hospital, yawning and stretching, wondering if the last eighteen hours had really happened.

"Did I imagine it, or did we get married yesterday?" I asked Dmitri, whose jaw was faintly black with whiskers, dark smudges under his eyes making it clear that while I had dozed uncomfortably on a chair, he had stayed vigilant, I assumed in support of Iakovos.

"We did indeed." He rubbed his face, the sound of his whiskers brushing against his hand sending a little sensual shiver down my back. "At least I think it was yesterday. It might have been two or three days ago. I'm not sure. Time has ceased to make sense to me."

"Come on, sexy former bachelor," I said, urging him forward when I saw Cove pull around to the entrance. "Let's go home and not have a wedding night."

"We couldn't if we wanted to. It's morning," he pointed out with pedantic sense that regardless irritated me. I chalked it up to being so tired I could hardly think straight.

"I could have one if I wanted," I said with injured dignity, climbing into the back of the car. "I simply choose not to do so. Despite you flaunting your jaw at me."

Dmitri, who had been rubbing his face tiredly again, paused and looked at me.

"It's a sexy, sexy jaw," I told him. "I feel like I'm drunk I'm so tired. How about you?"

"The same. I was going to drag myself into the shower so I could shave, but now—eh? Oh, Harry's fine, Cove. Baby is fine. Iakovos is near a mental and emotional breakdown, and swearing he's not only going to have a repeat vasectomy—he might just go for a full-out gelding just to ensure Harry doesn't change her mind again and want more kids. Not that I think she will after this one."

"They have a boy," I said, leaning against Dmitri. "A red-faced, splotchy-skinned boy, but they are both happy. Harry said she's mad because she was certain the baby was a girl, but she looked awfully happy."

"Happy," Dmitri agreed, and sagged into the seat.

"Yes, we are. Very happy." I must have drifted off to sleep, because the next thing I knew, Cove was telling us to wake up, and that we were home. There were two men lurking outside the building, but Dmitri glared at them and shoved me through the door to the building before they could do more than get a couple of shots of us.

Valentino was pleased to see us, and after I checked that Alexis—who had taken him home after the wedding, while the rest of us went to the hospital—had given him food and water, I staggered toward the bedroom.

Dmitri was behind me when I stopped in front of his door, and did an about-face.

He frowned at me. "You can't possibly want to do anything other than sleep. Tell me you don't expect me to stand with you admiring the sunrise on the Acropolis, because I'm afraid if you did, I might just break down and cry, and I don't want you seeing me crying over a sunrise. It'll haunt you forever."

I summoned up enough energy to chuckle. "I'm just going to say good-bye to my brother. Go to bed. I'll be there in five minutes or less."

He swayed for a moment, clearly hesitating. "Oh, to hell with it. Sleep is overrated," he said, and with an arm around me, we staggered through the kitchen to the other wing of the apartment.

I knocked on the door of the room where Chris was staying. He opened it after a few minutes, half his face covered in shaving cream.

"You two look like hell," he said, eyeing us. "I assume you haven't been off having wild, debauched sex and instead sat up all night to watch your cousin have his baby?"

"Bingo," I said, booping his nose, then giggling at the fact that I'd done so.

"What the hell?" he asked, looking faintly outraged. He sniffed the air. "Have you been drinking?"

"No," I said, giving him a haughty look. "We're just tired."

"Actually, I took a couple of pulls on Jake's flask, but that was hours ago," Dmitri said, waving a hand vaguely in the air. "Maybe days ago. I can't remember."

"We're very tired," I repeated, feeling that point needed to be made.

"But we wanted to wish Our Serene Highness a *bon voyage*," Dmitri added.

"And not cry at sunrises on the Acropolis," I added.

"Yes, that," Dmitri said, pointing at my mouth. I gently sucked on his fingertip.

"And that's about enough for me," Chris said, making shooing gestures. He paused long enough to hug me, kiss me on both cheeks, and then hold out his hand for Dmitri, who gravely shook it. "Go to bed before you both fall down. My flight leaves in a couple of hours, and assuming your assistant—"

"Former assistant," I said, smiling at Dmitri.

"Assuming Alexis is sober and awake enough to take me to the airport, I'll be fine. Happy marriage, Tee."

"Happy detecting, Cee," I answered, reverting to our childhood nicknames.

I have a vague memory of collapsing on the bed after that, minus my mother's dress, but still in the strapless bra, stockings, and petticoat. When I woke some six hours later, I lay mostly under Dmitri, whose chest and one leg were covering me, and who was snoring into the pillow above my head.

I thought of waking him up in a manner that I knew he'd enjoy, but decided the poor man needed his sleep, and instead got dressed, fed Valentino, and, once he'd eaten, dragged him away from his new favorite spot (in front of a massive fish tank that sat in the middle of the atrium).

"You need a walk, cat, and I need to clear my head," I told him, propping up a note on the kitchen counter that we would be back in half an hour. "I feel like my head is full of fog. Too many life-changing events in the last few days."

We toddled downstairs, and were about to exit the building when Spiros, one of the midday concierges, stopped me. "You might not want to do that," he said, coming around the desk to where I stopped to untwist Valentino's harness.

"Do what? Haven't you seen Valentino before? He likes walks. He's not an ordinary cat."

Spiros pulled me to the side window and pointed. "Pips."

"I beg your pardon?"

"Pips out there. Two of them. There was a third, but he left."

"There're still here? Damn." I bit my lip, reluctant to call off our walk. Now that Valentino had been removed from his observation perch next to the fish tank, he clearly wanted to have a stroll around the neighborhood. "Is there another exit?"

"One into the alley, and through the parking garage, but I suspect that the pip who left is watching those."

"Great." My shoulders slumped in defeat. "Now I'm a prisoner."

"Not necessarily." Spiros grinned. "If you would just step into the office ..."

Six minutes later, I exited the building, a big sun hat hiding my hair, my glasses tucked carefully into the inner pocket of the men's light jacket that Spiros had lent me from the lost and found box, and Valentino hidden in a large cloth carrier bag.

Upon Spiros's advice, I exited the building without glancing toward the photographers, and hurried off until we were clear of the building; then I put my glasses on, and apologized to Valentino as I de-bagged him.

Since it was almost lunchtime, there were a lot of people out and about, and we had a good wander around the neighborhood, Valentino garnering a few comments of how handsome he was. Just as we were about to head back, my phone rang.

"There's something wrong with a wife who leaves her husband on the morning after their wedding," a warm, delicious voice said into my ear.

"Not if that husband needed sleep, and you did."

"Sadly, that is true. I have a horrible feeling I embarrassed myself with your brother. Did I?"

"No, although he sent me a text a little bit ago saying he'd landed, and was just going to the bank, and he hoped that you weren't going to turn out to be a lush."

Dmitri made a strangled half laugh, half groan. "I don't blame him for that. Are you almost done with your walk?"

"Yes, we're half a block away. I have to put on my disguise before I get closer in case the paps see me."

"The what? Oh, Christ, are they still there? Where are you? I'll take care of them."

"It's OK. Spiros gave me a disguise. I just have to put Valentino back in the bag, then I'll—"

The words stopped dead on my lips when, as I was half a block away from the apartment building, a man veered in from the side and took the phone from my hand, calmly hanging it up before glaring at me. "I might have known you'd do something like this," Kardom said, his pale gray eyes narrowed and filled with ire. "And to think I offered you an honorable solution. Well, you have brought this on your own head."

"Give me that back! And what have I brought—" I snatched back my phone before looking at the newspaper he shoved at me. It had been folded back to a page that showed a very unflattering picture of me wearing the Feodorovna crown, a look of horror on my face, while next to me, Dmitri scowled. He, I noticed, looked downright gorgeous. Princess Weds Local Playboy read the headline. "They really have some nerve poking their noses—oh! Princess Juliane, with her empty title and emptier wallet, has wed one of Athens's most prominent and sought-after businessmen. Sources say the couple met only a few days previous to their marriage, fueling speculation that Dmitri Papaioannou hopes to benefit from the royal connection to the emerging country of Beck. Those bastards! Dmitri is not hoping any such thing! And how did they even find out about us getting married?"

"That would probably be my fault," Maggie said with an arch simper as she arrived next to Kardom. She made a show of examining a fingernail. "It seems your two friends—the ones I met at the party the first night we were here—were most happy to tell me everything they knew about you and your rich new husband. I may have told Kardom, who may have let it slip to Beck. ..."

My blood seemed to turn to ice in my veins. "What did you tell them?" I asked Kardom, pulling back when he tried to take my arm. "What lies have you convinced them are true now?"

"I didn't have to lie, as a matter of fact," he said with injured dignity. "I simply told them the truth—that Papaioannou International would be taking advantage of your position to secure lucrative deals and develop land to be sold away from the residents of Beck."

My heart sank. I closed my eyes for a few seconds, feeling every last shred of hope evaporating into nothing. "They'll never have me now. Not if they believe that complete and utter bullshit, and I have no doubt they will."

"Of course they will. It's the truth, after all," Kardom said smoothly.

I opened my eyes, too beat down to even argue with him.

"As for this Greek you married—" Kardom latched on to my arm as he tried to haul me over to a car. "Your marriage to him isn't legal. The one to me will be."

"Oh, for the love of all that's holy, give it up!" I yelled, anger giving me the strength to jerk my arm back. "Of course my marriage to him is legal!"

"Ah, but it turns out that the marriage license you took from me was false and, thus, illegal to use."

I gawked at him in outright disbelief. "Wait, you're admitting that you faked a marriage license in my name?"

"I didn't, no. However, your cousin in a dark wig and pair of glasses makes for a convincing impostor."

I stared in horror at him. I'd had a vague idea that Maggie had something to do with the license, but to have Kardom stand right there in front of me and confirm it took my breath away. "Why? You've evidently already bought off the entire Beck council. Why do you want to marry me so badly?"

His jaw tightened for a moment. "Insurance, my dear. I don't believe in risks without having ample safeguards in place. There are one or two … irregularities … in my current situation that cause me to believe it would be better for Beck to see our lines joined."

That made absolutely no sense to me. He had done what he'd set about to do—blackened my name until Beck would name him to the position that by rights should be mine. How was marrying me insurance?

"I don't understand what you want from me, but you aren't going to get anything," I said glumly. I wanted to sit right down and cry about what he'd done to my reputation. "I'm married. Legally married. So nothing you or Maggie can do will have an impact on that."

"Wanna bet?" Maggie asked archly.

I shook my head. "Not particularly. Not that I understand how you could betray me like that. I trusted you. I asked you for help with the magazine job."

"And you were thrilled to always keep me in your shadow, weren't you?"

My heart wept at the anger in her eyes.

"You moaned and groaned about being born a princess, and how horrible it was that people paid you attention and wanted to be around you. You even whined for years about how awful it was that Kardom wanted to marry you, and yet, all that time, you made sure I was kept in my place, just a lowly little cousin who didn't matter."

"Maggie!" I said on a gasp, stung by the accusations she flung at me. "I never treated you that way!"

"You wouldn't even let me have a few days in the limelight! You had to go and tell everyone who I really was just so I wouldn't get more than a tiny little taste of the preferential treatment you get every single day."

Was she mad? How could she say such things when she knew full well my life was not even remotely like that? "I trusted you," I said again, betrayal leaving a bad taste in my mouth. "You're my family."

"The wrong side of the family, though, aren't I? Not the royal side. Well, I've had it up to here with your bullshit," she said.

"Maggie, now is not the time for this," Kardom said, frowning at her. "You are deviating from my plan, and that I will not have."

"Your plan, your plan! You know what? You can shove your plan right up your ass," she snapped at him before pinning me back with a glare. "I'm just about as sick of you as I am of her. She's not going to marry you, all right?"

Kardom straightened his shoulders, giving Maggie a look of mingled hauteur and disgust. "It has become apparent that she is legally married to the Greek man she's been sleeping with, thank you. However, my plans allow for that contingency."

Maggie made a face at him before turning back to me. "Just so you know, cousin, Kardom was planning on threatening your boyfriend in order to force you to sign a statement giving up all claims to Beck, and telling them he had your blessing to become crown prince. That's about as lame an idea as forcing you to marry him, but that's the sort of mentality I've been forced to bear the last month."

"I will thank you to not speak of my plans in such disparaging—" Kardom stopped speaking when Maggie rounded on him.

"Shut it! You are done here, got it? Even as self-centered and stupid as Thyra is, she's not going to be afraid of some has-been who spent his whole life trying to make himself something he's not. And her rich husband certainly isn't going to worry about someone as insignificant as you."

Kardom took the insult well, I'll give him that. He adopted an even haughtier mien, and looked down his nose to say, "I have tolerated your insults because you have been a useful tool in the execution of my plans, but the time for you has passed."

"Blow it out your piehole," she snapped. Maggie slid her gaze my way, and my stomach tightened in response. "As for you, I should have known you would make sure the fact that you got married to that rich Greek was in all the papers. For someone who claims she hates attention, you sure seem to be right in front when the cameras come out."

It was my turn to straighten my shoulders. "That is the basest slander! I don't seek attention from anyone. Well, other than Dmitri, and I love him, so that is completely reasonable. But not the press!"

"And yet it was your friend who told the press. She told everyone, including me."

I shook my head, confused.

"Patricia something-or-other," Maggie said before I could protest.

"Patricia and Audrey are most certainly not friends," I told her, glancing around, wondering if I could make a dash for the safety of the lobby, even with the paparazzi lurking about the entrance.

"Oh, sure, you just happened to tell the mouthy Patricia about it, and she just happened to spill the details to the press. Uh-huh. I'm sure it was just like that. Christ, you can't even be honest about something so simple, can you?"

That made the decision for me. I edged away, saying, "I don't know why you've turned on me, or why you would throw away so many years of friendship, but I'm not going to stand here and listen to it any longer."

She grabbed my arm when I tried to walk away. "Oh, you're going to listen to everything I have to say. You owe that to me, just like you owe me all the money you've done me out of."

"I must protest—" Kardom started to say, but she spat a very rude word at him that had him sucking in his breath in outrage.

"Exactly what money do I owe you?" I inquired as politely as I could. Valentino, who had pressed close to my ankle, opened his mouth in a silent hiss at Maggie.

"Let's start with the money from the magazine article. I suppose you didn't bother turning it in now that you're rich."

"I'm not rich," I said, hurt that she'd think I'd take advantage of Dmitri that way. It was like she didn't know me at all … or maybe it was that I didn't know who she was anymore. "And I will give you half of the money I make from the article about Dmitri just as we agreed. I won't get paid until I turn it in, though. I planned on working on it on the weekend, since Dmitri and I wanted to have a few days as sort of a mini honeymoon."

"Of course you need a honeymoon with the man you've known less than a week," she said with sickening sweetness. "While the rest of us have to scrape and beg and put up with the most insufferably conceited of men just to get by, you are having a grand time with your rich husband."

"I object to being called conceited," Kardom said with a sniff. "I am a direct descendant of princes! Regardless of your lack of royal ancestry, if you are so unhappy taking advantage of my better nature, you are welcome to vacate the hotel room for which I am paying, not to mention cease charging food and other expenses to my account."

"You really are hung up on money, aren't you?" I asked Maggie, ignoring Kardom.

"If by 'hung up' you mean I want some? Yes, yes I do want money. I want what's mine. And you can stop pretending you like living like a pauper, because the truth is you sure as hell made sure you snapped up a rich, handsome bachelor as soon as you set eyes on him."

"A man who I thought was a waiter, and too poor to own a car," I pointed out, shaking my head. "You're so mercenary now. You never used to be that way."

"Oh, I was. You just never took the time to notice that I didn't pretend I didn't mind being poor, like you and Chris did."

"Well, now I know," I said, feeling like there wasn't much more I could say. "I'll send you a check just as soon as I turn in the article and get paid. Until then, I guess this is goodbye."

"You have no idea how right you are," she said, and, grabbing my arm with one hand, whipped out a small rectangular object the shape of a blocky cell phone and, before I could so much as blink, jammed it into my back.

Instantly, my body stiffened, my muscles locked so tight that I wanted to scream, but couldn't get my mouth to work. Pain burst all over my body, and I felt myself falling, my body slamming into the pavement with another wave of pain. I lay completely inert, my muscles still immobile, and my mind screaming with horror when I saw Maggie scoop up Valentino. She leaned down to look at me, her lips curving in a smile that seemed to be the epitome of evil. "I don't have time to wait for you to pay me the pittance you're making from the magazine. You get that rich husband of yours to pony up a hundred grand, and you can have the cat back. Otherwise, I'll send him to you in pieces. You got that, cousin?"

I lay on the pavement, my mind torn between the anguish of my body and the sheer horror of the thoughts of what Maggie would do to Valentino. I couldn't see him, but I could hear Kardom telling Maggie that she was stupid to attack me in full view of everyone, but his voice stopped as a car squealed away.

Two women who most likely had been watching from the safety of a shop emerged, asking me questions in Greek. Although my muscles were starting to relax, and I could move my hands and my legs a bit, I was still feeling the effects of the stun gun that Maggie had obviously used on me. I heard myself moaning and tried to roll over, one hand stretching out to where my phone had dropped when Maggie struck me down.

One of the Good Samaritans, a middle-aged woman with salt-and-pepper hair, picked up the phone and glanced at it before trying to hand it to me.

My fingers flexed, but couldn't grasp it. I tried to say Dmitri's name, but all that came out was garbled words, most of which were profane in the extreme. The woman tapped on the phone and held it to her ear. I prayed she was calling Dmitri.

Two minutes later the ladies had me sitting up. A shadow fell over me, and suddenly, Dmitri was there, holding me against him, murmuring things to my neck and hair, his hands running over my body to check for injuries.

"Maggie," I said, my tongue feeling like it belonged to someone else. "It was Maggie. She took Valentino. Dmitri, we have to get him back. She threatened ..." I couldn't go on. I had a policy of not crying in public, but being stunned must have knocked my inhibitions aside, because I clung to him and bawled like a baby.

And that, of course, brought the paparazzi at a run.

It took another few minutes before he got me to my feet, and by then, EMTs had arrived to check me out. A half hour later, I sat in the kitchen, both hands holding a cup of coffee, while Dmitri paced back and forth, barking orders into his phone, and periodically pausing to pull me into a hug to tell me it was going to be all right.

"No luck?" I asked when he ended the most recent call.

"The police won't give me access to the street cameras, no." The expression on his face was as grim as my spirits.

"Did you tell them that she threatened his life?" I clutched the coffee cup tighter. "Don't they realize that Maggie is unhinged and wouldn't stop at hurting an innocent cat? Oh, God, Dmitri! What are we going to do? We can't let her hurt him. He's probably scared and traumatized and who knows what else."

Tears burned hot in my eyes, making my throat ache.

Dmitri pulled me off the chair, his hands on my arms as he looked me in the eyes with a steady, unwavering gaze. "She won't hurt him. She knows we'll pay to get him back, and you said that above all else she wants money."

"I can't ... I don't have—"

"But I do, and I will pay whatever she wants for him."

"Thank you," I murmured, hugging him as tight as I could. "I don't know how I'll repay you, but I will."

"You will not. You married me, so now your cat is my cat, too, and no one messes with my cat."

I smiled into his collarbone, warmed by the anger in his voice almost as much as by his words. I tipped my head back. "I promised you that being married to me wasn't going to cost you anything. I'm sure not keeping that promise."

"About that," he said, his voice as hard as stone. I pulled myself back so I could look up at him. His eyes were a mossy green, glittering with emotion. "I've changed my mind."

"About being married to me?" I didn't think it was possible to feel worse than I already did at that moment, but his words struck me with the impact of a sledgehammer.

"Yes." He took a deep breath. "I don't want to be married to you just to keep you safe from your cousin. I want to be married to you because I want you to be my wife in more than just a legal sense. I want you to want to be my wife because you want to be married to me, and you can't live without me, and you will spend every second of every day doing things that make me the happiest man alive to have you in my life."

"I love you, too," I told him, and gently bit his chin.

He was moving in for a kiss, but at that moment, my phone rang. My hand shook with anger and fear when I answered it. "If you've hurt so much as one tiny little orange hair on Valentino's adorable head—"

"I told you that you could have him back if you ponied up the money. What use do I have for a cat, especially one that sits with its goddamned yellow eyes judging you, and looking at you like it smells something bad? Does your husband have the money?"

"Not in cash," I told her, startled. "Will you take a check?"

"For the love of—no! No checks! I want cash. Or, wait, a what-do-you-call-them, money transfer. Yeah, that's what I want. Into one of those banks that the embezzlers use, something that no one can trace."

"Hold on a minute," I told her, and pressed the mute button on my phone. "Maggie has gone insane."

Dmitri raised his eyebrows. "I wouldn't have called her the poster child of sanity and rational thought before, but what has she said now?"

"She has delusions of being some villain who has offshore bank accounts. Any minute now she's going to demand a private jet, and ten pizzas."

Dmitri made a face. "Do you want me to talk to her?"

"No." I took a deep breath. "She's my cousin. I'm going to stall her, and call around to see if I can find where Kardom was staying. I just bet you that she's sitting back in the hotel room he's paying for."

"Ah, well, as to that . . ." Dmitri gave a little embarrassed cough. "You don't have to call around. I know the hotel where he was staying."

"How do you know . . . oh." I didn't know whether I should be annoyed or amused. "You had someone checking him out."

"He drugged and kidnapped you. Of course I had him investigated. I wanted to determine if he was an actual threat, or if he was easily avoided."

"Let me guess—you decided the latter?"

Dmitri nodded. "Checkered as Kardom's reputation is, he hasn't used violence in the past, has no criminal record, nor could my people find any relationship with those involved in violent crimes. He doesn't appear to be overly reckless, so I feel confident that he's not going to risk his life attempting an attack on you. He's just a midlevel businessman who appears to be fixated on Beck."

"One who lies when it suits him. But despite Kardom killing any chance I have of being crown princess—remind me to tell you what he did that ensured we'll probably never even be able to step foot in the country again, let alone represent it—I've come to realize he's not the real villain of this piece." I pushed aside thoughts of Beck to focus on what was important, and I unmuted the phone to ask, "You still there?"

"Yes, but I'm getting sick and tired of you stalling. Either you give me the money that's due me, or I take out my frustrations on the little orange monster."

"It goes without saying that if I find you've harmed him, Dmitri and I will rain vengeance down on your head. However, since we don't want anything to happen to him, Dmitri is arranging for the money to be made available. But it's going to take half an hour. If you text us your bank info, he'll make the transfer happen." I lifted up my hand to show my crossed fingers.

Dmitri kept his gaze firmly on mine. I knew he wanted

badly to take over, but he recognized the fact that it was important to me to handle my own issues.

As if I couldn't love him any more, he had to be all supportive and thoughtful, the big oaf.

"All right, but that's as long as I'm going to wait. Just see to it that the money is ready then."

I ended the call and looked at Dmitri. He was already texting Cove, and took my hand, pulling me after him when he hurried out of the door.

Twenty long, excruciating minutes later, we stood outside the hotel room that Dmitri's investigators said Kardom had rented. Dmitri knocked at the door and spoke in Greek, one hand over the peephole.

There was a rattle of a lock; then the door opened. Dmitri rushed in, pushing Kardom aside in order to run through an opened doorway. It evidently led to Maggie's room, because I heard her squawk. I was hot on Dmitri's tail, bumping into him when he came to an abrupt halt.

She stood with her back to a bed, holding Valentino in one hand, and the stun gun in another, pressed to his neck. "Don't move, either of you, or I'll fill this cat so full of volts he'll be able to light up the whole hotel."

Before I could speak, Dmitri moved, throwing himself forward, reaching for the cat with one hand, while the other went for Maggie's wrist.

She screamed, and I heard a familiar hiss. Valentino bit her hand, leaping out of her hold to stand with his fur all puffed up. At the same time, there was a faint white-blue flash and a buzz; then Dmitri dropped, falling half on, half off the bed.

"Oh, you did not just do that!" I had bent to pick up Valentino, clutching him with one hand to my chest. With my other, I made a fist and punched Maggie in the eye. Her head snapped back, colliding with the wall with a painful thunk; then she slid down, her eyes fluttering.

"Dmitri! My darling, are you all right? Aww, I know, my brave Prince Charming. It hurts, huh? Just try to focus on breathing. It'll feel better as soon as your muscles stop trying to rip themselves out of your body. Here, Valentino, you go sit on Daddy and give him some love and snuggles while I find something to tie up Maggie."

I turned to find a belt or something that I could use to bind Maggie's hands, and saw Kardom in the doorway. I narrowed my eyes on him.

His gaze went from Maggie, to Dmitri, who recovered faster than me and was trying to push himself up, a steady stream of what I assumed were Greek oaths coming from his mouth. Kardom pursed his lips. "I don't suppose you—"

"No," I said, not even bothering to wait to hear what it was he wanted to ask. "You don't need me, Kardom. You won. You get Beck. So just go enjoy being a horrible man who cheated me out of my heritage. I don't care, so long as you leave us alone." That was a lie, but now was not the time to deal with my emotions.

Dmitri got himself into a sitting position, shook a fist at Kardom, then toppled over onto his side again.

While I helped him sit up again, Valentino strolled over to where Maggie was slumped, making faint moaning noises, turned so that his back was to her, and, to my great enjoyment, piddled on her.

Kardom quietly closed the door without any further comment.

SIXTEEN

"Are you sure you want to do this?" Chris's voice was unusually grave.

It perfectly matched the expression on Dmitri's face. "Thyra, I know you feel this is the right path to take, despite our many discussions on the subject—"

"They were arguments, pure and simple, but thank you for trying to make them sound nicer," I said, kissing him on the tip of his nose.

"Despite that, I feel obligated to remind you that I will be happy to put whatever resources I have at your disposal to clear up the situation. What you want to do is unnecessary and irreversible."

I nodded, tightening my fingers around his. We stood in a small office in what had once been a modest palace inhabited by my ancestors. Now it was home to the newly re-formed Beck government. My stomach made a few unpleasant flips at the idea of Kardom being somewhere in the building, but even the idea of him gloating at Chris and me couldn't stop me from doing what I knew I had to do. "I have to do it. It's only right."

Chris sighed. "Well, if you're going to, I might as well do it, too."

"You don't have to—" I started to protest, but he lifted a

hand. At that moment, the door opened to the office of the new prime minister. She stepped out, accompanied by all twelve ministers of the council, almost all of whom had been swayed by Kardom's underhanded methods to oust me from what should have been mine.

"Your Serene Highnesses, it is a pleasure to meet you at last." Prime Minister Nina Schoenberg nodded at Dmitri. "Mr. Papaioannou. I understand that you have a statement you wish to make before parliament is officially opened?"

"We do," Chris said. "My sister speaks for both of us. Thyra?"

I was momentarily surprised to note that Kardom wasn't with the ministers, and felt that was fate giving me a blessing for what must be done. I lifted my chin a little, and said, "My brother, Christian, and I are saddened that the government of Beck has opted to forgo recognition of our family and our heritage in favor of a distant cousin. However," I continued quickly when a pained expression passed over her face, "we are not here to decry the decision. Our family has been tied to Sonderburg-Beck for twelve generations, and in that time, from the first duke on, we have only ever wanted what was best for its citizens. Although my brother determined early on that he did not wish to be recognized as crown prince, he feels, as I do, that our family would want us to acknowledge just how unbreakable is the bond between Beck and us."

Dmitri gave my fingers a little squeeze of support, and then released my hand and moved back half a pace. I knew he was doing this to show the government that although they might have little respect for Chris and me, he had gallons of it. I made a mental note to pounce on him later and thank him for that show of support.

"For that reason, Chris and I feel that our family's prized possessions—Chris's order of St. Georg, and my tiara from the Grand Duchess Feodorovna—would benefit Beck in ways we are otherwise unable to ensure."

Chris handed over the two cases bearing my tiara and his order. The prime minister looked stunned for a moment when one of the ministers opened the leather cases. "These … these must be worth a fortune."

"We value them for much more than just their material worth," Chris said, looking every inch the crown prince even if he would shortly lose that title to Kardom. "They represent our family."

"Our heritage," I said.

"Our bond with Beck," he added.

"We give them to you freely, and only ask that you use the proceeds of their sale to further the programs that will directly benefit the citizens of Beck," I said, my throat going tight and painful with a sudden burn of unshed tears.

"This is most generous, most generous indeed," the prime minister said, her expression still one of astonishment. Several of the ministers murmured similar statements, but only Minister Martin met my gaze—and she merely smiled sadly, giving me a little thumbs-up sign.

I wanted to say more. I wanted to run down Kardom's shopping list of nefarious activities, pointing out not only that was he no stranger to lying and cheating to get what he wanted, but that the ministers who supported him were just as culpable, but I knew it would do no good.

I simply nodded, unable to speak for the ache in my throat, and turned on my heel, blindly reaching for Dmitri's hand.

We left without anyone saying anything else to us. That part of my life was well and truly over.

But I had Dmitri. And that thought made the future one of love and warmth and happiness despite the loss of Beck.

One morning, two days later, Dmitri looked up from where he was eating a handful of grapes and figs while perusing his laptop. "Good morning, my delectable—oof!"

I flung myself on him, kissing his face. "Why didn't you wake me up so we could play?"

He smiled, his eyes twinkling with wicked intent. "I decided you deserved a lie-in after the last couple of days.

However, there's nothing to say we can't go back to bed for a little ... nap."

His mouth was so hot on mine that I just let him kiss the bejeepers out of me before I remembered the thought that had been uppermost on my mind when I woke up. "I got a text from the editor at Noblesse. She loved the interview, and asked if I'd take on a column."

"Ah?" He eyed me, pouring a cup of coffee for me. "And do you want to do that?"

I ignored the little spike of pain that jabbed into me at the knowledge that now I had nothing else to do—other than be Dmitri's assistant. "I might as well, so long as the people I need to interview are wherever we are. I don't see why I can't help you and do the odd interview with whatever high mucky-mucks are about."

"It's your decision," he said in a noncommittal voice, which for some reason had me narrowing my eyes on him.

"Why do you look so odd?" I asked, noting immediately when his gaze skittered away to his laptop.

"Odd? First you say I'm the handsomest man you've ever seen—which is patently untrue, since you've seen my cousins—and now you think me odd?" He tsked and chucked Valentino under the chin. "And to think the honeymoon is over before it's even begun."

Valentino purred, and gently patted his hand before standing, his shepherd's crook tail bobbing while he marched off to go monitor the fish tank in the atrium.

"Don't give me that," I said, shaking a fig at him. "You're up to something. What is it, Dmitri?"

"Perhaps I'm just madly in love with my wife," he said, suddenly scooping me up against his chest and nuzzling my neck with exaggerated noises of delight.

I giggled, and pulled his shirt out of his pants.

"Or perhaps I'm smitten with the thought that I have my very own princess to ravish each night," he continued, his fingers sliding under my T-shirt to cup breasts that immediately demanded to be removed from the confines of my bra and placed against his palms.

I nipped his earlobe and wiggled suggestively against him.

"Then again, it may be that I have a present for you, and I know you're going to kick up a hell of a fuss even though it's fully my right to give you a wedding present."

"You gave me one," I said, biting his shoulder even as I stripped the shirt off that glorious chest. I spread my fingers across his pectorals, marveling that he was mine until the end of our days. "You gave me the Feodorovna necklace."

"Ah, but that was only part of the wedding present. What I have for you is a honeymoon present." His breath was hot on the spot on my neck that made my knees go weak. "One you are very much going to want."

"Oh, I certainly do want it," I said, boldly stroking the front of his fly. He was getting very bulgy there, and I started thinking several wicked thoughts, one involving silk scarves and massage oil, when suddenly he shifted to the side and brought out from the cupboard a familiar leather case.

"Let's get the argument over quickly, so I can ravish you as you deserve," he said, his lovely green eyes positively glowing with love.

I stared openmouthed at the case for a moment, then up to him. "You didn't."

"I did."

I blinked a couple of times and touched the top of the battered leather case. "But—"

"Princess," he said, pulling me back against his chest, giving me a swift kiss. "You didn't think I was going to let you give away your birthright, did you?"

"But I gave it to Beck. Chris and I both did."

"Yes, and can I say that your brother is almost as stubborn as you are about receiving gifts? He put up a hell of a fight, saying he'd repay me for the order a little bit at a time, but I told him if he did, he couldn't ever babysit for us when we needed some time away from our children."

I gawked at him, wondering if my brain had snapped under the strain of all his delicious maleness. "We don't have any children."

"Not yet, we don't, but the day is young," he said, waggling his eyebrows.

I shook my head, unable to respond to his obvious teasing. "You bought the tiara and order? You bought them? Just … bought them? Dmitri, that must have cost—"

"A lot," he said, then kissed me again, swung me up in his arms, and turned to start toward his bedroom. "But it's worth every cent to know it's back where it belongs. Now, my fair little serene one, about this honeymoon we have yet to take …"

A week later Dmitri came home to find me standing in front of the aquarium, watching the fish swim back and forth, little flashes of their color intriguing Valentino, who was tucked against my side.

I didn't see them. I didn't even realize I was standing there staring at them until my view was blocked by a familiar gorgeous Greek man. "Thyra? Are you all right?"

"What? Oh, yes, I'm fine. I just … I was just thinking. … Sorry, I didn't realize you'd come in. How was work?"

He took Valentino from my arms, gave his ears a little rub, then set him on the ground before leading me upstairs to the big deck that had the glorious view of the Acropolis. His voice rumbled around me in a manner that provided me with more happiness than I could ever express.

"Thyra?"

Once again I became aware he'd been talking and I hadn't heard a word. "Sorry?"

He gave me a piercing look, then turned me so I faced him, his thumb warm as it brushed a strand of hair from my cheek. "What's wrong, Princess? You look like your best friend has died."

I stared at him, my mind whirling, wanting to ask him, but not wanting to take any decisions away from him.

"How much do you like Greece?" The words were out before my brain could authorize them.

He looked about as stupefied as I felt. "How much do I like it? The country in general, or Athens, or the Mediterranean?"

"Would you consider spending time away from here?" I asked, waving a hand behind me.

"In the apartment?" His eyebrows rose. "Did Iakovos tell you I was looking at a house near his island?"

"No." I stared at him, this man I loved so much, and who filled my life with such joy. "He didn't. Dmitri—"

"This isn't about the tiara, is it? Thyra, I told you that it was my choice to buy it. There was no guilt involved. It belongs to you. It should be with you. And later, it will belong to our children, should we be blessed with them. So, you don't need to—"

I took a deep breath and let the words that had been dying to be blurted out for the last two hours do just that. "The prime minister of Beck contacted me. She said the government called a special meeting to discuss some facets of Kardom's business practices that had come to light when two of the ministers were asked to step down due to irregularities, and they want me to be crown princess. The prime minister said that they realize now that Kardom's claims were false, and now they investigated you and your cousins, and said that you have no history of predatory practices, and if I want the job, I can have it. It will mean living in Beck part of the year, and there won't be much of a living allowance, although they said we can have the summer palace if we do it up, because it's been used as a youth hostel for the last forty-five years, but the prime minister said she didn't think it would be a problem for us to split our time between Beck and Greece, and holy hellballs, Dmitri, they want me! They really want me! We're going to be a crown princess!"

He laughed when I whooped, spinning me around as I laughed and cried and tried to talk and kiss him all at the same time, the look in his olive-green eyes so warm that a little skitter of excitement rippled through me. Dear God, how I loved the man. "So long as you're always my princess, I don't mind sharing you with others. Now, tell me everything the prime minister said."

I did. It took an hour; then he made me go over the good parts again—how they kicked out a couple of the ministers and Kardom—before we made plans.

"Iakovos has been talking about setting up a European office. I'm sure he won't have an issue with us spending half the year in Beck," Dmitri mused, his big voice rumbling in his chest, beneath where I lay draped. "I think I'll keep this apartment, though. It's handy, and we can pop back when we like. And speaking of that, your cousin's hearing has been moved back a couple of weeks."

I stopped nibbling on his collarbone, and pushed myself back. "She's going to fight the assault charges?"

"Did you think she'd do anything else?" he asked, his hands gentle where they stroked my back.

I sighed. "No. But it's still not going to be pleasant once the press finds out."

"There's nothing they can say that will affect us. Now, I feel like we should celebrate this truly excellent news of yours. How about we rent a boat and sail along the coastline?"

I flinched at the mention of that. "I think it's going to take a while before I get on a boat again."

"Even though the repairs to my boat are covered by the insurance?" He shook his head. "And here I am, wanting badly to take you sailing … ah well. Perhaps my next princess will be more amenable. …"

TO: HARRY

Pictures attached of ceremony. Dmitri bought Valentino a little crown-shaped hat to wear. Chris almost had heart attack when the prime minister (in the red dress) tried on the tiara and went walking around with it on, but he managed to convince Dmitri to stuff it safely back into the bank. Summer palace is run-down, and filled with foxes, two badgers, and one very elderly cow. Valentino loves the place, and has bonded with the cow. Think we're going to have to keep her. We're staying in a hotel until the summer palace gets Wi-Fi, and the non-cow animals have been moved to a wildlife park on the border. We should be back in Greece next month for a few days to see you all and baby Atreo. Much love to everyone.

FROM: HARRY

Iakovos just got a text from Dmitri saying you just made him Margrave of Sonderburg-Beck, and we have to call him "my lord" now. Do you have any idea how he's going to hold that over Yacky and Theo's respective heads?

TO: HARRY

A NOTE FROM KATIE

My lovely one! I hope you enjoyed reading this book, which I handcrafted from the finest artisanal words just for you. If you are one of the folks who likes to review books, I'd love it if you posted a review for it on your favorite book spot. If you aren't a reviewing type, fear not, I will cherish you regardless.

I'd also like to encourage you to sign up for the exclusive readers' group newsletter wherein I share behind-the-scenes info about my books (and dogs, and love of dishy guys, and pretty much anything else that I think people would enjoy), sneak peeks of upcoming books, news of readers'-group-only contests, etc. You can join the fun by clicking on the SUBSCRIBE TO KATIE'S NEWSLETTER link on my website at www.katiemacalister.com

ABOUT THE AUTHOR

For as long as she can remember, Katie MacAlister has loved reading. Growing up in a family where a weekly visit to the library was a given, Katie spent much of her time with her nose buried in a book.

Two years after she started writing novels, Katie sold her first romance, *Noble Intentions*. More than fifty books later, her novels have been translated into numerous languages, been recorded as audiobooks, received several awards, and have been regulars on the *New York Times*, *USA Today*, and *Publishers Weekly* bestseller lists. Katie lives in the Pacific Northwest with two dogs, and can often be found lurking around online.

You are welcome to join Katie's official discussion group on Facebook, as well as connect with her via Twitter, Goodreads, and Instagram. For more information, visit her website at www.katiemacalister.com

Don't miss
It's All Greek to Me,
and *Ever Fallen in Love*,
the hilarious first two books the
Papaioannou Series!

CPSIA information can be obtained
at www.ICGtesting.com
Printed in the USA
LVHW022043210221
679522LV00004B/241